BOOKS BY MARY HIGGINS CLARK

Stillwatch

A Cry in the Night

The Cradle Will Fall

A Stranger Is Watching

Where Are the Children?

STILLWATCH

Mary Higgins Clark

SIMON AND SCHUSTER NEW YORK

This novel is a work of fiction. Names, characters, places and incidents either are products of the author's imagination or are used fictitiously. Any other resemblance to actual events or locales or persons, living or dead, is entirely coincidental.

Published by Simon and Schuster
A Division of Simon & Schuster, Inc.
Simon & Schuster Building
Rockefeller Center
1230 Avenue of the Americas
New York, New York 10020
SIMON AND SCHUSTER and colophon are registered trademarks
of Simon & Schuster, Inc.
Designed by Eve Kirch
Manufactured in the United States of America

1 3 5 7 9 10 8 6 4 2

Library of Congress Cataloging in Publication Data
Clark, Mary Higgins.
Stillwatch.
I. Title
PS3553.L287S7 1984 813′.54 84-14058
ISBN: 0-671-46952-5

To Pat Myrer, my agent
and
Michael V. Korda, my editor

For their inestimable expertise, support, help and encouragement I joyfully offer "the still small voice of gratitude."

1

Pat drove slowly, her eyes scanning the narrow Georgetown streets. The cloud-filled sky was dark; streetlights blended with the carriage lamps that flanked doorways; Christmas decorations gleamed against ice-crusted snow. The effect was one of Early American tranquillity. She turned onto N Street, drove one more block, still searching for house numbers, and crossed the intersection. That must be it, she thought—the corner house. Home Sweet Home.

She sat for a while at the curb, studying the house. It was the only one on the street that was unlighted, and its graceful lines were barely discernible. The long front windows were half-hidden by shrubbery that had been allowed to grow.

After the nine-hour drive from Concord her body ached every time she moved, but she found herself putting off the moment when she opened the front door and went inside. It's that damn phone call, she thought. I've let it get to me.

A few days before she'd left her job at the cable station in Boston, the switchboard operator had buzzed her: "Some kind of weirdo insists on talking to you. Do you want me to stay on the line?"

"Yes." She had picked up the receiver, identified herself and listened as a soft but distinctly masculine voice murmured, "Patricia Traymore, you must not come to Washington. You must not produce a program glorifying Senator Jennings. And you must not live in *that* house."

She had heard the audible gasp of the operator. "Who is this?" she asked sharply.

The answer, delivered in the same syrupy murmur, made her hands unpleasantly moist. "I am an angel of mercy, of deliverance—and of vengeance."

Pat had tried to dismiss the event as one of the many crank calls received at television stations, but it was impossible not to be troubled. The announcement of her move to Potomac Cable Network to do a series called *Women in Government* had appeared in many television-news columns. She had read all of them to see if there was any mention of the address where she would live, but there had been none.

The Washington Tribune had carried the most detailed story: "Auburn-haired Patricia Traymore, with her husky voice and sympathetic brown eyes, will be an attractive addition to Potomac Cable Network. Her profiles of celebrities on Boston Cable have twice been nominated for Emmys. Pat has the magical gift of getting people to reveal themselves with remarkable candor. Her first subject will be Abigail Jennings, the very private senior Senator from Virginia. According to Luther Pelham, news director and anchorman of Potomac Cable, the program will include highlights of the Senator's private and public life. Washington is breathlessly waiting to see if Pat Traymore can penetrate the beautiful Senator's icy reserve."

The thought of the call nagged at Pat. It was the cadence of the voice, the way he had said "*that* house."

Who was it who knew about the house?

The car was cold. Pat realized the engine had been off for minutes. A man with a briefcase hurried past, paused when he observed her sitting there, then went on his way. I'd better get moving before he calls the cops and reports a loiterer, she thought.

The iron gates in front of the driveway were open. She

stopped the car at the stone path that led to the front door and fumbled through her purse for the house key.

She paused at the doorstep, trying to analyze her feelings. She'd anticipated a momentous reaction. Instead, she simply wanted to get inside, lug the suitcases from the car, fix coffee and a sandwich. She turned the key, pushed the door open, found the light switch.

The house seemed very clean. The smooth brick floor of the foyer had a soft patina; the chandelier was sparkling. A second glance showed fading paint and scuff marks near the baseboards. Most of the furniture would probably need to be discarded or refinished. The good pieces stored in the attic of the Concord house would be delivered tomorrow.

She walked slowly through the first floor. The formal dining room, large and pleasant, was on the left. When she was sixteen and on a school trip to Washingon, she had walked past this house but hadn't realized how spacious the rooms were. From the outside the house seemed narrow.

The table was scarred, the sideboard badly marked, as if hot serving dishes had been laid directly on the wood. But she knew the handsome, elaborately carved Jacobean set was family furniture and worth whatever it would cost to restore.

She glanced into the kitchen and library but deliberately kept walking. All the news stories had described the layout of the house in minute detail. The living room was the last room on the right. She felt her throat tighten as she approached it. Was she crazy to be doing this—returning here, trying to recapture a memory best forgotten?

The living-room door was closed. She put her hand on the knob and turned it hesitantly. The door swung open. She fumbled and found the wall switch. The room was large and beautiful, with a high ceiling, a delicate mantel above the white brick fireplace, a recessed window seat. It was empty except for a concert grand piano, a massive expanse of dark mahogany in the alcove to the right of the fireplace.

The fireplace.

She started to walk toward it.

Her arms and legs began to tremble. Perspiration started from her forehead and palms. She could not swallow. The room was moving around her. She rushed to the French doors at the far end of the left wall, fumbled with the lock, yanked both doors open and stumbled onto the snow-banked patio.

The frosty air seared her lungs as she gulped in short, nervous breaths. A violent shudder made her hug her arms around her body. She began to sway and needed to lean against the house to keep from falling. Light-headedness made the dark outlines of the leafless trees seem to sway with her.

The snow was ankle-deep. She could feel the wetness seep through her boots, but she would not go back in until the dizziness receded. Minutes passed before she could trust herself to return to the room. Carefully she closed and double-locked the doors, hesitated and then deliberately turned around and with slow, reluctant steps walked to the fireplace. Tentatively she ran her hand down the rough whitewashed brick.

For a long time now, bits and pieces of memory had intruded on her like wreckage from a ship. In the past year she had persistently dreamed of being a small child again in this house. Invariably she would awaken in an agony of fear, trying to scream, unable to utter a sound. But coupled with the fear was a pervading sense of loss. The truth is in this house, she thought.

It was here that it had happened. The lurid headlines, gleaned from newspaper archives, flashed through her mind. "WISCONSIN CONGRESSMAN DEAN ADAMS MURDERS BEAUTIFUL SOCIALITE WIFE AND KILLS SELF. THREE-YEAR-OLD DAUGHTER FIGHTS FOR LIFE."

She had read the stories so many times, she knew them by heart. "A sorrowful Senator John F. Kennedy commented, 'I simply don't understand. Dean was one of my best friends. Nothing about him ever suggested pent-up violence.' "

What had driven the popular Congressman to murder and suicide? There had been rumors that he and his wife were on the verge of divorce. Had Dean Adams snapped when his wife made an irrevocable decision to leave him? They must have wrestled for the gun. Both their fingerprints, smudged and overlapping, were found on it. Their three-year-old daughter had been found lying against the fireplace, her skull fractured, her right leg shattered.

Veronica and Charles Traymore had told her that she was adopted. Not until she was in high school and wanted to trace her ancestry had she been given the whole truth. Shocked, she learned that her mother was Veronica's sister. "You were in a coma for a year and not expected to live," Veronica told her. "When you finally did regain consciousness you were like an infant and had to be taught everything. Mother—your grandmother—actually sent an obituary notice to the newspapers. That's how determined she was that the scandal wouldn't follow you all your life. Charles and I were living in England then. We adopted you and our friends were told you were from an English family."

Pat recalled how furious Veronica had been when Pat insisted on taking over the Georgetown house. "Pat, it's wrong to go back there," she'd said. "We should have sold that place for you instead of renting it all these years. You're making a name for yourself in television—don't risk it by raking up the past! You'll be meeting people who knew you as a child. Somebody might put two and two together."

Veronica's thin lips tightened when Pat insisted. "We did everything humanly possible to give you a fresh start. Go ahead, if you insist, but don't say we didn't warn you."

In the end they had hugged each other, both shaken and upset. "Come on," Pat pleaded. "My job is digging for the truth. If I hunt for the good and bad in other people's lives, how can I ever have any peace if I don't do it in my own?"

* * *

Now she went into the kitchen and picked up the telephone. Even as a child she had referred to Veronica and Charles by their first names, and in the past few years had virtually stopped calling them Mother and Dad. But she suspected that that annoyed and hurt them.

Veronica answered on the first ring. "Hi, Mother. I'm here safe and sound; the traffic was light all the way."

"Where is *here*?"

"At the house in Georgetown." Veronica had wanted her to stay at a hotel until the furniture arrived. Without giving her a chance to remonstrate, Pat rushed on. "It's really better this way. I'll have a chance to set up my equipment in the library and get my head together for my interview with Senator Jennings tomorrow."

"You're not nervous there?"

"Not at all." She could visualize Veronica's thin, worried face. "Forget about me and get ready for your cruise. Are you all packed?"

"Of course. Pat, I don't like your being alone for Christmas."

"I'll be too busy getting this program together even to think about it. Anyway, we had a wonderful early Christmas together. Look, I'd better unload the car. Love to both of you. Pretend you're on a second honeymoon and let Charles make mad love to you."

"Pat!" Disapproval and amusement mingled in her voice. But she managed one more piece of advice before hanging up. "Keep the double locks on!"

Buttoning her jacket, Pat ventured out into the chilly evening, and for the next ten minutes she tugged and hauled the luggage and cartons. The box of linens and blankets was heavy and ungainly; she had to rest every few steps on the way to the second floor. Whenever she tried to carry anything heavy her right leg felt as though it might give way. The carton with dishes and pans and groceries had to be hoisted up to the kitchen counter. I should have trusted the movers to arrive tomorrow on time, she thought—but she had learned to be skeptical of "firm" delivery dates. She had just finished hanging up her clothes and making coffee when the phone rang.

The sound seemed to explode in the quiet of the house. Pat jumped and winced as a few drops of coffee touched her hand. Quickly she put the cup on the counter and reached for the phone. "Pat Traymore."

"Hello, Pat."

She clutched the receiver, willing her voice to sound only friendly. "Hello, Sam."

Samuel Kingsley, Congressman from the 26th District of Pennsylvania, the man she loved with all her heart—the *other* reason she had decided to come to Washington.

2

Forty minutes later Pat was struggling with the clasp of her necklace when the peal of the door chimes announced Sam's arrival. She had changed to a hunter green wool dress with satin braiding. Sam had once told her that green brought out the red in her hair.

The doorbell rang again. Her fingers were trembling too much to fasten the catch. Grabbing her purse, she dropped the necklace into it. As she hurried down the stairs she tried to force herself to be calm. She reminded herself that during the eight months since Sam's wife, Janice, had died Sam hadn't called once.

On the last step she realized that she was again favoring her right leg. It was Sam's insistence that she consult a specialist about the limp that had finally forced her to tell him the truth about the injury.

She hesitated momentarily in the foyer, then slowly opened the door.

Sam nearly filled the doorway. The outside light caught the silver strands in his dark brown hair. Under unruly brows, his hazel eyes looked wary and quizzical. There were unfamiliar lines around them. But the smile when he looked at her was the same, warm and all-embracing.

They stood awkwardly, each waiting for the other to make the first move, to set the tone for the reunion. Sam was carrying a broom. Solemnly he handed it to her. "The Amish people are in my district. One of their customs is to carry a new broom and salt into a new home." He reached into his pocket for a salt cellar. "Courtesy of the House dining room." Stepping inside, he put his hands on her shoulders and leaned down to kiss her cheek. "Welcome to our town, Pat. It's good to have you here."

So this is the greeting, Pat thought. Old friends getting together. Washington is too small a town to try to duck someone from the past, so meet her head on and establish the rules. Not on your life, she thought. It's a whole new ball game, Sam, and this time I plan to win.

She kissed him, deliberately, leaving her lips against his just long enough to sense the intensity gathering in him, then stepped back and smiled easily.

"How did you know I was here?" she asked. "Have you got the place bugged?"

"Not quite. Abigail told me you were going to be in her office tomorrow. I called Potomac Cable for your phone number."

"I see." There was something intimate in the way Sam sounded when he mentioned Senator Jennings. Pat felt her heart give a queer twist and looked down, not wanting Sam to see the expression on her face. She made a business of fishing in her purse for her necklace. "This thing has a clasp that Houdini couldn't figure out. Will you?" She handed it to him.

He slipped it around her neck and she felt the warmth of his fingers as he fastened it. For a moment his fingers lingered against her skin.

Then he said, "Okay, that should stay put. Do I get the Cook's Tour of the house?"

"There's nothing to see yet. The moving van delivers tomorrow. This place will have a whole new look in a few days. Besides, I'm starving."

"As I remember, you always were." Now Sam's eyes betrayed genuine amusement. "How a little thing like you can put away hot-fudge sundaes and buttered biscuits and still not put on an ounce . . ."

Very smooth, Sam, Pat thought as she reached into the closet for her coat. You've managed to ticket me as a little thing with a big appetite. "Where are we going?" she asked.

"I made a reservation at Maison Blanche. It's always good."

She handed him her jacket. "Do they have a children's menu?" she asked sweetly.

"*What?* Oh, I see. Sorry—I thought I was paying you a compliment."

Sam had parked in the driveway behind her car. They walked down the path, his hand lightly under her arm. "Pat, are you favoring your right leg again?" There was concern in his tone.

"Just a touch. I'm stiff from the drive."

"Stop me if I'm wrong. But isn't this the house you own?"

She had told him about her parents the one night they had spent together. Now she nodded distractedly. She had often relived that night in the Ebb Tide Motel on Cape Cod. All she needed was the scent of the ocean, or the sight of two people in a restaurant, their fingers linked across the table, smiling the secret smile of lovers. And that one night had ended their relationship. In the morning, quiet and sad at breakfast, on their way to separate planes, they had talked it out and agreed they had no right to each other. Sam's wife, already confined to a wheelchair with multiple sclerosis, didn't deserve the added pain of sensing that her husband was involved with another woman. "And she'd know," Sam had said.

Pat forced herself back to the present and tried to change the subject. "Isn't this a great street? It reminds me of a painting on a Christmas card."

"Almost any street in Georgetown looks like a Christmas card at this time of year," Sam rejoined. "It's a lousy idea for you to try to dredge up the past, Pat. Let go of it."

They were at the car. He opened the door and she slipped

in. She waited until he was in the driver's seat and pulling away before she said, "I can't. There's something that keeps nagging me, Sam. I'm not going to have any peace until I know what it is."

Sam slowed for the stop sign at the end of the block. "Pat, don't you know what you're trying to do? You want to rewrite history, remember that night and decide it was all a terrible accident, that your father didn't mean to hurt you or kill your mother. You're just making it harder for yourself."

She glanced over and studied his profile. His features, a shade too strong, a hairbreadth too irregular for classic good looks, were immensely endearing. She had to conquer the impulse to slide over and feel the fine wool of his overcoat against her cheek.

"Sam, have you ever been seasick?" she asked.

"Once or twice. I'm usually a pretty good sailor."

"So am I. But I remember coming back on the *QE 2* with Veronica and Charles one summer. We hit a storm and for some reason I lost my sea legs. I don't ever remember being so miserable. I kept wishing I could be sick and have done with it. And you see, that's the way it's getting to be for me now. Things keep coming back to me."

He turned the car onto Pennsylvania Avenue. "What things?"

"Sounds . . . impressions . . . sometimes so vague; other times, especially when I'm just waking up, remarkably clear—and yet they fade before I can get hold of them. I actually tried hypnosis last year, but it didn't work. Then I read that some adults can remember accurately things that happened when they were as young as two. One study said the best way to recapture the memory is to reproduce the environment. Fortunately or unfortunately, that's something I can do."

"I still think it's a lousy idea."

Pat gazed out the car window. She had studied street maps to get a sense of the city and now tried to test herself on the accuracy of her impressions. But the car was moving too swiftly, and it was too dark to be sure of anything. They didn't speak.

The maître d' at Maison Blanche greeted Sam warmly and escorted them to a banquette.

"The usual?" Sam asked after they were seated.

Pat nodded, acutely aware of Sam's nearness. Was this his favorite table? How many other women had he brought here?

"Two Chivas Regals on the rocks with a splash of soda and a twist of lemon, please," Sam requested. He waited until the maître d' was out of earshot, then said, "All right—tell me about the last few years. Don't leave anything out."

"That's a tall order. Give me a minute to think." She would eliminate those first few months after they had agreed not to see each other, when she'd gotten through the day in a fog of sheer, hopeless misery. She could and did talk about her job, about getting an Emmy nomination for her program on the newly elected woman mayor of Boston, about her growing obsession to do a program about Senator Jennings.

"Why Abigail?" Sam asked.

"Because I think it's high time a woman was nominated for President. In two years there'll be a national election and Abigail Jennings should lead the ticket. Just look at her record: ten years in the House; in her third term in the Senate; member of the Foreign Relations Committee; the Budget Committee; first woman to be Assistant Majority Leader. Isn't it a fact that Congress is still in session because the President is counting on her to get the budget through the way he wants it?"

"Yes, it's true—and what's more, she'll do it."

"What do *you* think of her?"

Sam shrugged. "She's good. She's damn good, as a matter of fact. But she's stepped on a lot of important toes, Pat. When Abigail gets upset, she doesn't care who she blasts, and where and how she does it."

"I assume that's also true of the majority of the men on the Hill."

"Probably."
"Exactly."
The waiter came with menus. They ordered, deciding to share a Caesar salad. And that was another memory. That last day together Pat had made a picnic lunch and asked Sam what salad she should bring. "Caesar," he'd said promptly, "and lots of anchovies, please." "How can you eat those things?" she'd demanded. "How can you not? It's an acquired taste, but once you have it, you'll never lose it." She'd tried them that day and decided they were good.
He remembered too. As they handed back the menus, he commented, "I'm glad you didn't give up on the anchovies." He smiled. "Getting back to Abigail, I'm amazed she agreed to go along with the documentary."
"Frankly, I'm still amazed myself. I wrote to her about three months ago. I'd done a lot of research on her and was absolutely fascinated by what I uncovered. Sam, how much do you know about her background?"
"She's from Virginia. She took her husband's seat in Congress when he died. She's a workaholic."
"Exactly. That's the way everyone sees her. The truth is that Abigail Jennings comes from Upstate New York, *not* Virginia. She won the Miss New York State beauty contest but refused to go to Atlantic City for the Miss America pageant because she had a scholarship to Radcliffe and didn't want to risk wasting a year. She was only thirty-one when she was widowed. She was so in love with her husband that twenty-five years later she still hasn't remarried."
"She hasn't remarried, but she hasn't lived in a cloister either."
"I wouldn't know about that, but judging from the information I've gathered, the vast majority of her days and nights are strictly work."
"That's true."
"Anyhow, in my letter I wrote that I'd like to do a program that would give viewers the feeling of knowing her on a per-

sonal level. I outlined what I had in mind and got back about the frostiest rejection I've ever read. Then a couple of weeks ago Luther Pelham phoned. He was coming to Boston specifically to take me to lunch and wanted to talk about my coming to work for him. Over lunch he told me the Senator had showed him my letter; he'd already been mulling over the idea of a series called *Women in Government.* He knew and liked my work and felt I was right for the job. He also said that he wanted to make me a regular part of his seven-o'clock news program.

"You can imagine how I felt. Pelham is probably the most important commentator in the business; the network is as big as Turner's; the money's terrific. I'm to kick off the series with a documentary on Senator Jennings and he wants it as fast as possible. But I still don't know why the Senator changed her mind."

"I can tell you why. The Vice President may be on the verge of resigning. He's much sicker than people realize."

Pat laid down her fork and stared at him. "Sam, do you mean. . . ?"

"I mean the President has less than two years left in his second term. How better to make every woman in the country happy than by appointing the first woman Vice President?"

"But that means . . . if Senator Jennings is Vice President, they almost couldn't deny her the nomination for President next time."

"Hold on, Pat. You're going too fast. All I've said is that *if* the Vice President resigns, there's a damn good chance he'll be replaced by either Abigail Jennings or Claire Lawrence. Claire is practically the Erma Bombeck of the Senate—very popular, very witty, a first-rate legislator. She'd do an excellent job. But Abigail's been there longer. The President and Claire are both from the Midwest, and politically that isn't good. He'd rather appoint Abigail, but he can't ignore the fact that Abigail really isn't well known nationally. And she's made some powerful enemies in Congress."

"Then you believe Luther Pelham wants the documentary to let people see Abigail in a warmer, more personal way?"

"From what you've just told me, that's my guess. I think he wants to generate popular support for her. They were pretty cozy for a long time, and I'm sure he'd like to have his dear friend in the Vice President's chair."

They ate silently as Pat mulled the implications of what Sam had told her. Of course it explained the sudden job offer, the need for haste.

"Hey, remember me?" Sam finally said. "You haven't asked me what *I've* been doing these past two years."

"I've been following your career," she told him. "I toasted you when you were reelected—not that I was surprised. I wrote and tore up a dozen notes to you when Janice died. I'm supposed to have a way with words, but nothing sounded right. . . . It must have been very bad for you."

"It was. When it was obvious Janice didn't have much time, I cut my schedule to the bone and spent every possible minute with her. I think it helped."

"I'm sure it did." She had to ask: "Sam, why did you wait so long to call me? In fact, would you ever have called me if I hadn't come to Washington?"

The background sounds of the other diners' voices and the faint clinking of glasses, the tempting aromas of the food, the paneled walls and frosted-glass partitions of the attractive room faded as she waited for his answer.

"I did call you," he said, "a number of times, but I had the guts to break the connection before your phone rang. Pat, when I met you, you were about to become engaged. I spoiled that for you."

"With or without you it wouldn't have happened. Rob is a nice guy, but that's not enough."

"He's a bright young lawyer with an excellent future. You'd be married to him now if it weren't for me. Pat, I'm forty-eight years old. You're twenty-seven. I'm going to be a grandfather in three months. You know you would want to have children, and I simply don't have the energy to raise a new family."

"I see. Can I ask you something, Sam?"

"Of course."

"Do you love me, or have you talked yourself out of that too?"

"I love you enough to give you a chance to meet someone your own age again."

"And have you met someone *your* own age yet?"

"I'm not seeing anyone specifically."

"I see." She managed a smile. "Well, now that we have everything out in the open, why don't you buy me that nice gooey dessert I'm supposed to crave?"

He looked relieved. Had he expected her to badger him? she wondered. He seemed so tired. Where was all the enthusiasm he'd had a few years ago?

An hour later when he was dropping her at home, Pat remembered what she'd been meaning to discuss. "Sam, I had a crazy phone call at the office last week." She told him about it. "Do people in Congress get much hate mail or calls?"

He didn't seem especially concerned. "Not that many, and none of us takes them very seriously." He kissed her cheek and chuckled. "I was just thinking. Maybe I'd better talk to Claire Lawrence and see if she's been trying to scare off Abigail."

Pat watched him drive away, then closed and latched the door. The house reinforced her feeling of emptiness. The furniture will make a difference, she promised herself.

Something on the floor caught her eye: a plain white envelope. It must have been slipped under the door while she was out. Her name was printed in heavy black lettering that was sharply slanted from left to right. Probably someone from the realtor's office, she tried to tell herself. But the usual business name and address were missing from the upper left-hand corner, and the envelope was of the cheapest dime-store sort.

Slowly she ripped it open and pulled out the single sheet of paper. It read: "I TOLD YOU NOT TO COME."

3

The next morning the alarm went off at six. Pat slipped willingly out of bed. The lumpy mattress had not been conducive to sleep, and she had kept waking, aware of the creaking, settling sounds in the house and the thumping activity of the oil burner as it snapped off and on. Try as she would, she could not dismiss the note as the work of a harmless eccentric. Somebody was observing her.

The movers had promised to arrive by eight. She planned to move the files stored in the basement up to the library.

The basement was dingy, with cement walls and floor. Garden furniture was stacked neatly in the center. The storage room was to the right of the furnace room. A heavy padlock on its door was grimy with the accumulated soot of years.

When Charles had given her the key, he'd warned, "I don't know exactly what you'll find, Pat. Your grandmother instructed Dean's office to send all his personal effects to the house. We never did get around to sorting them."

For a moment it seemed as though the key would not work. The basement was damp, with a vague smell of mildew. She wondered if the lock had rusted. She moved the key back and forth slowly and then felt it turn. She tugged at the door.

Inside the storeroom, a stronger smell of mildew assailed her. Two legal-size filing cabinets were so covered with dust and cobwebs she could barely determine their color. Several heavy cartons, haphazardly piled, stood next to them. With her thumb she rubbed at the grime until the labels appeared: CONGRESSMAN DEAN W. ADAMS, BOOKS. CONGRESSMAN DEAN W. ADAMS, PERSONAL EFFECTS. CONGRESSMAN DEAN W. ADAMS, MEMORABILIA. The inserts on the file drawers read the same: CONGRESSMAN DEAN W. ADAMS, PERSONAL.

"Congressman Dean W. Adams," Pat said aloud. She repeated the name carefully. Funny, she thought, I really don't think of him as a Congressman. I only place him here in this house. What kind of Representative was he?

Except for the formal picture the newspapers used at the time of the deaths, she'd never seen even a snapshot of him. Veronica had shown her albums filled with pictures of Renée as a child, as a young woman at her debut, at her first professional concert, with Pat in her arms. It hadn't been hard to guess why Veronica had kept no reminder of Dean Adams around.

The key to the files was on the ring Charles had given her. She was about to unlock the first one when she began to sneeze. She decided it was crazy to try to examine anything in that cellar. Already her eyes were itching from the dust. I'll wait until it's all in the library, she thought. But first she would wash the outside of the cabinets and get the worst of the dust off the cartons.

It turned out to be a messy, exhausting job. There was no sink in the basement, and she trudged repeatedly upstairs to the kitchen, bringing down a pail of sudsy hot water and returning a few minutes later with both water and sponge blackened.

On the last trip she brought down a knife and carefully scraped the identifying labels from the cartons. Finally she removed the inserts from the fronts of the file drawers. Satisfied, she surveyed her work. The cabinets were olive green and still in decent condition. They would fit along the east wall of the library. The cartons could go there too. No one would have any reason to think they hadn't come from Boston. Veronica's influence again, she thought wryly. "Don't tell anyone, Pat. Think ahead, Pat. When you marry, do you want your children to know that the reason you limp was that your father tried to kill you?"

She had barely time to wash her hands and face before the movers arrived. The three men on the truck hauled in the furniture, unrolled carpets, unpacked china and crystal, brought up the contents of the storage room. By noon they had gone, manifestly pleased with their tip.

Alone again, Pat went directly to the living room. The transformation was dramatic. The fourteen-by-twenty-four-foot Oriental carpet with its brilliant designs of apricot, green, lemon and cranberry against a black background dominated the room. The green velvet love seat stood against the short wall at a right angle to the long apricot satin sofa. The matching high-backed wing chairs flanked the fireplace; the Bombay chest was to the left of the patio doors.

The room was well nigh a restoration of its former self. She walked through it, touching the tops of the tables, adjusting the angle of a chair or lamp, running her hands over the fabric of the upholstered pieces. What was she feeling? She couldn't be sure. Not fear exactly—though she had to force herself to pass the fireplace. What then? Nostalgia? But for what? Was it possible that some of those blurred impressions were memories of happy times spent in this room? If so, what else could she do to retrieve them?

At five minutes to three she stepped out of a cab in front of the Russell Senate Office Building. The temperature had dropped sharply in the last several hours and she was glad to enter the heated foyer. The security guards passed her through the metal detector and directed her to the elevator. A few minutes later she was giving her name to Abigail Jennings' receptionist.

"Senator Jennings is running a little behind," the young woman explained. "She has several constituents who stopped in to see her. It won't be long."

"I don't mind waiting." Pat selected a straight-backed chair and looked around. Abigail Jennings clearly had one of the most desirable of the senatorial offices. It was a corner unit and had a feeling of airiness and space that she knew was in short supply in the overcrowded building. A low railing separated the waiting area from the receptionist's desk. A corridor to the right led to a row of private offices. The walls were covered with framed news photos of the Senator. The small table by the leather couch held pamphlets explaining Senator Jennings' positions on pending legislation.

She heard the familiar voice, softly modulated by the faintest touch of a Southern accent, easing visitors out of an inner office. "I'm delighted you were able to stop by. I only wish we had more time. . . ."

The visitors were a well-dressed sixtyish couple, effusive in their thanks. "Well, at the fund-raiser you did say to stop in anytime, and I said, 'Violet, we're in Washington, let's just do it.' "

"You're sure you're not free for dinner?" the woman visitor interjected anxiously.

"I only wish I were."

Pat watched as the Senator steered her guests to the outer door, opened it and slowly closed it, forcing them out. Well done, she thought. She felt her adrenaline rise.

Abigail turned and paused, giving Pat an oppportunity to study her closely. Pat had forgotten how tall the Senator was—about five feet nine, with a graceful, erect carriage. Her gray tweed suit followed the lines of her body; broad shoulders accentuated a taut waistline; angular hips ended in slender legs. Her ash blond hair was cut short around the thin face dominated by extraordinary china-blue eyes. Her nose was shiny, her lips pale and undefined. She seemed to use absolutely no makeup, as though trying deliberately to understate her remarkable beauty. Except for the fine lines around her eyes and mouth, she looked the same as she had six years earlier.

Pat watched as the Senator's glance came to rest on her.

"Hello," the Senator said, moving quickly toward her. With a reproachful glance at the receptionist she said, "Cindy, you should have told me that Miss Traymore was here." Her chiding expression turned rueful. "Well, no harm done. Come inside, please, Miss Traymore. May I call you Pat? Luther has recommended you so highly I feel I know you. And I've seen some of the specials you've done in Boston. Luther ran them for me. They're splendid. And as you mentioned in your letter, we did meet some years ago. It was when I spoke at Wellesley, wasn't it?"

"Yes, it was." Pat followed the Senator into the inner office and looked around. "How lovely!" she exclaimed.

A long walnut console desk held a delicately painted Japanese lamp, an obviously valuable figurine of an Egyptian cat, a gold pen in a holder. The crimson leather chair, wide and comfortable with arched arms and intricate nailheads, was probably seventeenth-century English. An Oriental carpet had predominant tones of crimson and blue. The flags of the United States and the Commonwealth of Virginia were on the wall behind the desk. Blue silk tieback draperies softened the bleakness of the cloudy winter day beyond the windows. One wall was covered with mahogany bookshelves. Pat chose a chair nearest the Senator's desk.

The Senator seemed pleased at Pat's reaction to the office. "Some of my colleagues feel that the shabbier and more cluttered their offices appear, the busier and more down-to-earth their constituents will think they are. I simply can't work in confusion. Harmony in very important to me. I get a lot more accomplished in this atmosphere."

She paused. "There's a vote coming up on the floor within

the hour, so I guess we'd better get down to business. Has Luther told you that I really *hate* the idea of this special?"

Pat felt on safe ground. Many people resisted programs about themselves. "Yes, he has," she said, "but I honestly believe you'll be pleased with the result."

"That's the only way I'd even consider this. I'll be perfectly honest: I prefer to work with Luther and you rather than have another network decide to produce an unauthorized story. But even so, I wish the good old days were here when a politician could simply say 'I stand on my record.' "

"They're gone. At least, they are for the people who count."

Abigail reached into her desk drawer and pulled out a cigarette case. "I never smoke in public anymore," she observed. "Just once—*once,* mind you—a paper printed a picture of me with a cigarette in my hand. I was in the House then, and I got dozens of irate letters from parents in my district saying I was setting a bad example." She reached across the desk. "Do you . . . ?"

Pat shook her head. "No, thanks. My father asked me not to smoke till I was eighteen, and by then I'd lost interest."

"And you kept your word? No puffing away behind the garage or whatever?"

"No."

The Senator smiled. "I find that reassuring. Sam Kingsley and I share a great distrust of the media. You know him, don't you? When I told him about this program, he assured me you were different."

"That was kind of him," Pat said, trying to sound casual. "Senator, I suspect the shortest way to go about this is for you to tell me exactly why the idea of the program is so abhorrent to you. If I know in advance what you find objectionable we're bound to save a lot of time."

She watched as the Senator's face became thoughtful. "It's infuriating that no one is satisfied with my personal life. I've been a widow since I was thirty-one years old. Taking my husband's place in Congress after his death, then being elected myself and going on to the Senate—all of it has always made me feel I'm still partners with him. I love my job and I'm married to it. But of course I can't very well tearfully describe little Johnny's first day at school because I never had a child. Unlike Claire Lawrence, I can't be photographed with an army of grandchildren. And I warn you, Pat, I will not allow a picture of me in a bathing suit, high heels and a rhinestone crown to be used in this program."

"But you *were* Miss New York State. You can't ignore that."

"Can't I?" The incredible eyes flashed. "Do you know that shortly after Willard's death, some rag printed that picture of me being crowned Miss New York State with the caption *"And your real prize is to go to Congress for the South?"* The Governor almost changed his mind about appointing me to complete Willard's term. It took Jack Kennedy to persuade him that I'd been working side by side with my husband from the day he was elected. If Jack hadn't been so powerful, I might not be here now. No, thank you, Pat Traymore. No beauty-queen pictures. Start your special when I was a senior at the University of Richmond, just married to Willard and helping him campaign for the first seat in Congress. That's when my life began."

You can't pretend the first twenty years of your life don't exist, Pat thought. And why? Aloud she suggested, "I came across one picture of you as a child in front of your family home in Apple Junction. That's the kind of early background I plan to use."

"Pat, I never said that was *my* family home. I said I had *lived* there. In point of fact, my mother was the housekeeper for the Saunders family and she and I had a small apartment in the back. Please don't forget I'm the senior Senator from Virginia. The Jennings family has been prominent in Tidewater Virginia since Jamestown. My mother-in-law always called me Willard's Yankee wife. I've gone to great effort to be considered a Jennings from Virginia and to forget Abigail Foster from Upstate New York. Let's leave it that way, shall we?"

There was a knock at the door. A serious-looking, oval-faced man in his early thirties entered, wearing a gray suit with a faint pin stripe that accentuated the leanness of his body. Thinning blond hair carefully combed across his pate failed to conceal his bald spot. Rimless glasses added to the middle-aged effect. "Senator," he said, "they're about to take the vote. The fifteen-minute bell just went off."

The Senator stood up abruptly. "Pat, I'm sorry. Incidentally, this is Philip Buckley, my administrative assistant. He and Toby have put together some material for you—all sorts of stuff: press clippings, letters, photo albums, even some home movies. Why don't you look them over, and then let's talk again in the next few days?"

Pat could do nothing except agree. She would talk to Luther Pelham. Between them, they must convince the Senator that she could not sabotage the program. She realized Philip Buckley was studying her carefully. Did she detect a certain hostility in his manner?

"Toby will drive you home," the Senator continued hurriedly. "Where *is* he, Phil?"

"Right here, Senator. Keep your shirt on."

The cheerful voice came from a barrel-chested man who immediately gave Pat the impression of being an overage prizefighter. His big face was beefy, with the flesh beginning to puff under small, deep-set eyes. Fading sandy hair was abundantly mixed with gray. He was wearing a dark blue suit and holding a cap in his hands.

His hands—she found herself staring at them. They were the largest she had ever seen. A ring with an onyx an inch square accentuated the thickness of his fingers.

Keep your shirt on. Had he really said that? Aghast, she looked at the Senator. But Abigail Jennings was laughing.

"Pat, this is Toby Gorgone. He can tell you what his job is as he drives you home. I've never been able to figure it out and he's been with me for twenty-five years. He's from Apple Junction too, and besides me, he's the best thing that ever came out of it. And now I'm off. Come on, Phil."

They were gone. This special is going to be sheer hell to make, Pat thought. She had three solid pages of points she'd wanted to discuss with the Senator and had gotten to bring up exactly one. Toby had known Abigail Jennings since childhood. That she put up with his insolence was incredible. Maybe he'd answer some questions on the drive home.

She had just reached the reception area when the door was flung open and Senator Jennings rushed back in, followed by Philip. The relaxed manner was gone. "Toby, thank God I caught you," she snapped. "Where did you get the idea I'm not due at the Embassy until seven?"

"That's what you told me, Senator."

"That's what I *may* have told you, but you're supposed to double-check my appointments, aren't you?"

"Yes, Senator," Toby said genially.

"I'm due at *six.* Be downstairs at quarter to." The words were spat out.

"Senator, you'll be late for the vote," Toby said. "You'd better get a move on."

"I'd be late for everything if I didn't have eyes in the back of my head to double-check on you." This time the door slammed behind her.

Toby laughed. "We'd better get started, Miss Traymore."

Wordlessly, Pat nodded. She could not imagine one of the servants at home addressing either Veronica or Charles with such a familiarity or being so unconcerned about a reprimand. What circumstances had created such a bizarre relationship between Senator Jennings and her oxlike chauffeur?

She decided to find out.

4

Toby steered the sleek gray Cadillac Sedan de Ville through the rapidly gathering traffic. For the hundredth time he brooded on the fact that Washington in the late afternoon was a driver's nightmare. All the tourists in their rented cars who didn't realize that some of the streets became one-way on the dot of four created havoc for the people who worked here.

He glanced into the rearview mirror and liked what he saw. Patricia Traymore was all right. It had taken all three of them—himself, Phil and Pelham—to talk Abby into agreeing to this documentary. So Toby felt even more than usually responsible to see that it worked out.

Still, you couldn't blame Abby for being nervous. She was within an eyelash of everything she'd ever wanted. His eyes met Pat's in the mirror. What a smile that girl had! He'd heard Sam Kingsley tell Abigail that Pat Traymore had a way of making you tell things you never thought you'd share with another human being.

Pat had been considering what approach to take with Toby and had decided the straightforward one was the best. As the car stopped for a light on Constitution Avenue, she leaned forward. There was a chuckle in her voice as she said, "Toby, I have to confess I thought I wasn't hearing straight when you told the Senator to keep her shirt on."

He turned his head to look at her directly. "Oh, I shouldn't a said that first time you met me. I don't usually do that. It's just I knew Abby was uptight about this program business and on her way in for the vote, and a bunch of reporters were going to be all over her about why she wasn't going along with the rest of the party—so I figured if I got her to let down for a minute it'd do her good. But don't misunderstand. I respect the lady. And don't worry about her blowing up at me. She'll forget it in five minutes."

"You grew up together?" Pat prodded gently.

The light turned green. Smoothly the car moved forward; Toby maneuvered into the right lane ahead of a station wagon before answering. "Well, not exactly that. All the kids in Apple Junction go to the same school—'cept, of course, if they go to parochial school. But she was two years ahead of me, so we were never in the same classes. Then when I was fifteen I started doing yard work in the rich part of town. I guess Abby told you she lived in the Saunders house."

"Yes, she did."

"I worked for the people about four places away. One day I heard Abby screaming. The old guy who lived opposite the Saunderses' had taken in his head he needed a watchdog and bought a German shepherd. Talk about vicious! Anyway, the old guy left the gate open and the dog got out just as Abby was coming down the street. Made straight for her."

"And you saved her?"

"I sure did. I started shouting and distracted him. Bad luck for me I'd dropped my rake, 'cause I got half chewed to rags before I got a grip on his neck. And then"—Toby's voice filled with pride—"and then, no more watchdog."

With one hand, Pat slipped her tape recorder out of her shoulder bag and turned it on. "I can see why the Senator must feel pretty strongly about you," she commented. "The Japanese believe that if you save someone's life you become somehow responsible for them. Do you suppose that happened to you? It sounds to me as though you feel responsible for the Senator."

"Well, I don't know. Maybe that did happen, or maybe she stuck her neck out for me when we were kids." The car stopped. "Sorry, Miss Traymore. We should a made that light, but the jerk ahead of me is reading street signs."

"It doesn't matter. I'm not in any hurry. The Senator stuck her neck out for you?"

"I said *maybe* she did. Look, forget it. The Senator doesn't like me to talk about Apple Junction."

"I'll bet she talks about how you helped her," Pat mused. "I can imagine how *I'd* feel if an attack dog was charging at me and someone threw himself in between."

"Oh, Abby was grateful, all right. My arm was bleeding, and she wrapped her sweater around it, then insisted on coming to the emergency room with me and even wanted to sit in while they sewed it. After that we were friends for life."

Toby looked over his shoulder. "*Friends,*" he repeated emphatically, "not boyfriend-girlfriend. Abby's out of my league. I don't have to tell you that. There was no question of any of that stuff. But sometimes in the afternoon she'd come over and talk while I was working around the yard. She hated Apple Junction as much as I did. And when I was flunking English, she tutored me. I never did have any head for books. Show me a piece of machinery and I'll take it apart and put it together in two minutes, but don't ask me to diagram a sentence.

"Anyhow, Abby went off to college and I drifted down to New York and got married and it didn't take. And I took a job running numbers for some bookies and ended up in hot water. After that I started chauffeuring for some fruitcake on Long Island. By then Abby was married and her husband was the Congressman and I read that she'd been in an automobile accident because her chauffeur had been drinking. So I thought, What the hell. I wrote to her and two weeks later her husband hired me and that was going on twenty-five years ago. Say, Miss Traymore, what number are you? We're on N Street now."

"Three thousand," Pat said. "It's the corner house on the next block."

"*That* house?" Too late, Toby tried to cover the shock in his voice.

"Yes. Why?"

"I used to drive Abby and Willard Jennings to that house for parties. Used to be owned by a Congressman named Dean Adams. Did they tell you about him killing his wife and committing suicide?"

Pat hoped her voice was calm. "My father's lawyer arranged the rental. He mentioned there had been a tragedy here many years ago, but he didn't go into it."

Toby pulled up to the curb. "Just as well to forget it. He even tried to kill his kid—she died later on. Cute little thing. Her name was Kerry, I remember. What can you do?" He shook his head. "I'll just park by the hydrant for a minute. Cops won't bother as long as I don't hang around."

Pat reached for the handle of the door, but Toby was too quick for her. In an instant he was out the driver's side, around the car and holding the door open, putting a hand under her arm. "Be careful, Miss Traymore. Plenty icy here."

"Yes, I see that. Thank you." She was grateful for the early dusk, afraid that her expression might send some signal to Toby. He might not have a head for books but she sensed he was extremely perceptive. She had thought of this house only in the context of that one night. Of course there had been parties here. Abigail Jennings was fifty-six. Willard Jennings had been eight or nine years her senior. Pat's father would have been in his early sixties now. They had been contemporaries in those Washington days.

Toby was reaching into the trunk. She longed to ask him about Dean and Renée Adams, about "the cute little kid, Kerry." But not now, she cautioned herself.

Toby followed her into the house, two large cartons in his arms. Pat could see that they were heavy, but he carried them easily. She led him into the library and indicated the area next to the boxes from the storeroom. She blessed the instinct that had made her scrape off the labels with her father's name.

But Toby barely glanced at the boxes. "I'd better be off, Miss Traymore. This box"—he pointed—"has press clippings, photo albums, that sort of thing. The other one has letters from constituents—the personal kind, where you can see the sort of help Abby gives them. It had some home movies too, mostly of when her husband was alive. The usual stuff, I guess. I'll be glad to run the movies for you anytime and tell you who's in them and what was going on."

"Let me sort them out and I'll get back to you. Thanks, Toby. I'm sure you're going to be a big help in this project. Maybe between us, we'll put together something the Senator will be happy about."

"If she's not, we'll both know it." Toby's beefy face lit up in a genial smile. "Good night, Miss Traymore."

"Why not make it 'Pat'? After all, you do call the Senator 'Abby.' "

"I'm the only one who can call her that. She hates it. But who knows? Maybe I'll get a chance to save your life too."

"Don't hesitate for a minute if the opportunity comes your way." Pat reached out her hand and watched it disappear into his.

When he had left, she stood in the doorway, lost in thought. She would have to learn not to show any emotion when Dean Adams was mentioned. She had been lucky that Toby had brought up his name while she was still in the protective darkness of the car.

From the shadow of the house directly opposite, another observer watched Toby drive away. With angry curiosity he studied Pat as she stood in the doorway. His hands were thrust into the pockets of his skimpy overcoat. White cotton pants, white socks and white rubber-soles blended into the snow that was banked against the house. His bony wrists tightened as he closed his fingers into fists, and tension rippled through the muscles in his arms. He was a tall, gaunt man with a stiff, tense stance and a habit of holding his head unnaturally back. His hair, a silvery gray that seemed incongruous over a peculiarly unlined face, was combed forward over his forehead.

She was here. He had seen her unloading her car last night. In spite of his warnings, she was going ahead with that program. That was the Senator's car, and those boxes probably had some kind of records in them. And she was going to stay in that house.

The memory of that long-ago morning sprang into his mind: the man lying on his back, wedged between the coffee table and sofa; the woman's eyes, staring, unfocused; the little girl's hair matted with dried blood . . .

He stood there silently, long after Pat had closed the door, as if he were unable to tear himself away.

Pat was in the kitchen broiling a chop when the phone began to ring. She didn't expect to hear from Sam but . . . With a quick smile she reached for the receiver. "Hello."

A whisper. "Patricia Traymore."

"Yes. Who is this?" But she knew that syrupy, whispering voice.

"Did you get my letter?"

She tried to make her voice calm and coaxing. "I don't know why you're upset. Tell me about it."

"Forget your program on the Senator, Miss Traymore. I don't want to punish you. Don't make me do it. But you must remember the Lord said, 'Whoever harms one of these my little ones, better a millstone be put around his neck and he be drowned in the depth of the sea.' "

The connection went dead.

5

It was only a crank call—some wacko who probably thought women belonged in the kitchen, not in public office. Pat recalled the character in New York who used to parade on Fifth Avenue with signs quoting Scripture about women's duty to obey their husbands. He had been harmless. So was this caller. She wouldn't believe it was anything more than that.

She brought a tray into the library and ate dinner while she sorted out Abigail's records. Her admiration for the Senator increased with every line she read. Abigail Jennings had meant it when she said she was married to her job. Her constituents *are* her family, Pat thought.

Pat had an appointment with Pelham at the network in the morning. At midnight she went to bed. The master bedroom suite of the house consisted of a large bedroom, a dressing room and bath. The Chippendale furniture with its delicate inlays of fruitwood had been easy to place. It was obvious that it had been purchased for this house. The highboy fitted between the closets; the mirrored dresser belonged in the alcove, the bed with its elaborately carved headboard on the long wall facing the windows.

Veronica had sent a new spring and mattress, and the bed felt wonderfully comfortable. But the trips to the basement to clean the filing cabinets had taken their toll on her leg. The familiar nagging pain was more acute than usual, and even though she was very tired it was hard to fall asleep. Think about something pleasant, she told herself as she stirred restlessly and turned on her side. Then in the dark she smiled wryly. She'd think about Sam.

The offices and studio of the Potomac Cable Network were just off Farragut Square. As she went in, Pat remembered what the news director at the Boston station had told her: "There's no question you should take the job, Pat. Working for Luther Pelham is a once-in-a-lifetime break. When he left CBS for Potomac, it was the biggest upset in the industry."

At the lunch with Luther in Boston, she'd been astonished at the frank stares of everyone in the dining room. She had become used to being recognized in the Boston area and having people come to her table for autographs. But the way virtually every pair of eyes was absolutely riveted on Luther Pelham was something else. "Can you go anywhere without being the center of attention?" she'd asked him.

"Not too many places, I'm happy to say. But you'll find out for yourself. Six months from now, people will be following *you* when you walk down the street and half the young women in America will be imitating that throaty voice of yours."

Exaggerated, of course, but certainly flattering. After the second time she called him "Mr. Pelham," he'd said, "Pat, you're on the team. I have a first name. Use it."

Luther Pelham had certainly been charming, but on that occasion he had been offering her a job. Now he was her boss.

When she was announced, Luther came to the reception area to greet her. His manner was effusively cordial, the familiar well-modulated voice exuding hearty warmth: "Great to have you here, Pat. I want you to meet the gang." He took her around the newsroom and introduced her. Behind the pleasantries, she sensed the curiosity and speculation in the eyes of her new co-workers. She could guess what they were thinking.

Would she be able to cut the mustard? But she liked her immediate impressions. Potomac was rapidly becoming one of the largest cable networks in the country, and the newsroom whirred with activity. A young woman was giving on-the-hour headlines live from her desk; a military expert was taping his bi-weekly segment; staff writers were editing copy from the wire services. She well knew that the apparently calm exterior of the personnel was a necessary ploy. Everyone in the business lived with constant underlying tension, always on guard, waiting for something to happen, fearful that somehow a big story might be fumbled.

Luther had already agreed that she could write and edit at home until they were ready for actual taping. He pointed out the cubicle that had been reserved for her, then led her into his private office, a large oak-paneled corner room.

"Make yourself comfortable, Pat," he directed. "There's a call I have to return."

While he was on the phone, Pat had a chance to study him closely. He was certainly an impressive and handsome man. His thick, carefully barbered stone gray hair contrasted with his youthful skin and probing dark eyes. She knew he had just had his sixtieth birthday. The party his wife had given at their Chevy Chase estate had been written up in all the columns. With his aquiline nose and long-fingered hands that tapped impatiently on the desk top, he reminded her of an eagle.

He hung up the phone. "Have I passed inspection?" His eyes were amused.

"With flying colors." Why was it, she wondered, that she always felt at ease in a professional situation and yet so often had a sense of alienation in personal relationships?

"Glad to hear it. If you weren't sizing me up, I'd be worried. Congratulations. You made a great impression on Abigail yesterday."

A quick pleasantry and then he was down to business. She liked that and wouldn't waste his time leading up to the problem. "I was very impressed with her. Who wouldn't be?" Then she added significantly—"for as long as I had the chance to be with her."

Pelham waved his hand as though to remove an unpleasant reality. "I know. I know. Abigail is hard to pin down. That's why I told them to put together some of her personal material for you. Don't expect much cooperation from the lady herself because you won't get it. I've scheduled the program for the twenty-seventh."

"The twenty-seventh? December twenty-seventh!" Pat heard her voice rising. "Next Wednesday! That would mean all the taping, editing and scoring will have to be done in a week!"

"Exactly," Luther confirmed. "And you're the one who can do it."

"But why the rush?"

He leaned back, crossed his legs and smiled with the relish of a bearer of momentous news. "Because this isn't going to be just another documentary. Pat Traymore, you have the chance to be a kingmaker."

She thought of what Sam had told her. *"The Vice President?"*

"The Vice President," he confirmed, "and I'm glad you have your ear to the ground. That triple bypass last year hasn't done the job for him. My spies at the hospital tell me he has extensive heart damage and if he wants to live he's going to have to change his lifestyle. That means he's virtually certain to resign—and now. To keep all factions of the party happy, the President will go through the motions of having the Secret Service check out three or four serious contenders for the job. But the inside bet is that Abigail has the best shot at it. When we air this program we want to motivate millions of Americans to send telegrams to the President in Abigail's behalf. That's what the program must do for her. And think about what it can do for *your* career."

Sam had talked about the *possibility* of the Vice President's resignation and Abigail's candidacy. Luther Pelham clearly believed both were imminent *probabilities.* To be at the right place at the right time, to be there when a story was breaking—it was the dream of every newswoman. "If words leaks out about how sick the Vice President is . . ."

"It's more than leaking out," Luther told her. "I'm carrying it on my newscast tonight, including the rumors that the President is considering a woman replacement."

"Then the Jennings program could sweep the ratings next week! Senator Jennings isn't that well known to the average voter. Everyone's going to want to find out about her."

"Exactly. Now you can understand the need to put it together fast and make it something absolutely extraordinary."

"The Senator . . . If we make this program as bloodless as she seems to want, you won't get fourteen telegrams, never mind millions. Before I proposed this documentary I did some extensive surveying to find out what people think about her."

"And?"

"Older people compared her to Margaret Chase Smith. They called her impressive, gutsy, intelligent."

"What's wrong with that?"

"Not one of the older people felt they knew her as a human being. They think of her as being distant and formal."

"Go on."

"The younger people have a different approach. When I told them about the Senator being Miss New York State, they thought it was great. They want to know more about it. Remember, if Abigail Jennings is chosen to be Vice President, she'll be second in command of the whole country. A number of people who know she is from the Northeast resent the fact that she never talks about it. I think she's making a mistake. And we'll compound it if we ignore the first twenty years of her life."

"She'll never let you mention Apple Junction," Luther said flatly. "So let's not waste time on that. She told me that when she resigned her Miss New York State title, they wanted to lynch her there."

"Luther, she's wrong. Do you seriously think anyone in Apple Junction gives a damn anymore that Abigail didn't go to Atlantic City to try to become Miss America? Right now I'll bet every adult there is bragging that he or she knew Abigail when. As for resigning the title, let's face it head on. Who wouldn't sympathize with an answer like Abigail saying it had been a lark entering the contest but she found she hated the idea of parading around in a bathing suit and having people judge her like a side of beef? Beauty contests are passé now. We'll make her look good for realizing it before anyone else did."

Luther drummed his fingers on the desk. Every instinct told him Pat was right, but Abigail had been definite on this point. Suppose they talked her into doing some material on her early life and it backfired? Luther was determined to be the power that put Abigail across as Vice President. Of course the party leaders would exact a promise from Abigail not to expect to run for the number one spot next time, but hell, those promises were made to be broken. He'd keep Abigail front and center until the day came when she was sitting in the Oval Office—and she'd owe it to him. . . .

He suddenly realized that Pat Traymore was watching him calmly. Most of the people he hired were trying not to swallow their own spit in the first private session in this office. The fact that she seemed totally at ease both pleased and annoyed him. He had found himself doing a lot of thinking about her in the two weeks since he'd offered her the job. She was smart; she'd asked all the right questions about her contract; she was damn good-looking in an interesting, classy kind of way. She was a born interviewer; those eyes and that raspy voice gave her a kind of sympathetic, even naive quality that created a "tell all" atmosphere. And there was a smoldering sexiness about her that was especially intriguing.

"Tell me how you see the overall approach to her personal life," he ordered.

"First Apple Junction," Pat said promptly. "I want to go there myself and see what I can find. Maybe some shots of the town, of the house where she lived. The fact that her mother was a housekeeper and that she went to college on scholarship is a plus. It's the American dream, only for the first time we're applying it to a national leader who happens to be a woman."

She pulled her notebook from her purse. Flipping it open, she continued. "Certainly we'll emphasize the early years when she was married to Willard Jennings. I haven't run the films yet, but it looks as though we'll pick up quite a bit of both their public and private lives."

Luther nodded affirmatively. "Incidentally, you'll probably see a fair amount of Jack Kennedy in those pictures. He and Willard Jennings were close friends. That's when Jack was a Senator, of course. Willard and Abigail were a part of the pre-Camelot years. People don't realize that about her. Leave in as many clips as you can find of them with any of the Kennedys. Did you know that when Willard died, Jack escorted Abigail to the memorial service?"

Pat jotted a few words on her pad. "Didn't Senator Jennings have any family?" she asked.

"I guess not. It never came up." Luther impatiently reached for the cigarette case on his desk. "I keep trying to give up these damn weeds." He lit one and for the moment looked somewhat relaxed. "I only wish I'd headed to Washington at that time," he said. "I thought New York was where the action was. I've done all right, but those were great Washington years. Crazy, though, how many of those young men died violently. The Kennedy brothers. Willard in a plane crash. Dean Adams a suicide . . . You've heard about him?"

"Dean Adams?" She made her voice a question.

"Murdered his wife," Luther explained. "Killed himself.

Nearly killed his kid. She did die eventually. Probably better off, too. Brain-damaged, no doubt. He was a Congressman from Wisconsin. Nobody could figure the reason. Just went nuts, I guess. If you come across any pictures of him or his wife in a group shot, edit them out. No one needs to be reminded of that."

Pat hoped her face didn't betray distress. Her tone remained determinedly brisk as she said, "Senator Jennings was one of the moving forces in getting the Parental Kidnapping Prevention Act passed. There are some wonderful letters in her files. I thought I'd look up some of the families she's reunited and pick the best one for a segment on the program. That will counteract Senator Lawrence and her grandchildren."

Luther nodded. "Fine. Give me the letters. I'll get someone around here to do the legwork. And by the way, in your outline you didn't have anything about the Eleanor Brown case. I absolutely want that in. You know she came from Apple Junction too—the school principal there asked Abigail to give her a job after she'd been caught shoplifting."

"My instinct is to let that alone," Pat said. "Think about it. The Senator gave a convicted girl a new start. That much is fine. Then Eleanor Brown was accused of stealing seventy-five thousand dollars in campaign funds. She swore she was innocent. Essentially it was the Senator's testimony that convicted her. Did you ever see that girl's pictures? She was twenty-three when she went to prison for the embezzlement but looked about sixteen. People have a natural inclination to feel sorry for the underdog—and the whole purpose of this program is to make everyone love Abigail Jennings. In the Eleanor Brown case, she comes through as the heavy."

"That case shows that some legislators don't cover up for the crooks on their staff. And if you want Abigail's image softened, play up the fact that thanks to her, that kid got off a lot lighter than anyone else I know who stole that much money. Don't waste your sympathy on Eleanor Brown. She faked a nervous breakdown in prison, was transferred to a psychiatric hospital, was paroled as an outpatient and took off. She was some cool cookie. What else?"

"I'd like to go to Apple Junction tonight. If there's anything worthwhile there, I'll call you and we'll arrange for a camera crew. After that, I want to follow the Senator through a day in her office, plan some shots and then tape her there a day or two later."

Luther stood up—a signal that the meeting was over. "All right," he said. "Fly up to . . . What is the place . . . Apple Junction? What a hell of a name! See if you can get good copy. But play it low key. Don't let the natives get the idea they're going to be on camera. The minute they think you might have them on the program, they'll start using all the big words they know and planning what leisure suit to wear." He twisted his face into a worried frown, made his voice nasal. "Myrtle, get the lighter fluid. There's a gravy stain on my jacket."

"I'm sure I'll find some pretty decent people there." Pat forced a faint smile to take the implied rebuke out of her words.

Luther watched her leave, noting the burgundy-and-gray tweed suit, obviously a designer original; the burgundy leather boots with the small gold Gucci trademark; the matching shoulder bag; the Burberry over her arm.

Money. Patricia Traymore had family money. You could always tell. Resentfully, Luther thought of his own humble beginnings on a farm in Nebraska. They hadn't had indoor plumbing until he was ten. No one could sympathize more than he with Abigail about not wanting to resurrect the early years.

Had he done the right thing in allowing Pat Traymore to have her way in this? Abigail would be sore—but she'd probably be a lot sorer when she found out they hadn't told her about the trip.

Luther turned on his intercom. "Get me Senator Jennings' office." Then he hesitated. "No, hold it; don't bother."

He put down the phone and shrugged. Why start trouble?

6

Pat felt the sidelong glances of the people in the newsroom as she left Pelham's office. Deliberately she set her face in a half-smile and made her step brisk. He'd been very cordial; he had risked Senator Jennings' anger by letting her go to Apple Junction. He had expressed his faith in her ability to put the program together on a breakneck schedule.

Then what's the matter? she wondered. I should feel great.

Outside, it was a cold, bright day. The streets were clear, and she decided to walk home. It was a couple of miles, but she wanted the exercise. Why not admit it? she thought. It's what Pelham just said about the Dean Adams mess; it's what Toby said yesterday. It's the feeling of everyone stepping back when Dean Adams' name is mentioned, of no one wanting to admit having known him. What had Luther said about her? Oh, yes—he thought the child had died, and it was better that way; she was probably brain-damaged.

I'm not brain-damaged, Pat thought as she tried to avoid a spray of dirty slush. But I *am* damaged. My leg is the least of it. I hate my father for what he did. He killed my mother and he tried to kill me.

She had come here thinking she only wanted to understand what had caused him to crack up. Now she knew better. She had to face the anger she had been denying all these years.

It was a quarter to one when she got home. It seemed to her

that the house was taking on a certain comfortable aura. The antique marble table and Serapi rug in the foyer made the faded paint seem insignificant. The kitchen counters were cheerful now with canisters; the oval wrought-iron table and matching soda-parlor chairs fitted exactly into the area beneath the windows and made it easy to ignore the worn spots on the aging tiles.

Quickly she fixed a sandwich and tea while phoning for a plane reservation. She was fully seven minutes on "hold" listening to a particularly poor selection of canned music before a clerk finally came on the line. She arranged for a four-forty flight to Albany and a rental car.

She decided to use the few hours before flight time to begin going through her father's effects.

Slowly she pulled aside the flaps of the first box and found herself staring down at the dust-covered picture of a tall, laughing man with a child on one shoulder. The child's eyes were wide with delight; her mouth half-open and smiling. Her palms were facing each other as though she might have just clapped them. Both man and child were in swimsuits by the water's edge. A wave was crashing behind them. It was late afternoon. Their shadows on the sand were elongated.

Daddy's little girl, Pat thought bitterly. She had seen children on their fathers' shoulders, hanging on to their necks or even twining their fingers in their hair. Fear of falling was a basic instinct. But the child in this picture, the child she had been, clearly had trusted the man holding her, trusted him not to let her fall. She laid the picture on the floor and continued emptying the box.

When she had finished, the carpet was covered with memorabilia from the private office of Congressman Dean Adams. A formal portrait of her mother at the piano. She was beautiful, Pat thought—I resemble him more. There was a collage of snapshots of Pat as a baby and toddler that must have hung on his office wall; his appointment diary, dark green leather with his initials in gold; his silver desk set, now so terribly tarnished; the framed diploma from the University of Wisconsin, a B.A. in English with high honors; his law-school degree from the University of Michigan, proclaiming him an LL.B; a citation from the Episcopal Bishops' Conference for generous and unstinting work for minorities; a Man of the Year plaque from the Madison, Wisconsin, Rotary Club. He must have been fond of seascapes. There were several excellent old prints of sailing vessels, billowing over turbulent waters.

She opened the appointment book. He had been a doodler; almost every page contained swirls and geometric figures. So that's where I got the habit, Pat thought.

Her eyes kept returning to the picture of herself and her father. She looked so blissfully happy. Her father was looking up at her with so much love. His grip on her arm was so firm.

The telephone broke the spell. She scrambled to her feet, alarmed to realize that it was getting late, that she'd have to put all this away and pack a few things in a bag.

"Pat."

It was Sam.

"Hi." She bit her lip.

"Pat, I'm on the run as usual. I've got a committee meeting in five minutes. There's a dinner at the White House Friday night honoring the new Canadian Prime Minister. Would you like to go with me? I'll have to phone your name in to the White House."

"The White House! That would be wonderful. I'd love to go." She swallowed fiercely, trying to suppress the quiver in her voice.

Sam's tone changed. "Pat, is anything wrong? You sound upset. You're not crying, are you?"

At last she could control the tremor in her voice. "Oh, no. Not at all. I guess I'm just getting a cold."

7

At the Albany airport, Pat picked up her rental car, pored over a road map with the Hertz attendant and worked out the best route to Apple Junction, twenty-seven miles away.

"Better get going, Miss," the clerk warned. "We're supposed to have a foot of snow tonight."

"Can you suggest the best place to stay?"

"If you want to be right in town, the Apple Motel is it." He smirked. "But it's nothing fancy like you'd find in the *Big* Apple. Don't worry about phoning ahead for a reservation."

Pat picked up the car key and her bag. It didn't sound promising, but she thanked the clerk all the same.

The first flakes were falling as she pulled into the driveway of the dreary building with the flickering neon sign APPLE MOTEL. As the Hertz attendant had predicted, the VACANCY sign was on.

The clerk in the tiny, cluttered office was in his seventies. Wire-framed glasses drooped on his narrow nose. Deep lines creased his cheeks. Clumps of gray-white hair sprouted from his skull. His eyes, rheumy and faded, brightened in surprise when Pat pushed open the door.

"Do you have a single for the next night or two?" she asked.

His smile revealed a worn, tobacco-stained dental plate. "Long as you want, Miss; you can have a single, a double, even the Presidential suite." A braying laugh followed.

Pat smiled politely and reached for the registration card. Deliberately she omitted filling the blank spot after PLACE OF BUSINESS. She wanted to have as much chance as possible to look around for herself before the reason for her presence here became known.

The clerk studied the card, his curiosity disappointed. "I'll put you in the first unit," he said. "That way you'll be near the office here in case the snow gets real heavy. We have a kind of dinette." He gestured toward three small tables against the rear wall. "Always have juice and coffee and toast to get you started in the morning." He looked at her shrewdly. "What brings you here, anyway?"

"Business," Pat said, then added quickly, "I haven't had dinner yet. I'll just drop my bag in my room and maybe you can tell me where I can find a restaurant."

He squinted at the clock. "You better hurry. The Lamplighter closes at nine and it's near eight now. Just go out the drive, turn left and go two blocks, then turn left again on Main. It's on the right. Can't miss it. Here's your key." He consulted the registration card. "Miss Traymore," he concluded, "I'm Travis Blodgett. I own the place." Pride and apology blended in his voice. A slight wheeze suggested emphysema.

Except for a dimly lit movie marquee, the Lamplighter was the only establishment open in the two blocks embracing the business district of Apple Junction. A greasy, hand-printed menu posted on the front door announced the day's special, sauerbraten and red cabbage for $3.95. Faded linoleum lay underfoot just inside. Most of the checkered cloths on the dozen or so tables were partially covered with unpressed napkins—probably, she guessed, to hide stains caused by earlier diners. An elderly couple were munching on dark-looking meat from overfilled plates. But she had to admit the smell was tantalizing, and she realized she was very hungry.

The sole waitress was a woman in her mid-fifties. Under a

fairly clean apron, a thick orange sweater and shapeless slacks mercilessly revealed layers of bulging flesh. But her smile was quick and pleasant. "You alone?"

"Yes."

The waitress looked uncertainly around, then led Pat to a table near the window. "That way you can look out and enjoy the view."

Pat felt her lips twitch. The view! A rented car on a dingy street! Then she was ashamed of herself. That was exactly the reaction she would expect of Luther Pelham.

"Would you care for a drink? We have beer or wine. And I guess I'd better take your order. It's getting late."

Pat requested wine and asked for a menu.

"Oh, don't bother with a menu," the waitress urged. "Try the sauerbraten. It's really good."

Pat glanced across the room. Obviously that was what the old couple were eating. "If you'll give me about half as much . . ."

The waitress smiled, revealing large, even white teeth.

"Oh, sure." She lowered her voice. "I always fill those two up. They can only afford to eat out once a week, so I like to get a decent meal into them."

The wine was a New York State red jug wine, but it was pleasant. A few minutes later the waitress came out of the kitchen carrying a plate of steaming food and a basket of homemade biscuits.

The food was delicious. The meat had been marinated in wines and herbs; the gravy was rich and tangy; the cabbage pungent; the butter melted into the still-warm biscuits.

My God, if I ate like this every night, I'd be the size of a house, Pat thought. But she felt her spirits begin to lift.

When Pat had finished, the waitress took her plate and came over with the coffeepot. "I've been looking and looking at you," the woman said. "Don't I know you? Haven't I seen you on television?"

Pat nodded. So much for poking around on my own, she thought.

"Sure," the waitress continued. "You're Patricia Traymore. I saw you on TV when I visited my cousin in Boston. *I know why you're here!* You're doing a program on Abby Foster—I mean Senator Jennings."

"You knew her?" Pat asked quickly.

"Knew her! I should say I did. Why don't I just have coffee with you?" It was a rhetorical question. Reaching over to the next table for an empty cup, she sank heavily into the chair opposite Pat. "My husband does the cooking; he can take care of closing up. It was pretty quiet tonight, but my feet hurt anyhow. All this standing . . ."

Pat made appropriate sympathetic sounds.

"Abigail Jennings, huh. Ab-by-gail Jennings," the waitress mused. "You gonna put folks from Apple Junction in the program?"

"I'm not sure," Pat said honestly. "Did you know the Senator well?"

"Not well, exactly. We were in the same class at school. But Abby was always so quiet; you could never figure what she was thinking. Girls usually tell each other everything and have best friends and run in cliques. Not Abby. I can't remember her having even one close friend."

"What did the other girls think about her?" Pat asked.

"Well, you know how it is. When someone is as pretty as Abby was, the other kids are kind of jealous. Then everybody got the feeling she thought she was too good for the rest of us, so that didn't make her any too popular either."

Pat considered her for a moment. "Did *you* feel that way about her, Mrs. . . . ?"

"Stubbins. Ethel Stubbins. In a way I guess I did, but I kind of understood. Abby just wanted to grow up and get out of here. The debating club was the only activity she joined in school. She didn't even dress like the rest of us. When everyone else was going around in sloppy joe sweaters and penny loafers, she wore a starched blouse and heels to school. Her mother was the cook at the Saunders house. I think that bothered Abby a lot."

"I understood her mother was the housekeeper," Pat said.

"The *cook,*" Ethel repeated emphatically. "She and Abby had a little apartment off the kitchen. My mother used to go to the Saunders place every week to clean, so I know."

It was a fine distinction: saying your mother had been the housekeeper rather than the cook. Pat shrugged mentally. What could be more harmless than Senator Jennings' upgrading her mother's job a notch? She debated. Sometimes taking notes or using a recorder had the immediate effect of causing an interviewee to freeze. She decided to take the chance.

"Do you mind if I record you?" she asked.

"Not at all. Should I talk louder?"

"No, you're fine." Pat pulled out her recorder and placed it on the table between them. "Just talk about Abigail as you remember her. You say it bothered her that her mother was a cook?" She had a mental image of how Sam would react to that question. He would consider it unnecessary prying.

Ethel leaned her heavy elbows on the table. "Did it ever! Mama used to tell me how nervy Abby was. If anyone was coming down the street, she used to walk up the path to the front steps just as though she owned the place and then when no one was looking, she'd scoot around to the back. Her mother used to holler at her, but it didn't do any good."

"Ethel. It's nine o'clock."

Pat looked up. A squat man with pale hazel eyes set in a cheerful round face was standing at the table, untying a long white apron. His eyes lingered on the recorder.

Ethel explained what was happening and introduced Pat. "This is my husband, Ernie."

Clearly Ernie was intrigued by the prospect of contributing to the interview. "Tell how Mrs. Saunders caught Abby coming in the front door and told her to know her place," he suggested. "Remember, she made her walk back to the sidewalk and come up the driveway and go around to the back door."

"Oh, yeah," Ethel said. "That was lousy, wasn't it? Mama said she felt sorry for Abby until she saw the look on her face. Enough to freeze your blood, Mama said."

Pat tried to imagine a young Abigail forced to walk to the servants' entrance to show that she "knew her place." Again she had the feeling of intruding on the Senator's privacy. She wouldn't pursue that topic. Refusing Ernie's offer of more wine, she suggested, "Abby—I mean the Senator—must have been a very good student to get a scholarship to Radcliffe. Was she at the head of her class?"

"Oh, she was terrific in English and history and languages," Ethel said, "but a real birdbrain in math and science. She hardly got by in them."

"Sounds like me," Pat smiled. "Let's talk about the beauty contest."

Ethel laughed heartily. "There were four finalists for Miss Apple Junction. Yours truly was one of them. Believe it or not, I weighed one hundred eighteen pounds then, and I was darn cute."

Pat waited for the inevitable. Ernie did not disappoint her. "You're still darn cute, honey."

"Abby won hands down," Ethel continued. "Then she got into the contest for Miss New York State. You could have knocked everyone over with a feather when she won *that!* You know how it is. Sure, we knew she was beautiful, but we were all so used to seeing her. Was this town ever excited!"

Ethel chuckled. "I must say Abby kept this town supplied with gossip all that summer. The big social event around here was the country-club dance in August. All the rich kids from miles around went to it. None of *us,* of course. But that year Abby Foster was there. From what I hear, she looked like an angel in a white marquisette gown edged with layers of black Chantilly lace. And guess who took her? Jeremy Saunders! Just home after graduating from Yale. And he was practically engaged to Evelyn Clinton! He and Abby held hands all night and he kept kissing her when they danced.

"The next day the whole town was buzzing. Mama said Mrs. Saunders must have been spitting nails; her only son falling for the cook's daughter. And then"—Ethel shrugged—"it just ended. Abby resigned her Miss New York State crown and took off for college. Said she knew she'd never become Miss America, that she couldn't sing or dance or act for the talent part and there was no way she wanted to parade around in Atlantic City and come back a loser. A lot of people had chipped in for a wardrobe for her to wear to the Miss America contest. They felt pretty bad."

"Remember Toby threw a punch at a couple of guys who said Abby let the folks around here down?" Ernie prompted Ethel.

"Toby Gorgone?" Pat asked quickly.

"The same," Ernie said. "He was always nuts about Abby. You know how kids talk in locker rooms. If any guy said anything fresh about Abby in front of Toby, he was sorry fast."

"He works for her now," Pat said.

"No kidding?" Ernie shook his head. "Say hello to him for me. Ask him if he's still losing money on the horses."

It was eleven o'clock before Pat got back to the Apple Motel, and by then Unit One was chilly. She quickly unpacked—there was no closet, only a hook on the door—undressed, showered, brushed her hair and, propping up the narrow pillows, got into bed with her notebook. As usual, her leg was throbbing—a faint ache that began in her hip and shot down her calf.

She glanced over the notes she had taken during the evening. According to Ethel, Mrs. Foster had left the Saunders home right after the country-club dance and gone to work as a cook in the county hospital. Nobody ever did know whether she'd quit or been fired. But the new job must have been hard on her. She was a big woman—"You think *I'm* heavy," Ethel had said, "you should've seen Francey Foster." Francey had died a long time ago and no one had seen Abigail after that. Indeed, few had seen her for years before that.

Ethel had waxed eloquent on the subject of Jeremy Saunders—"Abigail was lucky she didn't marry him. He never amounted to a hill of beans. Lucky for him he had the family money: otherwise he'd probably have starved. They say his father tied up everything in trusts, even made Evelyn the executor of his will. Jeremy was a big disappointment to him. He always looked like a diplomat or an English lord and he's just a bag of wind."

Ethel had insinuated that Jeremy was a drinker, but suggested that Pat call him: "He'd probably love company. Evelyn spends most of her time with their married daughter in Westchester."

Pat turned out the light. Tomorrow morning she would try to visit the retired principal who'd asked Abigail to give Eleanor Brown a job, and she'd attempt to make an appointment with Jeremy Saunders.

It snowed during the night, some four or five inches, but the plows and sanders had already been through by the time Pat had coffee with the proprietor of the Apple Motel.

Driving around Apple Junction was a depressing experience. The town was a particularly shabby and unattractive one. Half the stores were closed and had fallen into disrepair. A single strand of Christmas lights dangled across Main Street. On the side streets, houses were jammed together, their paint peeling. Most of the cars parked in the street were old. There seemed to be no new building of any kind, residential or business. There were few people out; a sense of emptiness pervaded the atmosphere. Did most of the young people flee like

Abigail as soon as they were grown? she wondered. Who could blame them?

She saw a sign reading THE APPLE JUNCTION WEEKLY and on impulse parked and went inside. There were two people working, a young woman who seemed to be taking a want ad over the phone and a sixtyish man who was making an enormous clatter on a manual typewriter. The latter, it developed, was Edwin Shepherd, the editor-owner of the paper and perfectly happy to talk to Pat.

He could add very little to what she already knew about Abigail. However, he willingly went to the files to hunt up issues that might refer to the two contests, local and state, that Abigail had won.

In her research Pat had already found the picture of Abigail in her Miss New York State sash and crown. But the full-length shot of Abigail with the banner MISS APPLE JUNCTION was new and unsettling. Abigail was standing on a platform at the county fair, the three other finalists around her. The crown on her head was clearly papier-mâché. The other girls had pleased, fluttery smiles—Pat realized that the girl on the end was the youthful Ethel Stubbins—but Abigail's smile was cold, almost cynical. She seemed totally out of place.

"There's a shot of her with her maw inside," Shepherd volunteered, and turned the page.

Pat gasped. Could Abigail Jennings, delicate-featured and bone-slender, possibly be the offspring of this squat, obese woman? The caption read: PROUD MOTHER GREETS APPLE JUNCTION BEAUTY QUEEN.

"Why not take those issues?" Edwin Shepherd asked. "I've got more copies. Just remember to give us credit if you use anything on your program."

It would be awkward to refuse the offer, Pat realized. I can just see using *that* picture, she thought as she thanked the editor and quickly left.

A half-mile down Main Street, the town changed dramatically. The roads became wider, the homes stately, the grounds large and well tended.

The Saunders house was pale yellow with black shutters. It was on a corner, and a long driveway curved to the porch steps. Graceful pillars reminded Pat of the architecture of Mount Vernon. Trees lined the driveway. A small sign directed deliveries to the service entrance in the rear.

She parked and went up the steps, noticing that on closer inspection the paint was beginning to chip and the aluminum storm windows were corroded. She pushed the button and from somewhere far inside could hear the faint sound of chimes. A thin woman with graying hair wearing a half-apron over a dark dress answered the door. "Mr. Saunders is expecting you. He's in the library."

Jeremy Saunders, wearing a maroon velvet jacket, was settled in a high-backed wing chair by the fire. His legs were crossed, and fine dark blue silk hose showed below the cuffs of his midnight-blue trousers. He had exceptionally even features and handsome wavy white hair. A thickened waistline and puffy eyes alone betrayed a predilection for drink.

He stood up and steadied himself against the arm of the chair. "Miss Traymore!" His voice was so pointedly well bred as to suggest classes in elocution. "You didn't tell me on the phone that you were *the* Patricia Traymore."

"Whatever that means," Pat said, smiling.

"Don't be modest. You're the young lady who's doing a program on Abigail." He waved her to the chair opposite his. "You *will* have a Bloody Mary?"

"Thank you." The pitcher was already half-empty.

The maid took her coat.

"Thank you, Anna. That will be all for now. Perhaps a little later Miss Traymore will join me in a light lunch." Jeremy Saunders' tone became even more fatuous when he spoke to the servant, who silently left the room. "You can close the door if you will, Anna!" he called. "Thank you, my dear."

Saunders waited until the latch clicked, then sighed. "Good help is impossible to find these days. Not as it was when Francey Foster was presiding over the kitchen and Abby was serving the table." He seemed to relish the thought.

Pat did not reply. There was a gossipy kind of cruelty about the man. She sat down, accepted the drink and waited. He raised one eyebrow. "Don't you have a tape recorder?"

"Yes, I do. But if you prefer I won't use it."

"Not at all. I prefer that every word I say be immortalized. Perhaps someday there'll be an Abby Foster—forgive me, a *Senator Abigail Jennings*—Library. People will be able to push a button and hear me tell of her rather chaotic coming of age."

Silently Pat reached into her shoulder bag and pulled out the recorder and her notebook. She was suddenly quite sure that what she was about to hear would be unusable.

"You've followed the Senator's career," she suggested.

"Breathlessly! I have the utmost admiration for Abby. From the time she was seventeen and began offering to help her mother with household duties, she had won my utmost respect. She's ingenious."

"Is it ingenious to help your mother?" Pat asked quietly.

"Of course not. If you *want* to *help* your mother. On the other hand, if you offer to serve only because the handsome young scion of the Saunders family is home from Yale, it does color the picture, doesn't it?"

"Meaning you?" Pat smiled reluctantly. Jeremy Saunders had a certain sardonic, self-deprecating quality that was not unattractive.

"You've guessed it. I see pictures of her from time to time, but you can never trust pictures, can you? Abby always photographed very well. How does she look in person?"

"She's absolutely beautiful," Pat said.

Saunders seemed disappointed. He'd love to hear that the Senator needs a face lift, Pat reflected. Somehow she could not believe that even as a very young girl Abigail would have been impressed by Jeremy.

"How about Toby Gorgone?" Saunders asked. "Is he still playing his chosen role as bodyguard and slave to Abby?"

"Toby works for the Senator," Pat replied. "He's obviously devoted to her, and she seems to count on him very much." *Bodyguard and slave,* she thought. It was a good way to describe Toby's relationship to Abigail Jennings.

"I suppose they're still pulling each other's chestnuts out of the fire."

"What do you mean by that?"

Jeremy raised his hand in a gesture of dismissal. "Nothing, really. He probably told you how he saved Abby from the jaws of the attack dog our eccentric neighbor kept."

"Yes, he did."

"And did he tell you that Abigail was his alibi the night he may have gone joyriding in a stolen car?"

"No, he didn't, but joyriding doesn't seem to be a very serious offense."

"It is when the police car chasing the 'borrowed' vehicle goes out of control and mows down a young mother and her two children. Someone who looked like him had been observed hanging around the car. But Abigail swore that she had been tutoring Toby in English, right here in this house. It was Abigail's word against an uncertain witness. No charge was brought and the joyrider was never caught. Many people found the possible involvement of Toby Gorgone quite credible. He's always been obsessed with machinery, and that was a new sports car. It makes sense he'd want to give it a spin."

"Then you're suggesting the Senator may have lied for him?"

"I'm suggesting nothing. However, people around here have long memories, and Abigail's fervent deposition—taken under oath, of course—is a matter of record. Actually, nothing much could have happened to Toby even if he had been in the car.

He was still a juvenile, under sixteen. Abigail, however, was eighteen and if she had perjured herself would have been criminally culpable. Oh, well, Toby may very well have spent that evening diligently drilling on participles. Has his grammar improved?"

"It sounded all right to me."

"You couldn't have spoken to him very long. Now, fill me in on Abigail. The endless fascination she evokes in men. With whom is she involved now?"

"She's not involved with anyone," Pat said. "From what she tells me, her husband was the great love of her life."

"Perhaps." Jeremy Saunders finished the last of his drink. "And when you consider that she had absolutely no background—a father who drank himself to death when she was six, a mother content among the pots and pans . . ."

Pat decided to try another tack to get some sort of usable material. "Tell me about this house," she suggested. "After all, Abigail grew up here. Was it built by your family?"

Jeremy Saunders was clearly proud of both house and family. For the next hour, pausing only to refill his glass and then to mix a new pitcher of drinks, he traced the history of the Saunderses from "not quite the *Mayflower*—a Saunders was supposed to be on that historic voyage, but fell ill and did not arrive till two years later"—to the present. "And so," he concluded, "I sadly relate that I am the last to bear the Saunders name." He smiled. "You are a most appreciative listener, my dear. I hope I haven't been too long-winded in my recitation."

Pat returned the smile. "No, indeed. My mother's family were early settlers and I'm very proud of them."

"You must let me hear about *your* family," Jeremy said gallantly. "You will stay for lunch."

"I'd be delighted."

"I prefer having a tray right here. So much cozier than the dining room. Would that do?"

And so much nearer the bar, Pat thought. She hoped she could soon steer the subject back to Abigail.

Her opportunity came as she made a pretense of sipping the wine Jeremy insisted they have with the indifferently served chicken salad.

"It helps to wash it down, my dear," he told her. "I'm afraid when my wife is away, Anna doesn't put her best foot forward. Not like Abby's mother. Francey Foster took pride in everything she prepared. The breads, the cakes, the soufflés . . . Does Abby cook?"

"I don't know," Pat said. Her voice became confidential. "Mr. Saunders, I can't help feeling that you are angry at Senator Jennings. Am I wrong? I had the impression that at one time you two cared a great deal about each other."

"Angry at her? Angry?" His voice was thick, his words slurred. "Wouldn't *you* be angry at someone who set out to make a fool of you—and succeeded magnificently?"

It was happening now—the moment that came in so many of her interviews when people let down their guard and began to reveal themselves.

She studied Jeremy Saunders. This sleekly overfed, drunken man in his ridiculous formal getup was mulling a distasteful memory. There was pain as well as anger in the guileless eyes, the too soft mouth, the weak, puffy chin.

"Abigail," he said, his tone calmer, "United States Senator from Virginia." He bowed elaborately. "My dear Patricia Traymore, you have the distinction of addressing her former fiancé."

Pat tried unsuccessfully to hide her surprise. "You were *engaged* to Abigail?"

"That last summer she was here. Very briefly, of course. Just long enough for her overall scheme. She'd won the state beauty contest but was smart enough to know she wouldn't go any further in Atlantic City. She'd tried to get a scholarship to Radcliffe, but her math and science marks weren't scholarship level. Of course, Abby had no intention of day-hopping to the local college. It was a terrible dilemma for her, and I still wonder if Toby didn't have a hand in planning the solution.

"I had just been graduated from Yale and was due to go into my father's business—a prospect which did not intrigue me; I was about to become engaged to the daughter of my father's best friend—a prospect which did not excite me. And here was Abigail right in my own home, telling me what I could become with her at my side, slipping into my bed in the dark of the night, while poor, tired Francey Foster snored away in their service apartment. The upshot was that I bought Abigail a beautiful gown, escorted her to the country-club dance and proposed to her.

"When we came home we woke our parents to announce the joyous news. Can you imagine the scene? My mother, who delighted in ordering Abigail to use the back door, watching all her plans for her only son dissolving. Twenty-four hours later, Abigail left town with a certified check from my father for ten thousand dollars and her bags filled with the wardrobe the town people had donated. She was already accepted by Radcliffe, you see. She only lacked the money to attend that splendid institution.

"I followed her there. She was quite explicit in letting me know that everything my father was saying about her was accurate. My father to his dying day never let me forget what a fool I'd made of myself. In thirty-five years of married life, whenever Evelyn hears Abigail's name she becomes quite shrewish. As for my mother, the only satisfaction she could get was to order Francey Foster out of the house—and that was cutting off her nose to spite her face. We never had a decent cook after that."

When Pat tiptoed out of the room, Jeremy Saunders was asleep, his head bobbing on his chest.

It was nearly a quarter to two. The day was clouding up again, as though more snow might be in the offing. As she drove toward her appointment with Margaret Langley, the retired school principal, she wondered how accurate Jeremy Saunders' version of Abigail Foster Jennings' behavior as a young woman had been. Manipulator? Schemer? Liar?

Whatever, it didn't jibe with the reputation for absolute integrity that was the cornerstone of Senator Abigail Jennings' public career.

8

At a quarter of two, Margaret Langley took the unusual step of making a fresh pot of coffee, knowing full well that the burning discomfort of gastritis might plague her later.

As always when she was upset, she walked into her study, seeking comfort in the velvety green leaves of the plants hanging by the picture window. She'd been in the midst of rereading the Shakespeare sonnets with her after-breakfast coffee when Patricia Traymore phoned asking permission to visit.

Margaret shook her head nervously. She was a slightly stooped woman of seventy-three. Her gray hair was finger-waved around her head, with a small bun at the nape of her neck. Her long, rather horsey face was saved from homeliness by an expression of good-humored wisdom. On her blouse she wore the pin the school had given her when she retired—a gold laurel wreath entwined around the number 45 to signify the years she'd served as teacher and principal.

At ten minutes past two she was beginning to hope that Patricia Traymore had changed her mind about stopping in when she saw a small car coming slowly down the road. The driver paused at the mailbox, probably checking the house number. Reluctantly Margaret went to the front door.

Pat apologized for being late. "I took a wrong turn somewhere," she said, gladly accepting the offer of coffee.

Margaret felt her anxiety begin to subside. There was something very thoughtful about this young woman, the way she so carefully scraped her boots before stepping onto the polished floor. She was so pretty, with that auburn hair and those rich brown eyes. Somehow Margaret had expected her to be terribly aggressive. When she explained about Eleanor, maybe Patricia Traymore would listen. As she poured the coffee she said as much.

"You see," Margaret began, and to her own ears her voice sounded high-pitched and nervous, "the problem at the time the money disappeared in Washington was that everyone talked about Eleanor as though she were a hardened thief. Miss Traymore, did you ever hear the value of the object she supposedly stole when she was a high school senior?"

"No, I don't think so," Pat answered.

"*Six dollars.* Her life was ruined because of a six-dollar bottle of perfume! Miss Traymore, haven't you ever started to walk out of a store and realized you were holding something you meant to buy?"

"A few times," Pat agreed. "But surely no one is convicted of shoplifting for being absentminded about a six-dollar item."

"You are if there's been a wave of shoplifting in town. The shopkeepers were up in arms, and the district attorney had vowed to make an example of the next person caught."

"And Eleanor was the next person?"

"Yes." Fine beads of perspiration accentuated the lines in Margaret's forehead. Alarmed, Pat noticed that her complexion was becoming a sickly gray.

"Miss Langley, don't you feel well? May I get you a glass of water?"

The older woman shook her head. "No, it will pass. Just give me a minute." They sat silently as the color began to return to Miss Langley's face. "That's better. I guess just talking about Eleanor upsets me. You see, Miss Traymore, the judge made an example of Eleanor; sent her to the juvenile home for thirty days. After that she was changed. Different. Some people can't take that kind of humiliation. You see, nobody believed her except me. I know young people. She wasn't daring. She was the kind who never chewed gum in class or talked when the teacher was out of the room or cheated on a test. She wasn't only good. She was *timid.*"

Margaret Langley was holding something back. Pat could sense it. She leaned forward, her voice gentle. "Miss Langley, there's a little more to the story than you're telling."

The woman's lip quivered. "Eleanor didn't have enough money to pay for the perfume. She explained that she was going to ask them to wrap it and put it aside. She was going to a birthday party that night. The judge didn't believe her."

Neither do I, Pat thought. She was saddened she couldn't accept the explanation that Margaret Langley so passionately believed. She watched as the former principal put her hand on her throat as though to calm a rapid pulsebeat. "That sweet girl came here so many evenings," Margaret Langley continued sadly, "because she knew I was the one person who absolutely believed her. When she was graduated from our school, I wrote and asked Abigail if she could find a job for her in her office."

"Isn't it true that the Senator gave Eleanor that chance, trusted her, and then Eleanor stole campaign funds?" Pat asked.

Margaret's face became very tired. The tone of her voice flattened. "I was on a year's sabbatical when all that happened. I was traveling in Europe. By the time I got home, it was all over. Eleanor had been convicted and sent to prison and had a nervous breakdown. She was in the psychiatric ward of the prison hospital. I wrote to her regularly, but she never answered. Then, from what I understand, she was paroled for reasons of poor health, but only on condition she attend a clinic as an outpatient twice a week. One day she just disappeared. That was nine years ago."

"And you never heard from her again?"

"I . . . No . . . uh . . ." Margaret stood up. "I'm sorry—

wouldn't you like a little more coffee? There's plenty in the pot. I'm going to have some. I shouldn't, but I will." With an attempt at a smile Margaret walked into the kitchen. Pat snapped off the recorder. She *has* heard from Eleanor, she thought, and can't bring herself to lie. When Miss Langley returned, Pat asked softly, "What do you know about Eleanor now?"

Margaret Langley set down the coffeepot on the table and walked over to the window. Would she hurt Eleanor by trusting Pat Traymore? Would she in effect point out a trail that might lead to Eleanor?

A lone sparrow fluttered past the window and settled forlornly on the icy branch of an elm tree near the driveway. Margaret made up her mind. She would trust Patricia Traymore, show her the letters, tell her what she believed. She turned and met Pat's gaze and saw the concern in her eyes. "I want to show you something," she said abruptly.

When Margaret Langley returned to the room, she held in each hand a folded sheet of notepaper. "I've heard from Eleanor twice," she said. "This letter"—she extended her right hand—"was written the very day of the supposed theft. Read it, Miss Traymore; just read it."

The cream stationery was deeply creased as though it had been handled many times. Pat glanced at the date. The letter was eleven years old. Pat skimmed the contents quickly. Eleanor hoped that Miss Langley was enjoying her year in Europe; Eleanor had received a promotion and loved her job. She was taking painting classes at George Washington University and they were going very well. She had just returned from an afternoon in Baltimore. She'd had an assignment to sketch a water scene and decided on Chesapeake Bay.

Miss Langley had underlined one paragraph. It read:

I almost didn't get there. I had to run an errand for Senator Jennings. She'd left her diamond ring in the campaign of-

fice and thought it had been locked in the safe for her. But it wasn't there, and I just made my bus.

This was proof? Pat thought. She looked up, and her eyes met Margaret Langley's hopeful gaze. "Don't you see?" Margaret said. "Eleanor wrote to me the very night of the supposed theft. Why would she make up that story?"

Pat could find no way to soften what she had to say. "She could have been setting up an alibi for herself."

"If you're trying to give yourself an alibi, you don't write to someone who may not get the letter for months," she said spiritedly. Then she sighed. "Well, I tried. I just hope you'll have the goodness not to rake up that misery again. Eleanor apparently is trying to make some sort of life for herself and deserves to be let alone."

Pat looked at the other letter Margaret was holding. "She wrote you after she disappeared?"

"Yes. Six years ago this came."

Pat took the letter. The typeface was worn, the paper cheap. The note read:

Dear Miss Langley. Please understand that it is better if I have no contact with anyone from the past. If I am found, I will have to go back to prison. I swear to you I never touched that money. I have been very ill but am trying to rebuild my life. Some days are good. I can almost believe it is possible to become well again. Other times I am so frightened, so afraid that someone will recognize me. I think of you often. I love and miss you.

Eleanor's signature was wavering, the letters uneven—a stark contrast to the firm and graceful penmanship of the earlier letter.

It took all Pat's persuasive powers to coax Margaret Langley to let her take the letters. "We are planning to include the case in this program," she said, "but even if Eleanor is recognized and someone turns her in, perhaps we can have her parole reinstated. Then she wouldn't have to hide for the rest of her life."

"I would love to see her again," Margaret whispered. Now tears brightened her eyes. "She's the nearest thing I ever had to a child of my own. Wait—let me show you her picture."

On the bottom shelf of the bookcase were stacks of yearbooks. "I have one for every year I was in school," she explained. "But I keep Eleanor's on top." She riffled through the pages. "She graduated seventeen years ago. Isn't she sweet-looking?"

The girl in the photo had fine, mousy hair; soft, innocent eyes. The caption read:

> Eleanor Brown—Hobby: painting. Ambition: secretary. Activities: choir. Sport: roller skating. Prediction: right-hand gal for executive, marry young, two kids. Favorite thing: Evening in Paris perfume.

"My God," Pat said, "how cruel."

"Exactly. That's why I wanted her to leave here."

Pat shook her head, and her glance caught the other yearbooks. "Wait a minute," she said, "by any chance do you have the book Senator Jennings is in?"

"Of course. Let's see—that would be over here somewhere."

The second book Margaret Langley checked was the right one. In this photo Abigail's hair was in a pageboy on her shoulders. Her lips were parted slightly as though she had obediently followed the photographer's direction to smile. Her eyes, wide and thick-lashed, were calm and inscrutable. The caption read:

> Abigail Foster ("Abby")—Hobby: attending state legislature. Ambition: politics. Activities: debating. Prediction:

will become state assemblywoman from Apple Junction. Favorite thing: any book in the library.

"State assemblywoman," Pat exclaimed; "that's great!"

A half-hour later she left, the Senator's yearbook under her arm. As she got into the car, she decided that she'd send a camera crew to get some background footage of the town, including Main Street, the Saunders home, the high school and the highway with the bus to Albany. Under the footage she'd have Senator Jennings speak briefly about growing up there and her early interest in politics. They'd close that segment with the picture of the Senator as Miss New York State, then her yearbook picture and her explanation that going on to Radcliffe instead of Atlantic City was the most important decision of her life.

With the unfamiliar and disquieting feeling that somehow she was glossing over the full story, Pat drove around town for an hour and marked locations for the camera crew. Then she checked out of the Apple Motel, drove to Albany, turned in the rental car and with relief got on the plane back to Washington.

9

Washington is beautiful, Pat thought, from any view, at any hour. By night the spotlights on the Capitol and monuments seem to impart a sense of tranquil agelessness. She'd been gone from here only thirty hours, yet felt as though days had passed since she'd left. The plane landed with a slight bump and taxied smoothly across the field.

As she opened the door to her house, Pat heard the phone ringing and scrambled to answer it. It was Luther Pelham. He sounded edgy.

"Pat, I'm glad I've reached you. You never did let me know where you were staying in Apple Junction. When I finally tracked you down, you had checked out."

"I'm sorry. I should have phoned you this morning."

"Abigail is making a major speech before the final vote on the budget tomorrow. She suggested you spend the entire day at her office. She gets in at six-thirty."

"I'll be there."

"How did you do in the hometown?"

"Interesting. We can get some sympathetic footage that won't raise the Senator's hackles."

"I'd like to hear about it. I've just finished dinner at the Jockey Club and can be at your place in ten minutes." The phone clicked in her ear.

She had barely time to change into slacks and a sweater before he arrived. The library was cluttered with the Senator's material. Pat brought him back to the living room and offered him a drink. When she returned with it, he was studying the candelabrum on the mantel. "Beautiful example of Sheffield," he told her. "Everything in the room is beautiful."

In Boston, she had had a studio apartment similar to those of other young professionals. It had not occurred to her that the costly furnishings and accessories in this house might arouse comment.

She tried to sound casual. "My folks are planning to move into a condominium soon. We have an attic full of family stuff and Mother told me it's now or never if I want it."

Luther settled on the couch and reached for the glass she placed in front of him. "All I know is that at your age I was living at the Y." He patted the cushion beside him. "Sit here and tell me all about Our Town."

Oh, no, she thought. There'll be no passes tonight, Luther Pelham. Ignoring the suggestion, she sat on the chair across the table from the couch and proceeded to give Luther an accounting of what she had learned in Apple Junction. It was not edifying.

"Abigail may have been the prettiest girl in those parts," she concluded, "but she certainly wasn't the most popular. I can understand now why she's nervous about stirring things up there. Jeremy Saunders will bad-mouth her till the day he dies. She's right to be afraid that calling attention to her being Miss New York State will get the old-timers again talking about how they contributed their two bucks to dress her up for Atlantic City and then she bugged out. Miss Apple Junction! Here, let me show you the picture."

Luther whistled when he saw it. "Hard to believe that blimp could be Abigail's mother." He thought better of the remark. "All right. She has a valid reason for wanting to forget Apple Junction and everyone in it. I thought you told me you could salvage some human-interest stuff."

"We'll cut it to the bone. Background shots of the town, the school, the house where she grew up; then interview the school principal, Margaret Langley, about how Abigail used to go to Albany to sit in on the legislature. Wind up with her school picture in the yearbook. It's not much, but it's something. The Senator's got to be made to understand she's not a UFO who landed on earth at age twenty-one. Anyhow, she agreed to cooperate in this documentary. We didn't give her creative control of it, I hope."

"Certainly not creative control, but some veto power. Don't forget, Pat. We're not just doing this *about* her; we're doing it *with* her, and her cooperation in letting us use her personal memorabilia is essential."

He stood up. "Since you insist on keeping that table between us . . ." He walked around it, and came over to her, put his hands on hers.

Quickly she jumped to her feet, but she was not fast enough. He pulled her against him. "You're a beautiful girl, Pat." He lifted her chin. His lips pressed down on hers. His tongue was insistent.

She tried to pull away, but his grip was viselike. Finally she managed to dig her elbows into his chest. "Let go of me."

He smiled. "Pat, why don't you show me the rest of the house?"

There was no mistaking his meaning. "It's pretty late," she said, "but on the way out you can poke your head into the library and dining room. I do sort of wish you'd wait until I've had a chance to get pictures hung and whatever."

"Where's your bedroom?"

"Upstairs."

"I'd like to see it."

"As a matter of fact, even when it's fixed up, I'd like you to think of the second floor of this house the way you had to think about the second floor of the Barbizon for Women in your salad days in New York: off-limits for gentlemen callers."

"I'd rather you didn't joke, Pat."

"I'd rather we treat this conversation as a joke. Otherwise I can put it another way. I don't sleep on the job nor do I sleep off the job. Not tonight. Not tomorrow. Not next year."

"I see."

She preceded him down the hall. In the foyer she handed him his coat.

As he put it on, he gave her an acid smile. "Sometimes people who have your kind of insomnia problem find it impossible to handle their responsibilities," he said. "They often discover they're happier at some backwoods station than in the big time. Does Apple Junction have a cable station? You might want to check it out, Pat."

Promptly at ten to six, Toby let himself in the back door of Abigail's house in McLean, Virginia. The large kitchen was filled with gourmet equipment. Abigail's idea of relaxing was to spend an evening cooking. Depending on her mood, she'd prepare six or seven different kinds of hors d'oeuvre or fish and meat casseroles. Other nights she'd make a half-dozen different sauces, or biscuits and cakes that would melt in your mouth. Then she'd pop everything into the freezer. But when she gave a party she never admitted that she'd prepared everything herself. She hated any association with the word "cook."

Abigail herself ate very little. Toby knew she was haunted by the memory of her mother, poor old Francey, that groaning tub of a woman whose trunklike legs settled into fat ankles and feet so wide it was hard to find shoes to fit them.

Toby had an apartment over the garage. Nearly every morning he'd come in and start the coffeepot and squeeze fresh juice. Later on, after he had Abby settled in her office, he'd have a big breakfast, and if she wasn't going to need him, he'd find a poker game.

Abigail came into the kitchen, still fastening a crescent-shaped gold pin on her lapel. She was wearing a purple suit that brought out the blueness of her eyes.

"You look great, Abby," he pronounced.

Her smile was quick and instantly gone. Whenever Abby had a big speech planned in the Senate she was like this—nervous as a cat before it, ready to be irritated at anything that went wrong. "Let's not waste time on coffee," she snapped.

"You've got plenty of time," Toby assured her. "I'll have you there by six-thirty. Drink your coffee. You know how crabby you get without it."

Later he left both cups in the sink, knowing Abby would be irritated if he took time to rinse them out.

The car was at the front entrance. When Abby went to get her coat and briefcase, he hurried outside and turned on the heater.

By six-ten they were on the parkway. Even for a day when she was making a speech, Abby was unusually tense. She'd gone to bed early the night before. He wondered if she'd been able to sleep.

He heard Abby sigh and snap her briefcase closed. "If I don't know what I'm going to say by now I might as well forget it," she commented. "If this damn budget doesn't get voted on soon, we'll still be in session on Christmas Day. But I *won't* let them ax any more of the entitlement programs."

Toby watched in the rearview mirror as she poured some coffee from a thermos. From her attitude he knew she was ready to talk.

"Did you get a good rest last night, Senator?" Once in a while, even when they were alone, he threw in the "Senator." It reminded her that no matter what, he knew his place.

"No, I didn't. I started thinking about this program. I was stupid to let myself get talked into it. It's going to backfire. I feel it in my bones."

Toby frowned. He had a healthy respect for Abby's bones. He still hadn't told Abby that Pat Traymore lived in the Dean

Adams house. She'd get real superstitious about that. This wasn't the time for her to lose her cool. Still, at some point she'd have to know. It was bound to come out. Toby was starting to get a lousy feeling about the program himself.

Pat had set the alarm for five o'clock. In her first television job, she'd discovered that being calm and collected kept her energy directed to the project at hand. She could still remember the burning chagrin of rushing breathlessly to interview the Governor of Connecticut and realizing she'd forgotten her carefully prepared questions.

After the Apple Motel, it had felt good to be in the wide, comfortable bed. But she'd slept badly, thinking about the scene with Luther Pelham. There were plenty of men in the television-news business who made the obligatory pass, and some of them were vengeful when rejected.

She dressed quickly, choosing a long-sleeved black wool dress with a suede vest. Once again it looked as though it would be one of the raw, windy days that had characterized this December.

Some of the storm windows were missing, and the panes on the north side of the house rattled as the wind shrieked against them.

She reached the landing of the staircase.

The shrieking sound intensified. But now it was a child screaming. *I ran down the stairs. I was so frightened, and I was crying. . . .*

A momentary dizziness made her grasp the banister. It's starting to happen, she thought fiercely. It *is* coming back.

En route to the Senator's office she felt distracted, out of sync. She could not rid herself of the overwhelming fear that was the result of the fleeting memory.

Why should she experience fear now?

How much had she seen of what happened that night?

* * *

Philip Buckley was waiting for her in the office when she arrived. In the gloom of the early morning, his attitude toward her seemed even more cautiously hostile than before. What is he afraid of? Pat wondered. You'd think I was a British spy in a Colonial camp. She told him that.

His small, cold smile was humorless. "If we thought you were a British spy, you wouldn't be anywhere near this Colonial camp," he commented. "The Senator will be here any minute. You might want to have a look at her schedule today. It will give you some idea of her workload."

He looked over her shoulder as she read the crammed pages. "Actually we'll have to put off at least three of these people. It's our thought that if you simply sit in the Senator's office and observe, you'll be able to decide what segments of her day you might want to include in the special. Obviously, if she has to discuss any confidential matters, you'll be excused. I've had a desk put in her private office for you. That way you won't be conspicuous."

"You think of everything," Pat told him. "Come on, how about a nice big smile? You'll have to have one for the camera when we start to shoot."

"I'm saving my smile for the time when I see the final edited version of the program." But he did look a little more relaxed.

Abigail came in a few minutes later. "I'm so glad you're here," she said to Pat. "When we couldn't reach you, I was afraid you were out of town."

"I got your message last night."

"Oh. Luther wasn't sure if you'd be available."

So that was the reason for the small talk, Pat decided. The Senator wanted to know where she'd been. She wasn't going to tell her. "I'm going to be your shadow until the program's completed," she said. "You'll probably get sick of having me around."

Abigail didn't look placated. "I must be able to reach you quickly. Luther told me you had some questions to go over with me. With my schedule the way it is, I don't often know about free time until just before it's available. Now let's get to work."

Pat followed her into the private office and tried to make herself inconspicuous. In a few moments the Senator was in deep discussion with Philip. One report that he placed on her desk was late. Sharply, she demanded to know why. "I should have had that last week."

"The figures weren't compiled."

"Why?"

"There simply wasn't time."

"If there isn't time during the day, there's time in the evening," Abigail snapped. "If anyone on my staff has become a clock-watcher, I want to know about it."

At seven o'clock the appointments started. Pat's respect for Abigail grew with each new person who came into the office. Lobbyists for the oil industry, for environmentalists, for veterans' benefits. Strategy sessions for presenting a new housing bill. A representative from the IRS to register specific objections to a proposed exemption for middle-income taxpayers. A delegation of senior citizens protesting the cutbacks in Social Security.

When the Senate convened, Pat accompanied Abigail and Philip to the chamber. Pat was not accredited to the press section behind the dais and took a seat in the visitors' gallery. She watched as the Senators entered from the cloakroom, greeting one another along the way, smiling, relaxed. They came in all sizes—tall, short; cadaver-slender, rotund; some with manes of hair, some carefully barbered, some bald. Four or five had the scholarly appearance of college professors.

There were two other women Senators, Claire Lawrence of Ohio and Phyllis Holzer of New Hampshire, who had been elected as an independent in a stunning upset.

Pat was especially interested in observing Claire Lawrence. The junior Senator from Ohio wore a three-piece navy knit suit that fitted comfortably over her size 14 figure. Her short salt-and-pepper hair was saved from severity by the natural wave that framed and softened her angular face. Pat noted the genuine pleasure with which this woman was greeted by her colleagues, the burst of laughter that followed her murmured greetings. Claire Lawrence was eminently quotable; her quick wit had a way of taking the rancor out of inflammatory issues without compromising the subject at hand.

In her notebok, Pat jotted *"humor"* and underlined the word. Abigail was rightly perceived to be serious, intense. A few carefully placed light moments should be included in the program.

A long, insistent bell was calling the Senate to order. The senior Senator from Arkansas was presiding in place of the ailing Vice President. After a few short pieces of business had been completed, the Presiding Officer recognized the senior Senator from Virginia.

Abigail stood up and without a trace of nervousness carefully put on blue-rimmed reading glasses. Her hair was pulled back into a simple chignon that enhanced the elegant lines of her profile and neck.

"Two of the best-known sentences in the Bible," she said, "are 'The Lord giveth and the Lord taketh away. Blessed be the name of the Lord.' In recent years our government, in an exaggerated and ill-considered manner, has given and given. And then it has taken away and taken away. But there are few to bless its name.

"Any responsible citizen would, I trust, agree that an overhaul of the entitlement programs has been necessary. But now it is time to examine what we have done. I maintain that the surgery was too radical, the cuts too drastic. I maintain that this is the time for restoration of many necessary programs. Entitlement by definition means 'to have a claim to.' Surely no one in this august chamber will dispute that every human being in this country has a rightful claim to shelter and food. . . ."

Abigail was an excellent speaker. Her address had been carefully prepared, carefully documented, sprinkled with enough specific anecdotes to keep the attention of even these professionals.

She spoke for an hour and ten minutes. The applause was sustained and genuine. When the Senate recessed, Pat saw that the Majority Leader hurried over to congratulate her.

Pat waited with Philip until the Senator finally broke away from her colleagues and the visitors who crowded around her. Together they started back to the office.

"It was good, wasn't it?" Abigail asked, but there was no hint of question in her voice.

"Excellent, Senator," Philip said promptly.

"Pat?" Abigail looked at her.

"I felt sick that we couldn't record it," Pat said honestly. "I'd love to have had excerpts of that speech on the program."

They ate lunch in the Senator's office. Abigail ordered only a hard-boiled egg and black coffee. She was interrupted four times by urgent phone calls. One was from an old campaign volunteer. "Sure, Maggie," Abigail said. "No, you're not interrupting me. I'm always available to you—you know that. What can I do?"

Pat watched as Abigail's face became stern and a frown creased her forehead. "You mean the hospital told you to come get your mother when the woman can't even raise her head from the pillow? . . . I see. Have you any nursing homes in mind? . . . Six months' wait. And what are you supposed to do in those six months . . . Maggie, I'll call you back."

She slammed the phone down on the hook. "This is the kind of thing that drives me wild. Maggie is trying to raise three kids on her own. She works at a second job on Saturdays and now she's told to take home a senile, bedridden mother. Philip, track down Arnold Pritchard. And I don't care if he's having a two-hour lunch somewhere. Find him now."

Fifteen minutes later the call Abigail was waiting for came through. "Arnold, good to talk to you. . . . I'm glad you're fine. . . . No, I'm not fine. In fact, I'm pretty upset. . . ."

Five minutes later Abigail concluded the conversation by saying, "Yes, I agree. The Willows sounds like a perfect place. It's near enough so that Maggie can visit without giving up her whole Sunday to make the trip. And I know I can count on you, Arnold, to make sure the old girl gets settled in. . . . Yes, send an ambulance to the hospital for her this afternoon. Maggie will be so relieved."

Abigail winked at Pat as she hung up the phone. "This is the aspect of the job that I love," she said. "I shouldn't take time to call Maggie myself, but I'm going to. . . ." She dialed quickly. "Maggie, hello. We're in good shape . . ."

Maggie, Pat decided, would be a guest on the program.

There was an environmental-committee hearing between two and four. At the hearing, Abigail got into a verbal duel with one of the witnesses and quoted from her report. The witness said, "Senator, your figures are dead wrong. I think you've got the old quotes, not the revised ones."

Claire Lawrence was also on the committee. "Maybe I can help," she suggested. "I'm pretty sure I have the latest numbers, and they do change the picture somewhat. . . ."

Pat observed the rigid thrust of Abigail's shoulders, the way she clenched and unclenched her hands as Claire Lawrence read from her report.

The studious-looking young woman seated behind Abigail was apparently the aide who had compiled the inaccurate report. Several times Abigail turned to look at her during Senator Lawrence's comments. The girl was clearly in an agony of embarrassment. Her face was flushed; she was biting her lips to keep them from trembling.

Abigail cut in the instant Senator Lawrence stopped speaking. "Mr. Chairman, I would like to thank Senator Lawrence for her help, and I would also like to apologize to this committee for the fact that the figures given to me were inaccurate and wasted the valuable time of everyone here. I promise you it will never happen again." She turned again to her aide. Pat could read Abigail's lips: "You're fired." The girl slipped out of her chair and left the hearing room, tears running down her cheeks.

Inwardly Pat groaned. The hearing was being televised—anyone seeing the exchange would surely have felt sympathy for the young assistant.

When the hearing was over, Abigail hurried back to her office. It was obvious that everyone there knew what had happened. The secretaries and aides in the outer office did not lift their heads as she roared through. The hapless girl who had made the error was staring out the window, futilely dabbing at her eyes.

"In here, Philip," Abigail snapped. "You too, Pat. You might as well get a full picture of what goes on in this place."

She sat down at her desk. Except for the paleness of her features and the tight set of her lips, she appeared totally composed. "What happened, Philip?" she asked, her tone level.

Even Philip had lost his usual calm. He gulped nervously as he started to explain. "Senator, the other girls just talked to me. Eileen's husband walked out on her a couple of weeks ago. From what they tell me, she's been in a terrible state. She's been with us three years, and as you know, she's one of our best aides. Would you consider giving her a leave of absence until she pulls herself together? She loves this job."

"Does she, indeed? Loves it so much she lets me make a fool of myself in a televised hearing? She's finished, Philip. I want her out of here in the next fifteen minutes. And consider yourself lucky you're not fired too. When that report was late, it was up to you to dig for the real reason for the problem. With all the brainy people hungry for jobs, *including mine,* do you think I intend to leave myself vulnerable because I'm surrounded by deadwood?"

"No, Senator," Philip mumbled.

"There are no second chances in this office. Have I warned my staff about that?"

"Yes, Senator."

"Then get out of here and do as you're told."

"Yes, Senator."

Wow! Pat thought. No wonder Philip was so on guard with her. She realized the Senator was looking over at her.

"Well, Pat," Abigail said quietly, "I suppose you think I'm an ogre?" She did not wait for an answer. "My people know if they have a personal problem and can't handle their job, their responsibility is to report it and arrange for a leave of absence. That policy is in effect to prevent this sort of occurrence. When a staff member makes a mistake, it reflects on me. I have worked too hard, for too many years, to be compromised by anyone else's stupidity. And Pat, believe me, if they'll do it once, they'll do it again. And now, for God's sake, I'm due on the front steps to have my picture taken with a Brownie troop!"

10

At a quarter to five, a secretary timidly knocked on the door of Abigail's office. "A call for Miss Traymore," she whispered.

It was Sam. The reassuring heartiness of his voice boosted Pat's spirits immediately. She had been unsettled by the unpleasant episode, by the abject misery in the young woman's face.

"Hello, Sam." She felt Abigail's sharp glance.

"My spies told me you're on the Hill. How about dinner?"

"Dinner . . . I can't, Sam. I've got to work tonight."

"You also have to eat. What did you have for lunch? One of Abigail's hard-boiled eggs?"

She tried not to laugh. The Senator was clearly listening to her end of the conversation.

"As long as you don't mind eating fast and early," she compromised.

"Fine with me. How about if I pick you up outside the Russell building in half an hour?"

When Pat hung up, she looked over at Abigail.

"Have you reviewed all the material we gave you?—the films?" Abigail demanded.

"No."

"Some of them?"

"No," Pat admitted. Oh, boy, she thought. I'm glad I don't work for you, lady.

"I had thought you might come back to my place for dinner and we could discuss which ones you might be interested in using."

Again a pause. Pat waited.

"However, since you haven't seen the material, I think it would be wiser if I use tonight for some reading I must do." Abigail smiled. "Sam Kingsley is one of the most eligible bachelors in Washingon. I didn't realize you knew him so well."

Pat tried to make her answer light. "I really don't." But she couldn't help thinking that Sam was finding it hard to stay away from her.

She glanced out the window, hoping to hide her expression. Outside it was almost dark. The Senator's windows overlooked the Capitol. As the daylight faded, the gleaming domed building framed by the blue silk draperies resembled a painting. "How lovely!" she exclaimed.

Abigail turned her head toward the window. "Yes, it is," she agreed. "That view at this time of day always reminds me of what I'm doing here. You can't imagine the satisfaction of knowing that because of what I did today an old woman will be cared for in a decent nursing home, and extra money may be made available for people who are trying to eke out an existence."

There was an almost sensual energy in Abigail Jennings when she spoke about her work, Pat thought. She means every word.

But it also occurred to her that the Senator had already dismissed from her memory the girl she had fired a few hours earlier.

Pat shivered as she hurried down the few steps from the Senate office building to the car. Sam leaned over to kiss her cheek. "How's the hotshot filmmaker?"

"Tired," she said. "Keeping up with Senator Jennings is not the recipe for a restful day."

Sam smiled. "I know what you mean. I've worked with Abigail on a fair amount of legislation. She never wears down."

Weaving through the traffic, he turned onto Pennsylvania Avenue. "I thought we'd go to Chez Grandmère in Georgetown," he said. "It's quiet, the food is excellent and it's near your place."

Chez Grandmère was nearly empty. "Washington doesn't dine at quarter to six." Sam smiled as the maître d' offered them their choice of tables.

Over a cocktail Pat told him about the day, including the scene in the hearing room. Sam whistled. "That was a rotten break for Abigail. You don't need someone on your payroll to make you look bad."

"Could something like that actually influence the President's decision?" Pat asked.

"Pat, *everything* can influence the President's decision. One mistake can ruin you. Well, figure it out for yourself. If it weren't for Chappaquiddick, Teddy Kennedy might be President today. Then, of course, you have Watergate and Abscam, and way back, vicuña coats and home freezers. It never ends. Everything reflects on the man or woman who holds the office. It's a miracle Abigail survived that scandal about the missing campaign funds, and if she had tried to cover up for her aide, it would have been the end of her credibility. What was the girl's name?"

"Eleanor Brown." Pat thought of what Margaret Langley had said. *"Eleanor couldn't steal. She's too timid."*

"Eleanor always claimed she was innocent," she told Sam now.

He shrugged. "Pat, I was a county prosecutor for four years. You want to know something? Nine out of ten criminals swear they didn't do it. And at least eight out of nine of them are liars."

"But there is always that one who *is* innocent," Pat persisted.

"Very occasionally," Sam said. "What do you feel like eating?"

It seemed to her that she could watch him visibly unwind in the hour and a half they were together. I'm good for you, Sam, she thought. I can make you happy. You're equating having a child with the way it was when you were doing everything for Karen, because Janice was sick. It wouldn't be that way with me. . . .

Over coffee he asked, "How do you find living in the house? Any problems?"

She hesitated, then decided to tell him about the note she'd found slipped under the door and the second phone call. "But as you say, it's probably just some joker," she concluded.

Sam didn't return her attempt at a smile. "I said that one random call to the Boston station might not be important. But you're saying that in the last three days you've had a second phone call, and a note pushed under the door. How do you think this nut got your address?"

"How did *you* get it?" Pat asked.

"I phoned Potomac Cable and said I was a friend. A secretary gave me your phone number and street address here and told me when you were arriving. Frankly, I was a little surprised they were that casual about giving out so much information."

"I approved it. I'll be using the house as an office for this program, and you'd be surprised how many people volunteer anecdotes or memorabilia when they read about a documentary being prepared. I didn't want to take the chance of losing calls. I certainly didn't think I had anything to worry about."

"Then that creep could have gotten it the same way. By any chance do you have the note with you?"

"It's in my bag." She fished it out, glad to be rid of it.

Sam studied it, frowning in concentration. "I doubt whether anybody could trace this, but let me show it to Jack Carlson. He's an FBI agent and something of a handwriting expert. And you be sure to hang up if you get another call."

He dropped her off at eight-thirty. "You've got to get timers for the lamps," he commented as they stood at the door. "Anybody could come up here and put a note under the door without being noticed."

She looked up at him. The relaxed expression was gone, and the newly acquired creases around his mouth had deepened again. You've always had to worry about Janice, she thought. I don't want you worrying about me.

She tried to recapture the easy companionship of the evening. "Thanks for being the Welcome Wagon again," she said. "They're going to make you chairman of the Hospitality Committee on the Hill."

He smiled briefly and for that moment the tension disappeared from his eyes. "Mother taught me to be courtly to the prettiest girls in town." He closed his hands around hers. For a moment they stood silently; then he bent down and kissed her cheek.

"I'm glad you're not playing favorites," she murmured.

"What?"

"The other night you kissed me below my right eye—tonight the left."

"Good night, Pat. Lock the door."

Pat had barely reached the library when the telephone began to ring insistently. For a moment she was afraid to answer.

"Pat Traymore." To her own ears her voice sounded tense and husky.

"Miss Traymore," a woman's voice said, "I'm Lila Thatcher, your neighbor across the street. I know you just got home, but would it be possible for you to come over now? There's something quite important you should know."

Lila Thatcher, Pat thought. *Lila Thatcher.* Of course. She was the clairvoyant who had written several widely read books on ESP and other psychic phenomena. Only a few months ago she'd been celebrated for her assistance in finding a missing child.

"I'll be right there," Pat agreed reluctantly, "but I'm afraid I can't stay more than a minute."

As she threaded her way across the street, taking pains to avoid the worst of the melting slush and mud, she tried to ignore the sense of uneasiness.

She was sure she would not want to hear what Lila Thatcher was about to tell her.

11

A maid answered Pat's ring and escorted her to the living room. Pat didn't know what kind of person to expect—she'd visualized a turbaned Gypsy; but the woman who rose to greet her could be described simply as cozy. She was gently rounded and gray-haired, with intelligent, twinkling eyes and a warm smile.

"Patricia Traymore," she said, "I'm so glad to meet you. Welcome to Georgetown." Taking Pat's hand, she studied her carefully. "I know how busy you must be with the program you're preparing. I'm sure it's quite a project. How are you getting on with Luther Pelham?"

"Fine so far."

"I hope that continues." Lila Thatcher wore her glasses on a long silver chain around her neck. Absently she picked them up in her right hand and began to tap them against her left palm. "I have only a few minutes myself. I have a meeting in half an hour, and in the morning I have to catch an early flight to California. That's why I decided to phone. This is not the sort of thing I usually do. However, in conscience I can't go away without warning you. Are you aware that twenty-three years ago a murder-suicide took place in the house you're now renting?"

"I've been told that." It was the answer nearest the truth.

"It doesn't upset you?"

"Mrs. Thatcher, many of the houses in Georgetown must be about two hundred years old. Surely people have died in every one of them."

"It's not the same." The older woman's voice became quicker, a thread of nervousness running through it. "My husband and I moved into this house a year or so before the tragedy. I remember the first time I told him that I was beginning to sense a darkness in the atmosphere around the Adams home. Over the next months it would come and go, but each time it returned it was more pronounced. Dean and Renée Adams were a most attractive couple. He was quite splendid-looking, one of those magnetic men who instantly attract attention. Renée was different—quiet, reserved, a very private young woman. My feeling was that being a politician's wife was all wrong for her and inevitably the marriage became affected. But she was very much in love with her husband and they were both devoted to their child."

Pat listened motionless.

"A few days before she died, Renée told me she was going to go back to New England with Kerry. We were standing in front of your house, and I can't describe to you the sense of trouble and danger I experienced. I tried to warn Renée. I told her that if her decision was irrevocable, she should not wait any longer. And then it was too late. I never again felt even a suggestion of trouble concerning your house until this week. But now it's coming back. I don't know why but it's like last time. I sense the darkness involves you. Can you leave that house? *You shouldn't be there.*"

Pat chose her question carefully. "Do you have any reason, other than sensing this aura around the house, for warning me not to stay there?"

"Yes. Three days ago my maid observed a man loitering on the corner. Then she saw footprints in the snow along the side of this house. We thought there might be a prowler and notified the police. We saw footprints again yesterday morning after the fresh snowfall. Whoever is prowling about only goes as far as that tall rhododendron. Standing behind it anyone can watch your house without being observed from our windows or from the street."

Mrs. Thatcher was hugging herself now as if she were suddenly chilled. The flesh on her face had hardened into deep, grave lines. She stared intently at Pat and then, as Pat watched, her eyes widened; an expression of secret knowledge crept into them. When Pat left a few minutes later, the older woman was clearly upset and again urged Pat to leave the house.

Lila Thatcher knows who I am, Pat thought. I'm sure of it. She went directly to the library and poured a fairly generous brandy. "That's better," she murmured as warmth returned to her body. She tried not to think of the dark outside. But at least the police were on the lookout for a prowler. She tried to force herself to be calm. Lila had begged Renée to leave. If her mother had listened, had heeded the warning, could the tragedy have been averted? Should she take Lila's advice now and go to a hotel or rent an apartment? "I can't," she said aloud. "I simply can't." She had so little time to prepare the documentary. It would be unthinkable to waste any of that time relocating. The fact that, as a psychic, Lila Thatcher *sensed* trouble did not mean she could *prevent* it. Pat thought, If Mother had gone to Boston, Daddy would probably have followed her. If someone is determined to find me, he'll manage it. I'd have to be just as careful in an apartment as here. And I *will* be careful.

Somehow the thought that Lila might have guessed her identity was comforting. She cared about my mother and father. She knew me well when I was little. After the program is finished I can talk to her, probe her memory. Maybe she can help me piece it all together.

But now it was absolutely essential to begin reviewing the Senator's personal files and select some for the program.

The spools of film were jumbled together in one of the cartons Toby had brought in. Fortunately, they were all labeled. She began to sort them. Some were of political activities, campaign events, speeches. Finally she found the personal ones she was most interested in seeing. She started with the film labeled WILLARD AND ABIGAIL—HILLCREST WEDDING RECEPTION.

She knew they had eloped before his graduation from Harvard Law School. Abby had just finished her junior year at Radcliffe. Willard had run for Congress a few months after their wedding. She'd helped him campaign, then completed college at the University of Richmond. Apparently there had been a reception when he brought her to Virginia.

The film opened on the panorama of a festive garden party. Colorful umbrella-covered tables were arranged against the tree-shaded background. Servants moved among the clusters of guests—women in summer gowns and picture hats, men in dark jackets and white flannel trousers.

In the reception line on the terrace, a breathtaking young Abigail wearing a white silk tunic-style gown stood next to a scholarly-looking young man. An older woman, obviously Willard Jennings' mother, was to Abigail's right. Her aristocratic face was set in taut, angry lines. As the guests moved slowly past her, she introduced them to Abigail. Never once did she look directly at Abigail.

What was it the Senator had said? "My mother-in-law always considered me the Yankee who stole her son." Clearly, Abigail had not exaggerated.

Pat studied Willard Jennings. He was only slightly taller than Abigail, with sandy hair and a thin, gentle face. There was something rather endearingly shy about him, a diffidence in his manner as he shook hands or kissed cheeks.

Of the three, only Abigail seemed totally at ease. She smiled constantly, bent her head forward as if carefully committing names to memory, reached out her hand to show her rings.

If there were only a sound track, Pat thought.

The last person had been greeted. Pat watched as Abigail and Willard turned to each other. Willard's mother stared straight ahead. Now her face seemed less angry than thoughtful.

And then she smiled warmly. A tall auburn-haired man approached. He hugged Mrs. Jennings, released her, hugged her again, then turned to greet the newlyweds. Pat leaned forward. As the man's face came into full view, she stopped the projector.

The late arrival was her father, Dean Adams. He looks so young! she thought. He can't be more than thirty! She tried to swallow over the lump in her throat. Did she have a vague memory of him looking like this? His broad shoulders filled the screen. He was like a handsome young god, she thought, towering over Willard, exuding magnetic energy.

Feature by feature she studied the face, frozen on the screen, unwavering, open to minute examination. She wondered where her mother was, then realized that when this film was taken, her mother had still been a student at the Boston Conservatory, still planning a career in music.

Dean Adams was then a freshman Congressman from Wisconsin. He still had the healthy, open look of the Midwest in him, a larger-than-life outdoorsy aura.

She pushed the button and the figures sprang to life—Dean Adams joking with Willard Jennings, Abigail extending her hand to him. He ignored it and kissed her cheek. Whatever he said to Willard, they all began to laugh.

The camera followed them as they walked down the flagstone steps of the terrace and began to circulate among the guests. Dean Adams had his hand under the arm of the older Mrs. Jennings. She was talking to him animatedly. Clearly they were very fond of each other.

When the film ended, Pat reran it, marking off segments that might be used in the program. Willard and Abigail cutting the cake, toasting each other, dancing the first dance. She couldn't use any of the footage from the reception line—the displeasure on the face of the senior Mrs. Jennings was too obvious. And of course there was no question of using the film that involved Dean Adams.

What had Abigail felt that afternoon? she wondered. That beautiful whitewashed brick mansion, that gathering of Virginia gentry and she only a few years removed from the service apartment of the Saunders house in Apple Junction.

The Saunders house. Abigail's mother, Francey Foster. Where was she that day? Had she declined to be at her daughter's wedding reception, feeling she would seem out of place among these people? Or had Abigail made that decision for her?

One by one Pat began to view the other reels, steeling herself against the shock of watching her father regularly appear in those which had been taken on the estate.

Even without the dates, it would have been possible to arrange the films in a time sequence.

The first campaign: professional newsreels of Abigail and Willard hand in hand walking down the street, greeting passersby . . . Abigail and Willard inspecting a new housing development. The announcer's voice . . . "As Willard Jennings campaigned this afternoon for the seat to be made vacant by the retirement of his uncle, Congressman Porter Jennings, he pledged to continue the family tradition of service to the constituency."

There was an interview with Abigail. "How does it feel to spend your honeymoon campaigning?"

Abigail's reply: "I can't think of a better way than being at my husband's side helping him begin his career in public life."

There was a soft lilt in Abigail's voice, the unmistakable trace of a Southern accent. Pat did a rapid calculation. At that point Abigail had been in Virginia less than three months. She marked that segment for the program.

There were clips of five campaigns in all. As they progressed, Abigail increasingly played a major role in reelection efforts. Often her speech would begin "My husband is in Washington doing a job for you. Unlike many others, he is not taking time from the important work of the Congress to campaign for himself. I'm glad to be able to tell you just a few of his accomplishments."

The films of social events at the estate were hardest to watch. WILLARD'S 35TH BIRTHDAY. Two young couples posing with Abigail and Willard—Jack and Jackie Kennedy and Dean and Renée Adams . . . both recent newlyweds . . .

It was the first time Pat had seen a film of her mother. Renée was wearing a pale green gown; her dark hair fell loosely on her shoulders. There was a hesitancy about her, but when she smiled up at her husband, her expression was adoring. Pat found she could not bear to dwell on it. She was glad to let the film unwind. A few frames later, just the Kennedys and Jenningses were posing together. She made a note on her pad. That will be a wonderful clip for the program, she thought bitterly. The pre-Camelot days minus the embarrassment of Congressman Dean Adams and the wife he murdered.

The last film she viewed was of Willard Jennings' funeral. In it was a newsreel clip that opened outside the National Cathedral. The announcer's voice was subdued. "The funeral cortege of Congressman Willard Jennings has just arrived. The great and the near-great are gathered inside to bid a final farewell to the Virginia legislator who died when his chartered plane crashed en route to a speaking engagement. Congressman Jennings and the pilot, George Graney, were killed instantly.

"The young widow is being escorted by Senator John Fitzgerald Kennedy of Massachusetts. Congressman Jennings' mother, Mrs. Stuart Jennings, is escorted by Congressman Dean Adams of Wisconsin. Senator Kennedy and Congressman Adams were Willard Jennings' closest friends."

Pat watched as Abigail emerged from the first car, her face composed, a black veil covering her blond hair. She wore a simply cut black silk suit and a string of pearls. The handsome young Senator from Massachusetts gravely offered her his arm.

The Congressman's mother was obviously grief-stricken. When she was assisted from the limousine, her eyes fell on the flag-draped casket. She clasped her hands together and shook her head slightly in a gesture of agonized rejection. As Pat watched, her father slid his arm under Mrs. Jennings' elbow and clasped her hand in his. Slowly the procession moved into the cathedral.

She had seen as much as she could absorb in one evening. Clearly the human interest material she had been seeking was amply present in the old film clips. She turned out the lights in the library and went into the hall.

The hall was drafty. There had been no windows open in the library. She checked the dining room, kitchen and foyer. Everything was closed and locked.

But there was a draft.

A sense of apprehension made Pat's breath come faster. The door to the living room was closed. She put her hand on it. The space between the door and the frame was icy cold. Slowly she opened the door. A blast of cold air assaulted her. She reached for the chandelier switch.

The French doors to the patio were open. A pane of glass that had been cut from its frame was lying on the carpet.

And then she saw it.

Lolling against the fireplace, the right leg twisted under it, the white apron soaked with blood, was a Raggedy Ann doll. Sinking to her knees, Pat stared at it. A clever hand had painted downward curves on the stitched mouth, added tears to the cheeks and drawn lines on the forehead so that the typical Raggedy Ann smiling face had been transformed to a pain-filled weeping image.

She held her hand to her mouth to force back a shriek. Who had been here? Why? Half-hidden by the soiled apron was a sheet of paper pinned to the doll's dress. She reached for it; her fingers recoiling at the touch of the crusted blood. The same kind of cheap typing paper as the other note; the same small, slanted printing. *This is your last warning. There must not be a program glorifying Abigail Jennings.*

A creaking sound. One of the patio doors was moving. Was someone there? Pat jumped up. But it was the wind that was pushing the door back and forth. She ran across the room, yanked the doors together and turned the lock. But that was useless. The hand that had cut out the pane could reach through the empty frame, unlock the doors again. Maybe the intruder was still there, still hiding in the garden behind the evergreens.

Her hands shook as she dialed the police emergency number. The officer's voice was reassuring. "We'll send a squad car right away."

As she waited, Pat reread the note. This was the fourth time she'd been warned away from the program. Suddenly suspicious, she wondered if the threats were valid. Was it possible this was some kind of "dirty tricks" campaign to make the Senator's documentary a subject of gossip, to smear it with outlandish, distracting publicity?

What about the doll? Shocking to her because of the memory it evoked, but basically a Raggedy Ann with a garishly painted face. On closer examination, it seemed bizarre rather than frightening. Even the bloodied apron might be a crude attempt to horrify. If I were a reporter covering this story, I'd have a picture of that thing on the front page of tomorrow's newspaper, she thought.

The wail of the police siren decided her. Quickly she unpinned the note and left it on the mantelpiece. Rushing into the library, she dragged the carton from under the table and dropped the doll into it. The grisly apron sickened her. The doorbell was ringing—a steady, persistent peal. Impulsively she untied the apron, pulled it off and buried it deep in the carton. Without it the doll resembled a hurt child.

She shoved the carton back under the table and hurried to admit the policemen.

12

Two police cars, their dome lights blazing, were in the driveway. A third car had followed them. Don't let it be the press, she prayed. But it was.

Photographs were taken of the broken pane; the grounds were searched, the living room dusted for fingerprints.

It was hard to explain the note. "It was pinned to something," a detective pointed out. "Where did you find it?"

"Right here by the fireplace." That was true enough.

The reporter was from the *Tribune.* He asked to see the note.

"I'd prefer not to have it made public," Pat urged. But he was allowed to read it.

"What does 'last warning' mean?" the detective asked. "Have you had other threats?"

Omitting the reference to 'that house,' she told them about the two phone calls, about the letter she'd found the first night.

"This one isn't signed," the detective pointed out. "Where's the other one?"

"I didn't keep it. It wasn't signed either."

"But on the phone he called himself an avenging angel?"

"He said something like 'I am an angel of mercy, of deliverance, an avenging angel.'"

"Sounds like a real screwball," the detective commented.

He studied her keenly. "Funny he bothered to break in this time. Why not just slip an envelope under the door again?"

Dismayed, Pat watched the reporter scribbling in his notebook.

Finally the police were ready to go. The surfaces of all the living-room tables were smudged with fingerprint powder. The patio doors had been wired together so they couldn't be opened until the pane was replaced.

It was impossible to go to bed. Vacuuming the soot and grit from the living room, she decided, might help her unwind. As she worked, she couldn't forget the mutilated Raggedy Ann doll. *The child had run into the room . . . and tripped . . . the child fell over something soft, and its hands became wet and sticky . . . and the child looked up and saw . . .*

What did I see? Pat asked herself fiercely. What did I see?

Her hands worked unconsciously, vacuuming the worst of the greasy powder, then polishing the lovely old wooden tables with an oil-dampened chamois cloth, moving bric-a-brac, lifting and pushing furniture. The carpet had small clumps of slush and dirt from the policemen's shoes.

What did I see?

She began pushing the furniture back into place. No, not here; that table belongs on the short wall, that lamp on the piano, the slipper chair near the French doors.

It was only when she had finished that she understood what she had been doing.

The slipper chair. The movers had placed it too near the piano.

She'd run down the hall into the room. She'd screamed "Daddy, Daddy . . ." She'd tripped over her mother's body. Her mother was bleeding. She looked up, and then . . .

And then, only darkness . . .

It was nearly three o'clock. She couldn't think about it any more tonight. She was exhausted, and her leg ached. Her limp would have been obvious to anyone as she dragged the vacuum cleaner back to the storage closet and made her way upstairs.

At eight o'clock the telephone rang. The caller was Luther Pelham. Even coming out of the stupor of heavy sleep, Pat realized he was furious.

"Pat, I understand you had a break-in last night. Are you all right?"

She blinked, trying to force the sleep from her eyes and brain. "Yes."

"You made the front page of the *Tribune.* It's quite a caption. 'Anchorwoman's life threatened.' Let me read you the first paragraph:

" 'A break-in at her Georgetown home was the most recent in a series of bizarre threats received by television personality Patricia Traymore. The threats are tied to the documentary program "A Profile of Senator Abigail Jennings," which Miss Traymore will produce and narrate, to be aired next Wednesday night on Potomac Cable Television.'

"That's just the kind of publicity Abigail needs!"

"I'm sorry," Pat stammered. "I tried to keep the reporter away from the note."

"Did it ever occur to you to call *me,* instead of the police? Frankly, I gave you credit for more brains than you displayed last night. We could have had private detectives watch your place. This is probably some harmless nut, but the burning question in Washingon will be, Who hates Abigail so much?"

He was right. "I'm sorry," Pat repeated. Then she added, "However, when you realize your home has been broken into, and you're wondering if some nut may be six feet away on the patio, I think it's a fairly normal reaction to call the police."

"There's no use discussing it further until we can assess the damage. Have you reviewed Abigail's films?"

"Yes. I have some excellent material to edit."

"You didn't tell Abigail about being in Apple Junction?"

"No, I didn't."

"Well, if you're smart, you *won't!* That's all she needs to hear now!"

Without saying goodbye, Luther hung up.

It was Arthur's habit to go to the bakery promptly at eight for hot rolls and then pick up the morning paper. Today he reversed the procedure. He was so eager to see if the paper had anything about the break-in that he went to the newsstand first.

There it was, right on the front page. He read the story through, relishing every word, then frowned. Nothing had been said about the Raggedy Ann doll. The doll had been his means of making them understand that violence had been committed in that house and might be again.

He purchased two seeded rolls and walked the three blocks back to the leaning frame house and up to the dreary apartment on the second floor. Only half a mile away King Street had expensive restaurants and shops, but the neighborhood here was run-down and shabby.

The door of Glory's bedroom was open, and he could see she was already dressed in a bright red sweater and jeans. Lately she'd gotten friendly with a girl in her office, a brazen type who was teaching Glory about makeup and had persuaded her to cut her hair.

She did not look up, even though she must have heard him coming in. He sighed. Glory's attitude toward him was becoming distant, even impatient. Like last night when he'd tried to tell her what a hard time old Mrs. Rodriguez had had swallowing her medicine and how he'd had to break up the pill and give her a little bread with it to hide the taste. Glory had interrupted him. "Father, can't we ever talk about anything except the nursing home?" And then she'd gone to a movie with some of the girls from work.

He put the rolls on plates and poured the coffee. "Soup's on," he called.

Glory hurried into the kitchen. She was wearing her coat

and her purse was under her arm, as though she couldn't wait to leave.

"Hello," he said softly. "My little girl looks very pretty today."

Gloria didn't smile.

"How was the movie?" he asked.

"It was okay. Look, don't bother getting a roll or bun for me anymore. I'll have mine in the office with the others."

He felt crushed. He liked sharing breakfast with Glory before they left for work.

She must have sensed his disappointment, because she looked right at him and the expression in her eyes softened. "You're so good to me," she said, and her voice sounded a little sad.

For long minutes after she left, he sat staring into space. Last night had been exhausting. After all these years, to have been back in *that* house, in *that* room—to have placed Glory's doll on the exact spot where the child had lain . . . When he'd finished arranging it against the fireplace, the right leg crumpled under it, he had almost expected to turn around and see the bodies of the man and woman lying there again.

13

After Luther's call, Pat got up, made coffee and began editing the storyboards for the program. She had decided to plan two versions of the documentary, one including an opening segment about Abigail's early life in Apple Junction, the other starting at the wedding reception. The more she thought about it, the more she felt Luther's anger was justified. Abigail was skittish enough about the program without this upsetting publicity. At least I had the sense to hide the doll, she thought.

By nine o'clock she was in the library running off the rest of the films. Luther had already sent over edited segments of the Eleanor Brown case, showing Abigail leaving the courthouse after the Guilty verdict. Her regretful statement: "This is a very sad day for me. I only hope that now Eleanor will have the decency to tell where she has hidden that money. It may have been for my campaign fund, but far more important, it was the donations of people who believed in the goals I embrace."

A reporter asked: "Then, Senator, there is absolutely no truth to Eleanor's insistence that your chauffeur phoned her asking her to look for your diamond ring in the campaign-office safe?"

"My chauffeur was driving me that morning to a meeting in Richmond. The ring was on my finger."

And then the clip showed a picture of Eleanor Brown, a close-up that clearly revealed every feature of her small, colorless face, her timid mouth and shy eyes.

The reel ended with a scene of Abigail addressing college students. Her subject was Public Trust. Her theme was the absolute responsibility of a legislator to keep his or her own office and staff above reproach.

There was another segment Luther had already edited, a compilation of the Senator in airline-safety hearings, with excerpts from her speeches demanding more stringent regulations. Several times she referred to the fact that she had been widowed because her husband had entrusted his life to an inexperienced pilot in an ill-equipped plane.

At the end of each of those segments Luther had marked "*2-minute discussion between Senator J. and Pat T. on subject.*"

Pat bit her lip.

Both those segments were out of sync with what she was trying to do. What happened to my creative control of this project? she wondered. The whole thing is getting too rushed. No, the word is *botched.*

The phone rang as she began to go through Abigail's letters from constituents. It was Sam. "Pat, I read what happened. I've checked with the rental office for my place." Sam lived in the Watergate Towers. "There are several sublets available. I want you to take one on a monthly basis until this character is caught."

"Sam, I can't. You know the kind of pressure I'm under. I have a locksmith coming. The police are going to keep a watch on the place. I have all my equipment set up here." She tried to change the subject. "My real problem is what to wear to the White House dinner."

"You always look lovely. Abigail is going to be there as well. I bumped into her this morning."

A short time later, the Senator phoned to express her shock at the break-in. Then she got to the point. "Unfortunately, the suggestion that you are being threatened because of this program is bound to lead to all sorts of speculation. I really want to get this thing wrapped up, Pat. Obviously, once it's completed and aired, the threats will end even if they are simply from some sort of crank. Have you reviewed the films I gave you?"

"Yes, I have," Pat replied. "There's wonderful material and I've got it marked off. But I'd like to borrow Toby. There are some places where I need names and more specific background."

They agreed that Toby would come over within the hour. When Pat hung up she had the feeling that in Abigail Jennings' estimation she had become an embarrassment.

Toby arrived forty-five minutes later, his leathery face creased in a smile. "I wish I'd been here when that joker tried to get in, Pat," he told her. "I'd 've made mincemeat of him."

"I'll bet you would."

He sat at the library table while she ran the projector. "That's old Congressman Porter Jennings," Toby answered at one point. "He was the one who said he wouldn't retire if Willard didn't take over his seat. You know that Virginia aristocracy. Think they own the world. But I have to say that he bucked his sister-in-law when he supported Abigail to succeed Willard. Willard's mother, that old she-devil, pulled out all the stops to keep Abigail out of Congress. And between us, she was a lot better Congressman than Willard. He wasn't aggressive enough. You know what I mean?"

While waiting for Toby, Pat had reviewed the newspaper clippings about the Eleanor Brown case. The case seemed almost too simple. Eleanor said that Toby had phoned and sent her to the campaign office. Five thousand dollars of the money had been recovered in her storage area in the basement of her apartment building.

"How do you think Eleanor Brown expected to get away with such a flimsy story?" Pat now asked Toby.

Toby leaned back in the leather chair, crossing one thick leg over the other, and shrugged. Pat noticed the cigar in his breast pocket. Wincing inwardly, she invited him to smoke.

He beamed, sending his jowly face into a mass of creases. "Thanks a lot. The Senator can't stand the smell of cigar smoke. I don't dare have even a puff in the car no matter how long I'm waiting for her."

He lit the cigar and puffed appreciatively.

"About Eleanor Brown," Pat suggested. She rested her elbows on her knees, cupping her chin in her hands.

"The way I figure it," Toby confided, "Eleanor didn't think the money would be missed for a while. They've kind of tightened up the law since then, but it really used to be that you could have big money sit in the campaign-office safe for a couple of weeks—even longer."

"But seventy-five thousand dollars in cash?"

"Miss Traymore . . . Pat, you gotta understand how many companies contribute to both sides in a campaign. They want to be sure to be with the winner. Now, of course you can't hand cash to a Senator in the office. *That's* against the law. So what the big shot does is visit the Senator, let him or her know he's planning to make a big donation, and then takes a walk with the Senator's aide on the Capitol grounds and turns over the money there. The Senator never touches it, but *knows* about it. It's put right in the campaign funds. But because it's in cash, if the competition gets elected it isn't so obvious. You know what I mean?"

"I see."

"Don't get me wrong. It's legal. But Phil had taken some big donations for Abigail, and of course Eleanor knew about them. Maybe she had some boyfriend who wanted to make a killing and only borrowed the money. Then when they looked for it so fast, she had to come up with an excuse."

"She just doesn't seem that sophisticated to me," Pat observed, thinking of the high school yearbook picture.

"Well, like the prosecutor said, still water runs deep. I hate to rush you, Pat, but the Senator will be needing me."

"There are just one or two more questions."

The phone rang. "I'll make this fast." Pat picked it up. "Pat Traymore."

"How are you, my dear?" She instantly recognized the precise, overly cultivated voice.

"Hello, Mr. Saunders." Too late she remembered that Toby knew Jeremy Saunders. Toby's head jerked up. Would he associate the name Saunders with the Jeremy Saunders he'd known in Apple Junction?

"I tried to get you several times early last evening," Saunders purred. He was not drunk this time. She was sure of it.

"You didn't leave your name."

"Recorded messages can be heard by the wrong ears. Don't you agree?"

"Just a moment, please." Pat looked at Toby. He was smoking his cigar thoughtfully and seemed indifferent to the call. Maybe he hadn't put together the name Saunders with a man he hadn't seen in thirty-five years.

"Toby, this is a private call. I wonder if . . ."

He stood up quickly before she could finish. "Want me to wait outside?"

"No, Toby. Just hang up when I get to the kitchen extension?" Deliberately she spoke his name again so that Jeremy would hear and not begin talking until he was sure only Pat was on the line.

Toby accepted the receiver casually, but he was certain it was Jeremy Saunders. Why was he calling Pat Traymore? Had she been in touch with him? Abigail would hit the ceiling. From the other end of the phone he heard the faint sound of breathing. That stinking phony, he thought. If he tries to smear Abby . . . !

Pat's voice came on. "Toby, would you mind hanging up?"

"Sure, Pat." He made his voice hearty. He hung up the receiver with a definite click and didn't dare to try to ease it off the hook again.

"Toby," Jeremy Saunders said, his voice incredulous. "Don't tell me you're hobnobbing with Toby Gorgone."

"He's helping me with some of the background material on the program," Pat replied. She kept her voice low.

"Of course. He's been there every step of the way with our stateswoman, hasn't he? Pat, I wanted to call because I realize that the combination of vodka and your sympathy made me rather indiscreet. I do insist that our conversation remain totally confidential. My wife and daughter would not enjoy having the shabby little tale of my involvement with Abigail aired on national television."

"I have no intention of quoting anything you told me," Pat replied. "The *Mirror* might be interested in gossipy personal material, but I assure you, I'm not."

"Very good. I'm greatly relieved." Saunders' voice became friendlier. "I saw Edwin Shepherd at the club. He tells me he gave you a copy of the newspaper showing Abby as the beauty queen. I'd forgotten about that. I do hope you plan to use the picture of Miss Apple Junction with her adoring mother. *That* one's worth a thousand words!"

"I really don't think so," Pat said coldly. His presumption had turned her off. "I'm afraid I'll have to get back to work, Mr. Saunders."

She hung up and went back into the library. Toby was sitting in the chair where she'd left him, but there was something different about him. The genial manner was gone. He seemed distracted and left almost immediately.

After he had gone, she flung open the window to get rid of the cigar smell. But the odor hung in the room. She realized that once again she felt acutely uneasy and jumped at every sound.

Back at the office, Toby went directly to Philip. "How's it going?"

Philip raised his eyes heavenward. "The Senator is in a state about the story. She just gave Luther Pelham hell for ever talking her into that documentary. She'd kill it in a minute if the publicity weren't already out. How did it go with Pat Traymore?"

Toby wasn't ready to talk about Apple Junction, but he did ask Philip to look into the question of the rental of the Adams house, which was also on his mind.

He knocked on the door of Abigail's office. She was quiet now—too quiet. That meant she was worried. She had the afternoon edition of the paper. "Look at this," she told him.

A famous Washington gossip column's lead item began:

> Wags on Capitol Hill are placing bets on the identity of the person who threatened Patricia Traymore's life if she goes ahead with the documentary on Senator Jennings. Seems everyone has a candidate. The beautiful senior Senator from Virginia has a reputation among her colleagues as an abrasive perfectionist.

As Toby watched, Abigail Jennings, her face savage with fury, crumpled the paper in her hand and tossed it into a wastepaper basket.

14

Sam Kingsley snapped the last stud in his dress shirt and twisted his tie into a bow. He glanced at the clock on the mantel over his bedroom fireplace and decided he had more than enough time for a Scotch and soda.

His Watergate apartment commanded a sweeping view of the Potomac. From the side window of the living room he looked down at the Kennedy Center. Some evenings when he arrived late from the office, he'd go in and catch the second and third acts of a favorite opera.

After Janice died, there'd been no reason to keep the big house in Chevy Chase. Karen was living in San Francisco, and she and her husband spent their holidays with her in-laws in Palm Springs. Sam had given Karen her choice of dishes, silver, bric-a-brac and furniture and sold most of the rest. He had wanted to start with a clean slate in the hope that his pervading sense of weariness might subside.

Sam carried his glass to the window. The Potomac was shimmering from the lights of the apartment building and the floodlights of Kennedy Center. Potomac fever. He had it. So did most of the people who came here. Would Pat catch it as well? he wondered.

He was damn worried about her. His FBI friend Jack Carlson had flatly told him: "First she gets a phone call, then a note under the door, then another phone call and finally a break-in with a warning note left in her home. You figure out what might happen next time.

"You've got a full-blown psycho who's about to explode. That slanted printing is a dead giveaway—and compare these notes. They're written only a few days apart. Some of the letters on the second one are practically illegible. His stress is building to a breaking point. And one way or another, that stress seems to be directed at your Pat Traymore."

His Pat Traymore. In those last months before Janice died, he'd managed to keep Pat from his thoughts. He'd always be grateful for that. He and Janice had managed to recapture something of their early closeness. She had died secure in his love.

Afterward, he had felt drained, exhausted, lifeless, *old.* Too old for a twenty-seven-year-old girl and all that a life with her would involve. He simply wanted peace.

Then he'd read that Pat was coming to work in Washington and he'd decided to phone and invite her to dinner. There was no way he could avoid her, or want to avoid her, and he did not intend their first meeting to be constrained by the presence of others. So he'd asked her out.

He had soon realized that whatever was between them hadn't gone away, but was still simmering, waiting to blaze up—and that was what she wanted.

But what did *he* want?

"I don't know," Sam said aloud. Jack's warning rang in his ears: Suppose something happened to Pat?

The house phone rang. "Your car is here, Congressman," the doorman announced.

"Thank you. I'll be right down."

Sam put his half-empty glass on the bar and went into the bedroom to get his jacket and coat. His movements were brisk. In a few minutes he'd be with Pat.

* * *

Pat decided to wear an emerald satin gown with a beaded top to the White House dinner. It was an Oscar de la Renta that Veronica had insisted she purchase for the Boston Symphony Ball. Now she was glad she'd been talked into it. With it she wore her grandmother's emeralds.

"You don't look the part of the girl reporter," Sam commented when he picked her up.

"I don't know whether to take that as a compliment." Sam was wearing a navy blue cashmere coat and white silk scarf over his dinner jacket. What was it Abigail had called him? One of the most eligible bachelors in Washington?

"It was intended as one. No more phone calls or notes?" he asked.

"No." She had not yet told him about the doll and didn't want to bring it up now.

"Good. I'll feel better when that program is finished."

"*You'll* feel better."

In the limousine on the way to the White House, he asked her about her activities.

"Work," she said promptly. "Luther agreed with the film clips I selected and we've completed the storyboard. He's adamant about not crossing the Senator by including her early life. He's turning what's supposed to be a documentary into a paean of praise that's going to be journalistically unsound."

"And you can't do anything about it?"

"I could quit. But I didn't come down here to quit after the first week—not if I can help it."

They were at Eighteenth Street and Pennsylvania Avenue. "Sam, was there ever a hotel on that corner?"

"Yes, the old Roger Smith. They tore it down about ten years ago."

When I was little I went to a Christmas party there. I wore a red velvet dress and white tights and black patent leather slippers. I spilled chocolate ice cream on the dress and cried and Daddy said, "It's not your fault, Kerry."

The limousine was drawing up to the northwest gate of the White House. They waited in line as each car stopped for the security check. When it was their turn, a respectful guard confirmed their names on the guest list.

Inside, the mansion was festive with holiday decorations. The Marine Band was playing in the marble foyer. Waiters were offering champagne. Pat recognized familiar faces among the assembled guests: film stars, Senators, Cabinet members, socialites, a grande dame of the theater.

"Have you ever been here before?" Sam asked.

"On a school trip when I was sixteen. We took the tour and they told us that Abigail Adams used to hang her wash in what is now the East Room."

"You won't find any laundry there now. Come on. If you're going to have a career in Washington, you'd better get to know some people." A moment later he was introducing her to the President's press secretary.

Brian Salem was an amiable, rotund man. "Are you trying to push us off the front page, Miss Traymore?" he asked, smiling.

So even in the Oval Office the break-in had been discussed.

"Have the police any leads?"

"I'm not sure, but we all think it was just some sort of crank."

Penny Salem was a sharp-eyed, wiry woman in her early forties. "God knows Brian sees enough crank letters addressed to the President."

"I sure do," her husband agreed easily. "Anyone in public office is bound to step on toes. The more powerful you are, the madder somebody or some group gets at you. And Abigail Jennings takes positive stands on some mighty volatile issues. Oh, say, there's the lady now." He suddenly grinned. "Doesn't she look great?"

Abigail had just entered the East Room. This was one night she had not chosen to underplay her beauty. She was wearing an apricot satin gown with a bodice covered in pearls. A belled skirt complimented her small waist and slender frame. Her hair was loosely drawn back into a chignon. Soft waves framed her flawless features. Pale blue shadow accentuated the extraordinary eyes, and rose blush highlighed her cheekbones. A deeper apricot shade outlined her perfectly shaped lips.

This was a different Abigail, laughing softly, laying a hand for just an extra moment on the arm of an octogenarian ambassador, accepting the tributes to her appearance as her due. Pat wondered if every other woman in the room felt as she did—suddenly colorless and insignificant.

Abigail had timed her arrival well. An instant later, the music from the Marine Band shifted to a stirring "Hail to the Chief." The President and First Lady were descending from their private quarters. With them were the new Prime Minister of Canada and his wife. As the last notes of "Hail to the Chief" died out, the opening chords of the Canadian national anthem began.

A receiving line was formed. When Pat and Sam approached the President and First Lady, Pat realized that her heart was pounding.

The First Lady was far more attractive in person than in her pictures. She had a long, tranquil face with a generous mouth and pale hazel eyes. Her hair was sandy with traces of gray. There was an air of total self-confidence about her. Her eyes crinkled when she smiled, and her lips parted to reveal strong, perfect teeth. She told Pat that when she was a girl her ambition had been to get a job in television. "And instead"—she laughed, looking up at her husband—"I had no sooner let go of the daisy chain at Vassar than I found myself married."

"I was smart enough to grab her before anyone else did," the President said. "Pat, I'm glad to meet you."

It was a palpable emotion to feel the solid handshake of the most powerful man in the world.

"They're good people," Sam commented as they accepted champagne. "And he's been a strong President. It's hard to believe he's completing his second term. He's young, not sixty yet. It'll be interesting to see what he does with the rest of his life."

Pat was studying the First Lady. "I'd love to do a program on her. She seems comfortable in her own skin."

"Her father was Ambassador to England; her grandfather was Vice President. Generations of breeding and money coupled with a diplomatic background do have a way of instilling self-confidence, Pat."

In the State Dining Room, the tables were set with Limoges china, an intricate green pattern, rimmed with gold. Pale green damask cloths and napkins with centerpieces of red roses and ferns in low crystal containers completed the effect. "Sorry we're not sitting together," Sam commented, "but you seem to have a good table. And please notice where Abigail has been placed."

She was at the President's table between the President and the guest of honor, the Prime Minister of Canada. "I wish I had this on camera," Pat murmured.

She glanced at the first few items on the menu: salmon in aspic, suprême of capon in flamed brandy sauce, wild rice.

Her dinner partner was the Chairman of the Joint Chiefs of Staff. The others at the table included a college president, a Pulitzer Prize–winning playwright, an Episcopal bishop, the director of Lincoln Center.

She glanced around to see where Sam had gone. He was at the President's table directly across from Senator Jennings. They were smiling at each other. With a twinge of pain, Pat looked away.

Near the end of the dinner the President invited everyone to remember in prayer the Vice President, who was so seriously ill. He added, "More than any of us realized, he had been pursuing arduous fourteen-hour days without ever considering the toll they were taking on his health." When the tribute was completed, there was no doubt in anyone's mind that the Vice

President would never resume his duties. As he sat down, the President smiled at Abigail. There was something of a public benediction in that glance.

"Well, did you enjoy yourself?" Sam asked on the way home. "That playwright at your table seemed quite taken with you. You danced with him three or four times, didn't you?"

"When you were dancing with the Senator. Sam, wasn't it quite an honor for you to be at the President's table?"

"It's always an honor to be placed there."

An odd constraint came over them. It seemed to Pat that suddenly the evening had gone flat. Was that the true reason Sam had gotten the invitation for her—so that she'd meet Washington people? Did he simply feel he had a certain obligation to help launch her before he withdrew from her life again?

He waited while she unlocked the door, but declined a nightcap. "I've got to get in a long day tomorrow. I'm leaving for Palm Springs on the six-o'clock flight to spend the holiday with Karen and Tom at his family's place. Are you going to Concord for the holiday, Pat?"

She didn't want to tell him that Veronica and Charles had left for a Caribbean cruise. "This will be a working Christmas," she said.

"Let's have a belated celebration after the program is finished. And I'll give you your Christmas present then."

"That'll be fine." She hoped her voice sounded as casually friendly as his. She refused to reveal the emptiness she felt.

"You looked lovely, Pat. You'd be surprised at the number of people I heard commenting about you."

"I hope they were all my own age. Good night, Sam." She pushed the door open and went inside.

"Damn it, Pat!" Sam stepped into the foyer and spun her around. Her jacket fell from her shoulders as he pulled her to him.

Her hands slipped around his neck; her fingertips touched the collar of his coat, found the cool skin above it, twisted his thick, wavy hair. It was as she remembered—the faint good scent of his breath, the feel of his arms enveloping her, the absolute certainty that they belonged together. "Oh, my love," she whispered. "I've missed you so."

It was as if she had slapped him. In an involuntary movement, he straightened up and stepped back. Dumbfounded, Pat dropped her arms.

"Sam . . ."

"Pat, I'm, sorry . . ." He tried to smile. "You're just too damn attractive for your own good."

For a long minute they stared at each other. Then Sam grasped her shoulders. "Don't you think I'd like nothing better than to pick up where we left off that day? I'm not going to do it to you, Pat. You're a beautiful young woman. Within six months you'll have your pick of half a dozen men who can give you the kind of life you should have. Pat, my time is past. I damn near lost my seat in the last election. And you know what my opponent said? He said it's time for new blood. Sam Kingsley's been around too long. He's in a rut. Let's give him the rest he needs."

"And you believed it?"

"I believe it because it's true. That last year and a half with Janice left me empty—empty and drained. Pat, it's hard for me to decide where I stand on any issue these days. Choosing what tie to wear is a big effort, for God's sake, but there is one decision I can stick to. I'm not going to foul up your life again."

"Have you ever stopped to think how much you'll foul it up by not coming back into it?"

Unhappily they stared at each other. "I'm simply not going to let myself believe that, Pat." Then he was gone.

15

Glory was different now. She had begun setting her hair in the morning. She had new clothes, more colorful. The blouses had high ruffled necks instead of button-down collars. And recently she had bought some earrings, a couple of pairs. He'd never seen her wear earrings before.

Every day now she told him not to make her a sandwich for lunch, that she would eat out.

"All by yourself?" he'd asked.

"No, Father."

"With Opal?"

"I'm just eating out"—and there was that unfamiliar note of impatience in her voice.

She didn't want to hear about his work at all anymore. He'd tried a couple of times to tell her how even with the respirator, old Mrs. Gillespie was rasping and coughing and in pain. Glory used to listen so sympathetically when he told her about his patients and agree when he said it would be a mercy if the angels came for the very sick ones. Her agreement helped him carry out his mission.

He'd been so distracted with Glory that when he delivered Mrs. Gillespie to the Lord he'd been careless. He had thought she was asleep, but as he pulled out the respirator plug and prayed over her, she opened her eyes. She had understood what he was doing. Her chin had quivered, and she had whispered, "Please, please oh, . . . sweet Virgin, help me . . ." He'd watched the expression in her eyes change from terrified to glassy to vacant.

And Mrs. Harnick had seen him leaving Mrs. Gillespie's room.

Nurse Sheehan was the one who'd found Mrs. Gillespie. She hadn't accepted the old woman's death as the will of God. Instead she'd insisted that the respirator be checked to make sure it had been functioning properly. Later on he'd seen her with Mrs. Harnick. Mrs. Harnick was very much excited and pointing toward Mrs. Gillespie's room.

Everyone in the Home liked him except Nurse Sheehan. She was always reprimanding him, telling him that he was overstepping. "We have staff chaplains," she would say. "It's not your job to counsel people."

If he'd thought about Nurse Sheehan's being on duty today, he would never have gone near Mrs. Gillespie.

It was his worry over the Senator Jennings documentary that was consuming him, making it impossible for him to think straight. He had warned Patricia Traymore four times that she must not continue to prepare that program.

There would be no fifth warning.

Pat simply wasn't sleepy. After an hour of restless tossing, she gave up and reached for a book. But her mind refused to become involved with the Churchill biography she had been looking forward to reading.

At one o'clock she shut her eyes. At three o'clock she went downstairs to heat a cup of milk. She had left the downstairs foyer light on, but even so, the staircase was dark and she had to reach for the railing where the steps curved.

She used to sit on this step just out of sight of the people in the foyer and watch company come. I had a blue nightgown with flowers on it. I was wearing it that night . . . I had been sitting here and then I was frightened and I went back up to bed. . . .

And then . . . "I don't know," she said aloud. "I don't know."

Even the hot milk did not induce sleep.

At four o'clock she went downstairs again and brought up the nearly completed storyboard.

The program would open with the Senator and Pat in the studio seated in front of an enlarged picture of Abigail and Willard Jennings in their wedding reception line. Mrs. Jennings senior had been edited out of the reel. While the film of the reception ran, the Senator would talk about meeting Willard while she was attending Radcliffe.

At least, that way I get something in about the Northeast, Pat thought.

Then they'd show a montage of Willard's Congressional campaigns with Pat asking about Abigail's growing commitment to politics. Willard's thirty-fifth-birthday party would highlight the pre-Camelot years with the Kennedys.

Then would come the funeral, with Abigail escorted by Jack Kennedy. They'd eliminated the segment that showed her mother-in-law in a separate car. Then Abigail being sworn into Congress in black mourning attire, her face pale and grave.

Next came the footage about the embezzlement of the campaign funds and Abigail's commitment to airline safety. She sounds so strident and sanctimonious, Pat thought, and then you see the picture of that scared kid, Eleanor Brown. And it's one thing to be concerned about airline safety—another to keep pointing the finger at a pilot who also lost his life . . . But she knew she wouldn't be able to persuade Luther to change either segment.

The day after Christmas they would shoot Abigail in her office, with her staff and some carefully selected visitors. Congress had at last adjourned, and the shooting should go quickly.

At least Luther had agreed to a scene of Abigail in her own

home with friends. Pat had suggested a Christmas supper party with shots of Abigail arranging the buffet table. The guests would be some distinguished Washington personalities as well as a few of her office staff who could not be with their families on the holiday.

The last scene would be the Senator returning home at dusk, a briefcase under her arm. And then the wrap-up: "Like many of the millions of single adults in the United States, Senator Abigail Jennings has found her family, her vocation, her avocation in the work she loves."

Luther had written that line for Pat to deliver.

At eight o'clock Pat phoned Luther and asked him again to persuade the Senator to allow her early life to be included in the program. "What we have is dull," she said. "Except for those personal films, it's a thirty-minute campaign commercial."

Luther cut her off. "You've examined *all* the film?"

"Yes."

"How about photographs?"

"There were very few."

"Call and see if there are any more. No. I'll call. You're not very high on the Senator's list right now."

Forty-five minutes later she heard from Philip. Toby would be over around noon with photograph albums. The Senator believed Pat would find some interesting pictures in them.

Restlessly Pat wandered into the library. She had jammed the carton with the doll under the library table. She would use this time to go through more of her father's effects.

When she lifted the doll from the carton, she carried it to the window and examined it closely. A skillful pen had shaded the black button eyes, filled in the brows, given the mouth that mournful twist. In the daylight, it seemed even more pathetic. Was it supposed to represent her?

She put it aside and began to unpack the carton: the pictures of her mother and father; the packets of letters and papers; the photo albums. Her hands became soiled and dusty as she sorted the material into piles. Then she sat cross-legged on the carpet and began to go through it.

Loving hands had kept the mementos of Dean Adams' boyhood. Report cards were neatly pasted in sequence. A's and A-pluses. The lowest mark a B-plus.

He had lived on a farm fifty miles from Milwaukee. The house was a medium-sized white frame with a small porch. There were pictures of him with his mother and father. My grandparents, Pat thought. She realized she didn't know their names. The back of one of the pictures was marked *Irene and Wilson with Dean, age 6 months.*

She picked up a packet of letters. The rubber band snapped and they scattered on the carpet. Quickly she gathered and glanced through them. One especially caught her eye.

> *Dear Mom,*
> *Thank you. I guess those are the only words for all the years of sacrifice to put me through college and law school. I know all about the dresses you didn't buy, the outings you never attended with the other ladies in town. Long ago I promised I'd try to be just like Dad. I'll keep that promise. I love you. And remember to go to the doctor please. That cough sounded awfully deep.*
>
> *Your loving son,*
> *Dean*

An obituary notice for Irene Wagner Adams was beneath the letter. It was dated six months later.

Tears blurred Pat's eyes for the young man who had not been ashamed to express his love for his mother. *She too had experienced that generous love. Her hand in his. Her screaming delight when he came home. Daddy. Daddy. Swung high in the air and tossed up and strong hands catching her. She was rid-*

ing her tricycle down the driveway . . . her knee scraping along gravel . . . his voice saying, "This won't hurt much, Kerry. We have to make sure it's clean . . . What kind of ice cream should we get? . . ."

The doorbell rang. Pat swept the pictures and letters together and stood up. Half of them spilled from her arms as she tried to jam them into the carton. The doorbell rang again, this time more insistently. She scrambled to pick up the scattered photos and notes and hide them with the others. She started from the room and realized she'd forgotten to put away the pictures of her parents and the Raggedy Ann doll. Suppose Toby had come in here and seen them! She dropped them into the carton and shoved it under the table.

Toby was about to ring the bell again when she yanked open the door. Involuntarily, she stepped back as his bulky frame filled the doorway.

"I was just giving up on you!" His attempt to sound genial didn't come off.

"Don't give up on me, Toby," she said coldly. Who was he to be annoyed at having to wait a few seconds? He seemed to be studying her. She glanced down and realized how grimy her hands were and that she had been rubbing her eyes. Her face was probably smeared with dirt.

"You look like you were making mud pies." There was a puzzled, suspicious expression on his face. She didn't answer him. He shifted the package under his arm, and the oversized onyx ring moved back and forth on his finger. "Where do you want this stuff, Pat? In the library?"

"Yes."

He followed her so closely that she had the uneasy feeling he would crash into her if she stopped suddenly. Sitting cross-legged for so long had made her right leg numb, and she was favoring it.

"You limping, Pat? You didn't fall on the ice or anything, did you?"

You don't miss a trick, she thought. "Put the box on the table," she told him.

"Okay. I gotta get right back. The Senator wasn't happy about having to figure out where these albums were. I can see myself out."

She waited until she heard the front door close before she went to secure the bolt. As she reached the foyer, the door opened again. Toby seemed startled to see her standing there; then his face creased in an unpleasant smile. "That lock wouldn't keep out anyone who knew his way around, Pat," he said. "Be sure to use the dead bolt."

The Senator's additional material was a hodgepodge of newspaper clippings and fan letters. Most of the pictures were shots of her at political ceremonies, state dinners, ribbon-cutting ceremonies, inaugurations. As Pat turned the pages, several of them fluttered down to the floor.

The back pages of the album were more promising. She came upon an enlarged photo of a young Abigail and Willard seated on a blanket near a lake. He was reading to her. It was an idyllic setting; they looked like lovers on a Victorian cameo.

There were a few more snapshots that might fit into a montage. At last she had gone through everything and bent down to retrieve the pictures that had fallen. Underneath one of them was a folded sheet of expensive notepaper. She opened it. It read:

> *Billy darling. You were splendid in the hearings this afternoon. I am so proud of you. I love you so and look forward to a lifetime of being with you, of working with you. Oh, my dearest we really are going to make a difference in this world.*
>
> A.

The letter was dated May 13. Willard Jennings had been on his way to deliver the commencement address when he met his death on May 20.

What a terrific wrap-up that would make! Pat exulted. It would quiet anyone who thinks of the Senator as cold and uncaring. If she could only persuade Luther to let her read the note on the program. How would it sound? "Billy darling," she read aloud. "I'm so sorry . . ."

Her voice broke. What is the matter with me? she thought impatiently. Firmly, she began again. "Billy darling. You were splendid . . ."

16

On the twenty-third of December at 2 P.M. Senator Abigail Jennings sat in the library of her home with Toby and Philip and watched the telecast as the Vice President of the United States formally tendered his resignation to the Chief Executive.

Her lips dry, her fingernails digging into her palms, Abigail listened as the Vice President, propped on pillows in his hospital bed, ashen-faced and obviously dying, said in a surprisingly strong voice, "I had expected to withhold my decision until after the first of the year. However, I feel that it is my clear duty to vacate this office and have the line of succession to Chief Executive of this great country uncompromised. I am grateful for the confidence the President and my party expressed when I was twice chosen to be the Vice Presidential candidate. I am grateful to the people of the United States for having given me the opportunity to serve them."

With profound regret, the President accepted the resignation of his old friend and colleague. When asked if he had decided on a replacement, he said, "I have a few ideas." But he declined to respond to the names suggested by the press.

Toby whistled. "Well, it's happened, Abby."

"Senator, mark my words . . ." Philip began.

"Be quiet and listen!" she snapped. As the scene in the hospital room ended, the camera focused on Luther Pelham in the newsroom of Potomac Cable.

"A historic moment," Luther began. With dignified reticence he recounted a brief history of the Vice Presidency and then came to the point. "The time has come for a woman to be selected for the high office . . . a woman with the necessary experience and proved expertise. Mr. President, choose *her* now."

Abigail laughed sharply. "Meaning me."

The phone began to ring. "That will be reporters. I'm not in," she said.

An hour later the press was still camped outside Abigail's home. Finally she agreed to an interview. Outwardly she was calm. She said that she was busy with preparations for a Christmas supper for friends. When asked if she expected to be appointed Vice President, she said in an amused tone, "Now, you really can't expect me to comment on that."

Once the door closed behind her, her expression and manner changed. Even Toby did not dare to cross the line.

Luther phoned to confirm the taping schedule. Abigail's raised voice could be heard throughout the house. "Yes, I saw it. You want to know something? I probably have this in the bag right now, without that damn program hanging over my head. I told you it was a rotten idea. Don't tell *me* you only wanted to help me. You wanted to have me obligated to you, and we both know it."

Abigail's voice lowered, and Philip exchanged glances with Toby. "What did you find out?" he asked.

"Pat Traymore was up in Apple Junction last week. She stopped at the newspaper office and got some back issues. She visited Saunders, the guy who was sweet on Abby when she was a kid. He talked his head off to her. Then she saw the retired school principal who knew Abby. I was at Pat's house in Georgetown when Saunders phoned her."

"How much damage could any of those people do to the Senator?" Philip asked.

Toby shrugged. "It depends. Did you find out anything about the house?"

"Some," Philip told him. "We got to the realty company that has been renting it for years. They had a new tenant all lined up, but the bank handling the trust for the heirs said that someone in the family was planning to use it and it wouldn't be for rent again."

"Someone *in* the family?" Toby repeated. "*Who in* the family?"

"I would guess Pat Traymore," Philip said sarcastically.

"Don't get smart with me," Toby snapped. "I want to know *who* owns that place now, and *which* relative is using it."

With mixed emotions Pat watched Potomac Cable cover the Vice President's resignation. At the end of Luther's segment, the anchorman said that it was considered unlikely the President would name a successor before the New Year.

And we air the program on the twenty-seventh, Pat thought.

As Sam had predicted the first night she was in Washington, she might have a hand in the selection of the first woman Vice President.

Once again her sleep had been interrupted by troubled dreams. Did she really remember her mother and father so clearly, or was she confusing the films and pictures she had seen of them with reality? The memory of his bandaging her knee and taking her for ice cream was authentic. She was sure of that. But hadn't there also been times when she had pulled the pillow over her ears because of angry voices and hysterical weeping?

She was determined to finish reviewing her father's effects.

Doggedly she had examined the material and found herself increasingly concerned about the references to her mother. There were letters from her grandmother to Renée. One of them, dated six months before the tragedy, said: "*Renée, dear, the tone of your note troubles me. If you feel you are having onslaughts of depression again, please go into counseling immediately."*

It had been her grandmother, according to the newspaper articles, who had claimed that Dean Adams was an unstable personality.

She found a letter from her father to her mother written the year before their deaths:

> *Dear Renée,*
> *I am pretty upset that you want to spend the entire summer in New Hampshire with Kerry. You must know how much I miss you both. It is absolutely necessary for me to go to Wisconsin. Why not give it a try? We can rent a Steinway for you while you're there. I certainly understand that Mother's old spinet is hardly appropriate. Please, dear. For my sake.*

Pat felt as though she were trying to remove bandages from a festering wound. The nearer she got to the wound itself, the harder it was to pull the adhesive from it. The sense of pain, emotional and even physical, was increasingly acute.

One of the cartons was filled with Christmas ornaments and strings of lights. They gave her an idea. She would get a small Christmas tree. Why not? Where were Veronica and Charles now? She consulted their itinerary. Their ship would be putting in at St. John tomorrow. She wondered if she could phone them on Christmas Day.

The mail was a welcome respite. She had an abundance of cards and invitations from her friends in Boston. *"Come up just for the day if you possibly can." "We're all waiting for the program." "An Emmy for this one, Pat—not just the nomination."*

One letter had been forwarded from Boston Cable. The return-address sticker on the envelope read: CATHERINE GRANEY, 22 BALSAM PLACE, RICHMOND, VA.

Graney, Pat thought. That was the name of the pilot who died with Willard Jennings.

The letter was brief:

Dear Miss Traymore:
I have read that you are planning to prepare and narrate a program about Senator Abigail Jennings. As one who has had the opportunity to appreciate several of your fine documentaries, I feel it imperative to notify you that the program about Senator Abigail Jennings may become the subject of a lawsuit. I warn you, do not give the Senator the opportunity to discuss Willard Jennings' death. For your own sake, don't let her assert that pilot error cost her husband his life. That pilot, my husband, died too. And believe me, it is a bitter joke that she dares to affect the pose of a bereaved widow. If you wish to speak with me, you may call me at this number: 804-555-6841.

Pat went to the phone and dialed the number. It rang many times. She was about to hang up when she heard a hurried hello. It was Catherine Graney. The background was noisy, as though a crowd of people were there. Pat tried to make an appointment. "It will have to be tomorrow," the woman told her. "I run an antiques shop, and I'm having a sale today."

They agreed on a time, and she hurriedly gave Pat directions.

That afternoon Pat went shopping. Her first stop was an art shop. She left for reframing one of the old sailing prints that had come from her father's office. It would be her Christmas present to Sam.

"Have it for you in a week, Miss. That's a fine print. Worth some money if you ever want to sell it."

"I don't want to sell it."

She stopped in the specialty market near the house and ordered groceries, including a small turkey. At the florist's she bought two poinsettias and a garland of evergreen for the mantel. She found a Christmas tree that stood as high as her shoulders. The pick of the trees was gone, but this one was well enough shaped and the pine needles had a luxurious sheen.

By early evening she had finished decorating. The tree was set near the patio doors. The mantel was draped with evergreen. One poinsettia was on the low round table next to the couch, the other on the cocktail table in front of the love seat.

She had hung all the paintings. She had had to guess at placing them, but even so, the living room was now complete. A fire, she thought. There was always a fire.

She laid one, ignited the papers and kindling, and positioned the screen. Then she fixed an omelette and salad and brought the tray to the living room. Tonight she would simply watch television and relax. She felt she had been pushing too hard, that she should let memory unfold in its own way. She had expected this room to be repugnant to her, but despite the terror of that last night, she found it warm and peaceful. Did it harbor happy memories as well?

She turned on the set. The President and First Lady flashed on the screen. They were boarding *Air Force One* en route to their family home for Christmas. Once again the President was being badgered about his choice. "I'll tell you who she or he is by the New Year," he called. "Merry Christmas."

She. Had that been a deliberate slip? Of course not.

Sam phoned a few minutes later. "Pat, how is it going?"

She wished her mouth would not go dry at the sound of his voice. "Fine. Did you see the President on TV just now?"

"Yes, I did. Well, we're surely down to two people. He's committed himself to selecting a woman. I'm going to give Abigail a call. She must be chewing her nails."

Pat raised her eyebrows. "I would be, in her place." She twisted the tassel of her belt. "How's the weather?"

"It's hot as hell. Frankly, I prefer Christmas in a winter setting."

"Then you shouldn't have left. I was trooping around buying a Christmas tree and it was cold enough."

"What are your plans for Christmas Day? Will you be at Abigail's for the supper party?"

"Yes. I'm surprised you weren't invited."

"I was. Pat, it's good to be with Karen and Tom, but—well, this is Karen's family now, not mine. I had to bite my tongue at lunch not to tell off some pompous ass who had a laundry list of all the mistakes this Administration has made."

Pat couldn't resist. "Isn't Tom's mother fixing you up with her available friends or cousins or whatever?"

Sam laughed. "I'm afraid so. I'm not staying till New Year's. I'll be back a few days after Christmas. You haven't had any more threats, have you?"

"Not even one breathless phone call. I miss you, Sam," she added deliberately.

There was a pause. She could imagine his expression—worried, trying to find the right phrase. You care every bit as much about me as you did two years ago, she thought.

"Sam?"

His voice was constrained. "I miss you, too, Pat. You're very important to me."

What a fantastic way to put it. "And you're one of my very dearest friends."

Without waiting for his response, she hung up.

17

"Father, have you seen my Raggedy Ann doll?"

He smiled at Glory, hoping he didn't look nervous. "No, of course I haven't seen it. Didn't you have it in the closet in your bedroom?"

"Yes. I can't imagine . . . Father, are you sure you didn't throw it away?"

"Why would I throw it away?"

"I don't know." She got up from the table. "I'm going to do a little Christmas shopping. I won't be late." She looked worried, then asked, "Father, are you starting to feel sick again? You've been talking in your sleep the last few nights. I could hear you from my room. Is anything worrying you? You're not hearing those voices again, are you?"

He saw the fear in her eyes. He never should have told Glory about the voices. She hadn't understood. Worse, she had started to be nervous around him. "Oh, no. I was joking when I told you about them." He was sure she didn't believe him.

She put her hand on his arm. "You kept saying Mrs. Gillespie's name in your sleep. Isn't she the woman who just died in the nursing home?"

After Glory went out, Arthur sat at the kitchen table, his thin legs wound around the rungs of the chair, thinking. Nurse Sheehan and the doctors had questioned him about Mrs. Gillespie: had he looked in on her?

"Yes," he'd admitted. "I just wanted to see if she was comfortable."

"How many times did you look in on her?"

"Once. She was asleep. She was fine."

"Mrs. Harnick and Mrs. Drury both thought they saw you. But Mrs. Drury said it was at five after three, and Mrs. Harnick was sure it was later."

"Mrs. Harnick is wrong. I only stopped in once."

They had to believe him. Half the time Mrs. Harnick was almost senile. *But the rest of the time she was very sharp.*

He suddenly picked up the newspaper again. He'd taken the Metro home. An old woman carrying a shopping bag and leaning on a cane had been on the platform. He'd been about to go over and offer to help her with her bag when the express roared into the station. The crowd had surged forward and a young fellow, his arms filled with schoolbooks, had nearly knocked the old lady over as he rushed to get a seat.

He recalled how he had helped her into the train just before the doors closed. "Are you all right?" he had asked.

"Oh, yes. My, I was afraid I'd fall. Young people are so careless. Not like in my day."

"They are cruel," he said softly.

The young man got off at Dupont Circle and crossed the platform. He had followed him, managed to get next to him as he stood at the front of the crowd, right at the edge of the platform. As the train approached he had stepped behind him and jostled his arm so that one of the books began to slip. The young man grabbed for it. Off-balance as he was, it was easy to push him forward. The book and the young man landed on the tracks together.

The newspaper. Yes, here it was on page three: NINETEEN-YEAR-OLD STUDENT KILLED BY METRO. The account called the death an accident. A bystander had seen a book slip from the student's arm. He had bent forward to retrieve it and lost his balance.

The coffee cup in Arthur's hands had grown cold. He would make a fresh cup, then get to work.

There were so many helpless old people in the nursing home waiting for his attention. His mind had been on Patricia Traymore. That was why he hadn't been more careful about Mrs. Gillespie. Tomorrow he'd tell Glory he had to work late and he'd go back to Patricia Traymore's house.

He had to get in again.

Glory wanted her doll back.

At ten o'clock on the twenty-fourth Pat set off for Richmond. The sun had come out strong and golden, but the air was still very cold. It would be a frosty Christmas.

After leaving the highway she took three wrong turns and became thoroughly exasperated with herself. At last she found Balsam Place. It was a street of comfortable medium-sized Tudor-style houses. Number 22 was larger than its neighbors and had a carved sign ANTIQUES on the lawn.

Catherine Graney was waiting in the doorway. She was about fifty, with a square face, deep-set blue eyes and a sturdy, slim body. Her graying hair was straight and blunt-cut. She shook Pat's hand warmly. "I feel as though I know you. I go on buying trips to New England fairly often, and whenever I got the chance I watched your program."

The downstairs was used as a showroom. Chairs, couches, vases, lamps, paintings, Oriental carpets, china and fine glassware were all marked with tags. A Queen Anne breakfront held delicate figurines. A sleepy Irish setter, his dark red hair generously sprinkled with gray, was asleep in front of it.

"I live upstairs," Mrs. Graney explained. "Technically the shop is closed, but someone phoned and asked if she could stop in for a last-minute gift. You will have coffee, won't you?"

Pat took off her coat. She looked around, studying the contents of the room. "You have beautiful things."

"I like to think so." Mrs. Graney looked pleased. "I love

searching out antiques and restoring them. My workshop is in the garage." She poured coffee from a Sheffield pot and handed a cup to Pat. "And I have the pleasure of being surrounded by beautiful things. With that auburn hair and gold blouse, you look as though you belong on that Chippendale couch."

"Thank you." Pat realized she liked this outspoken woman. There was something direct and honest about her. It made it possible to get right to the point of the visit. "Mrs. Graney, you can understand that your letter was quite startling. But will you tell me why you didn't contact the network directly, instead of writing to me?"

Catherine Graney took a sip of coffee. "As I told you, I've seen a number of your documentaries. I sense integrity in your work, and I didn't think you would willingly help to perpetuate a lie. That's why I'm appealing to you to make sure that George Graney's name is not mentioned on the Jennings program, and that Abigail Jennings does not refer to 'pilot error' in connection with Willard's death. My husband could fly anything that had wings."

Pat thought of the already-edited segments for the program. The Senator had denounced the pilot—but had she actually mentioned his name? Pat wasn't sure. But she did remember some of the details of the accident. "Didn't the investigation findings indicate that your husband was flying too low?" she asked.

"The *plane* was flying too low and went into the mountain. When Abigail Jennings started using that crash as a means for getting her name in the paper as a spokesperson for airline safety regulations, I should have objected immediately."

Pat watched as the Irish setter, seeming to sense the tension in his mistress's voice, got up, stretched, ambled across the room and settled at her feet. Catherine leaned over and patted him.

"Why *didn't* you speak up immediately?"

"Many reasons. I had a baby a few weeks after the accident. And I suppose I wanted to be considerate of Willard's mother."

"Willard's mother?"

"Yes. You see, George used to fly Willard Jennings quite often. They became good friends. Old Mrs. Jennings knew that, and she came to me after the crash had been sighted—to *me,* not to her daughter-in-law—and we sat together and waited for the final word. She put a very generous sum of money in trust for my son's education. I didn't want to make her unhappy by using the weapon I could have used against Abigail Jennings. We both had our suspicions, but to her, scandal was anathema."

Three grandfather clocks simultaneously chimed the hour. It was one o'clock. The sun streamed into the room. Pat noticed that Catherine Graney twisted her gold wedding band as she spoke. Apparently, she had never remarried. "What weapon could you have used?" she asked.

"I could have destroyed Abigail's credibility. Willard was miserably unhappy with her and with politics. The day he died he was planning to announce that he was not seeking reelection and that he was accepting the presidency of a college. He wanted the academic life. The last morning he and Abigail had a terrible fight at the airport. She pleaded with him not to announce his resignation. And he told her, right in front of George and me—'Abigail, it won't make a damn bit of difference to you. We're finished.'"

"Abigail and Willard Jennings were on the verge of *divorce?*"

"This 'noble widow' business has always been a posture. My son, George Graney, Junior, is an Air Force pilot now. He never knew his dad. But I'm not going to have him embarrassed by any more of her lies. And whether I win the suit or not, I'll make the whole world realize what a phony she's always been."

Pat tried to choose her words carefully. "Mrs. Graney, I will certainly do what I can to see that your husband isn't referred to in a derogatory way. But I must tell you, I've been going through the Senator's private files and everything I see suggests that Abigail and Willard Jennings were very much in love."

Catherine Graney looked scornful. "I'd like to see the expression on old Mrs. Jennings' face if she ever heard *that!* Tell you what: on your way back, drive an extra mile and pass Hillcrest. That's the Jennings estate. And imagine how strongly a woman must have felt not to leave it—or one red cent—to her own daughter-in-law."

Fifteen minutes later, Pat was looking through high iron gates at the lovely mansion set on the crest of the snow-covered grounds. As Willard's widow, Abigail had had every right to think she might inherit this estate as well as his seat in Congress. As his divorced wife, on the other hand, she would have been the outcast once again. If Catherine Graney was to be believed, the tragedy Abigail spoke so movingly about had, in fact, been the stroke of fortune that twenty-five years ago saved her from oblivion.

18

"It looks good, Abby," Toby said genially.

"It should photograph well," she agreed. They were admiring the Christmas tree in Abigail's living room. The dining-room table was already set for the Christmas buffet.

"There are bound to be reporters hanging around tomorrow morning," she said. "Find out what time the early services are at the Cathedral. I should be seen there."

She didn't plan to leave a stone unturned. Ever since the President had said, "I'll announce *her*," Abigail had been sick with nervousness.

"I'm the better candidate," she'd said a dozen times. "Claire is from his own region. That's not good. If only we weren't involved with the damn program."

"It might help you," he said soothingly, though secretly he was as worried as she.

"Toby, it might help if I were running for elective office in a big field of candidates. But I don't think the President is going to see the damn thing and jump up and say '*She's* for me.' But he just might wait to see if there's negative reaction to it before he announces his decision."

He knew she was right. "Don't worry. Anyway, you can't pull out. The program's already in the listings."

She'd carefully selected the guests for the Christmas buffet supper. Among them she had two Senators, three Congressmen, a Supreme Court Justice and Luther Pelham. "I only wish Sam Kingsley weren't in California," she said.

By six o'clock, everything had been arranged. Abby had a goose cooking in the oven. She would serve it cold at the supper the next day. The warm, rich smell filled the house. It reminded Toby of being in the kitchen of the Saunders house when they were high school kids. That kitchen always smelled of good food roasting or baking. Francey Foster had been some cook. You had to give her that!

"Well, I guess I'll be on my way, Abby."

"Got a heavy date, Toby?"

"Not too heavy." The Steakburger waitress was beginning to bore him. Eventually they all did.

"I'll see you in the morning. Pick me up early."

"Right, Senator. Sleep well. You want to look your best tomorrow."

Toby left Abby fussing with some strands of tinsel that weren't hanging straight. He went back to his apartment, showered and put on slacks, a textured shirt and a sports jacket. The Steakburger kid had pretty definitely told him she didn't plan to cook tonight. He would take her out for a change and then they'd go back to her apartment for a nightcap.

Toby didn't enjoy spending his money on food—not when the ponies were so interesting. He pulled on his dark green knitted tie and was looking at himself in the mirror when the phone rang. It was Abby.

"Go out and get me a copy of *The National Mirror,*" she demanded.

"The *Mirror?*"

"You heard me—go out and get it. Philip just phoned. Miss Apple Junction and her elegant mother are on the front page. Who dug out that picture? Who?"

Toby gripped the phone. Pat Traymore had been in the

newspaper office at Apple Junction. Jeremy Saunders had phoned Pat Traymore. "Senator, if someone is trying to put the screws on you, I'll make mincement of them."

Pat was home by three-thirty and looked forward to an hour's nap. As usual, the extra exertion of standing and climbing to hang the pictures the night before had taken its toll on her leg. The dull, steady ache had been persistent during the drive from Richmond. But she'd scarcely entered the house when the phone rang. It was Lila Thatcher.

"I'm so glad I've caught you, Pat. I've been watching for you. Are you free this evening?"

"As a matter of fact . . ." Caught off guard, Pat could not think of a reasonable excuse. You can't lie easily to a psychic, she thought.

Lila interrupted. "*Don't* be busy. The Ambassador is having people in for his usual Christmas Eve supper and I phoned and told him I'd like to bring you. After all, you are one of his neighbors now. He'd be delighted."

The octogenarian retired Ambassador was perhaps the most distinguished elder statesmen of the District. Few world leaders visiting Washington failed to stop at the Ambassador's home.

"I'd love to go," Pat said warmly. "Thank you for thinking of me."

When she hung up, Pat went up to the bedroom. The guests at the Ambassador's home would be a dressy crowd. She decided to wear a black velvet suit with sable-banded cuffs.

She still had time to soak in a hot tub for fifteen minutes and then to take a nap.

As she lay back in the tub, Pat noticed that a corner of the bland beige wallpaper was peeling. A swatch of Wedgwood blue could be seen underneath. Reaching up, she peeled back a large piece of the top layer of paper.

That was what she remembered—that lovely violet and

Wedgwood blue. *And the bed had an ivory satin quilted spread,* she thought, *and we had a blue carpet on the floor.*

Mechanically she dried herself and pulled on a terry-cloth caftan. The bedroom was cool and already filled with late-afternoon shadows.

As a precaution, she set the alarm for four-thirty before drifting off to sleep.

The angry voices . . . the blankets pulled over her head . . . the loud noise . . . another loud noise . . . her bare feet silent on the stairs . . .

The insistent pealing of the alarm woke her. She rubbed her forehead trying to recall the shadowy dream. Had the wallpaper triggered something in her head? Oh, God, if only she hadn't set the alarm.

But it's coming closer, she thought. The truth comes closer each time. . . .

Slowly she got up and went to the vanity in the dressing room. Her face was strained and pale. A creaking sound down the hallway made her whirl around, her hand at her throat. But of course, it was just the house settling.

Promptly at five, Lila Thatcher rang the bell. She stood framed in the doorway, almost elfin with her rosy cheeks and white hair. She looked festive in an Autumn Haze mink coat with a Christmas corsage pinned on the wide collar.

"Have we time for a glass of sherry?" Pat asked.

"I think so." Lila glanced at the slender Carrara marble table and matching marble-framed mirror in the foyer. "I always loved those pieces. I'm glad to see them back."

"You know." It was a statement. "I thought so the other night."

She had set out a decanter of sherry and a plate of sweet biscuits on the cocktail table. Lila paused at the doorway of the living room. "Yes," she said, "you've done a very good job. Of course, it's been so long, but it is as I remember it. That wonderful carpet; that couch. Even the paintings," she murmured.

"No wonder I've been troubled. Pat, are you sure this is wise?"

They sat down and Pat poured the sherry. "I don't know if it's wise. I *do* know it's necessary."

"How much do you remember?"

"Bits. Pieces. Nothing that hangs together."

"I used to call the hospital to inquire about you. You were unconscious for months. When you were moved, we were given to understand that if you did pull through, you'd be permanently damaged. And then the death notice appeared."

"Veronica . . . my mother's sister and her husband adopted me. My grandmother didn't want the scandal following me . . . or them."

"And that's why they changed your first name as well?"

"My name is Patricia Kerry. I gather the Kerry was my father's idea. Patricia was my grandmother's name. They decided that as long as they were changing my last name they might as well start using my real first name too."

"So Kerry Adams became Patricia Traymore. What are you hoping to find here?" Lila took a sip of sherry and set down the glass.

Restlessly Pat got up and walked over to the piano. In a reflex action she reached toward the keyboard, then pulled her hands back.

Lila was watching her. "You play?"

"Only for pleasure."

"Your mother played constantly. You *know* that."

"Yes. Veronica has told me about her. You see, at first I only wanted to understand what happened here. Then I realized that ever since I can remember I've hated my father; hated him for hurting me so, for robbing me of my mother. I think I hoped to find some indication that he was sick, falling apart—I don't know what. But now, as I begin to remember little things, I realize it's more than that. I'm not the same person I would have become if . . ."

She gestured at the area where the bodies had been found.

". . . if all this hadn't happened. I need to link the child I was with the person I am. I've lost some part of myself back there. I have so many preconceived ideas—my mother was an angel, my father a devil. Veronica hinted that my father destroyed my mother's musical career and then her life. But what about *him?* She married a politician and then refused to share his life. Was that fair? How much was I a catalyst of the trouble between them? Veronica told me once that this house was *too small.* When my mother tried to practice, I'd wake up and start crying."

"Catalyst," Lila said. "That's exactly what I'm afraid you are, Pat. You're setting things in motion that are best left alone." She studied her. "You seem to have recovered very well from your injuries."

"It took a long time. When I finally regained consciousness, I had to be taught everything all over again. I didn't understand words. I didn't know how to use a fork. I wore the brace on my leg till I was seven."

Lila realized she was very warm. Only a moment before she'd felt cool. She didn't want to examine the reason for the change. She knew only that this room had not yet completed its scenario of tragedy. She stood up. "We'd better not keep the Ambassador waiting," she said briskly.

She could see in Pat's face the cheekbones and sensitive mouth of Renée, the wide-spaced eyes and auburn hair of Dean.

"All right, Lila, you've studied me long enough," Pat said. "Which one of them do I resemble?"

"Both," Lila said honestly, "but I think you are more like your father."

"Not in every way, please, God." Pat's attempt at a smile was a forlorn failure.

19

Well-hidden in the shadows of the trees and shrubs, Arthur observed Pat and Lila through the patio doors. He had been bitterly disappointed to see the lighted house, the car in the driveway. Maybe he wouldn't be able to search for the doll tonight. And he desperately wanted Glory to have it in time for Christmas. He tried to hear what the women were saying but could not catch more than an occasional word. They were both dressed up. Could they be going out? He decided to wait. Avidly he studied Patricia Traymore's face. She was so serious, her expression so troubled. Had she begun to heed his warnings? For her sake he hoped so.

He had been watching only a few minutes when they stood up. They *were* going out. Silently he crept along the side of the house and in a moment heard the sound of the front door opening. They did not take the car. They could not be going too far, maybe to a neighbor's house or a nearby restaurant. He would have to hurry.

Quickly he made his way back to the patio. Patricia Traymore had left the living-room lights on and he could see the strong new locks on the French doors. Even if he cut a pane he would not be able to get in. He had anticipated that and had planned what he would do. There was an elm tree next to the patio, one that would be easy to climb. A thick branch ran just under an upstairs window.

The night he left the doll he'd noticed that window was not completely closed at the top. It sagged as though it didn't hang properly. It would be easy to force it open.

A few minutes later he was stepping over the sill onto the floor. He listened intently. The room had a hollow feeling. Cautiously he turned on his flashlight. The room was empty and he opened the door to the hallway. He was sure he was alone in the house. Where should he begin searching?

He'd gone to so much trouble because of the doll. He'd almost been caught taking the vial of blood from the lab in the nursing home. He'd forgotten how much Glory loved her doll, how when he'd tiptoe into her room just to see if she was sleeping peacefully, she'd always had the doll clutched in her arms.

It was incredible to him that for the second time in a week he was inside this house again. The memory of that long ago morning was still so vivid: the ambulance, lights flashing, sirens blazing, tires screeching in the driveway. The sidewalk crowded with people, neighbors with coats thrown over expensive bathrobes; police cars barricading N Street; cops everywhere. A woman screaming. She was the housekeeper who'd found the bodies.

He and his fellow ambulance attendant from Georgetown Hospital had rushed into the house. A young cop was on guard at the door. "Don't hurry. They don't need you."

The man lying on his back, the bullet in his temple, must have died instantly. The gun was between him and the woman. She had pitched forward and the blood from the chest wound stained the rug around her. Her eyes were still open, staring, unfocused, as though she'd wondered what had happened, how it had happened. She couldn't have been more than thirty. Her dark hair was scattered over her shoulders. Her thin face had delicate nostrils and high cheekbones. A yellow silk robe billowed around her like an evening gown.

He'd been the first to bend over the little girl. Her red hair was so matted with dried blood it had turned auburn; her right leg was jutting from the flowered nightdress, the bone sticking up in a pyramid.

He'd bent closer. "Alive," he'd whispered. Bedlam. I.V. hooked up. They'd hung a bottle of O negative; clamped an oxygen mask on the small, still face; splinted the shattered leg. He'd helped swathe the head, his fingers smoothing her forehead, her hair curling around his fingers. Someone said her name was Kerry. "If it is God's will, I'll save you, Kerry," he'd whispered.

"She can't make it," the intern told him roughly, and pushed him out of the way. The police photographers snapped pictures of the little girl; of the corpses. Chalk marks on the carpet outlined the positions of the bodies.

Even then he'd felt the house was a place of sin and evil, a place where two innocent flowers, a young woman and her little girl, had been willfully violated. He'd pointed out the house to Glory once and told her all about that morning.

Little Kerry had remained in an intensive-care unit at Georgetown Hospital for two months. He'd looked in on her as often as he could. She never woke up, just lay there, a sleeping doll. He had come to understand that she was not supposed to live and had tried to find a way to deliver her to the Lord. But before he could act, she was moved to a long-term-care facility near Boston, and after a while he read that she'd died.

His sister had had a doll. "Let me help take care of it," he'd pleaded. "We'll pretend it's sick and I'll make it well." His father's heavy, callused hand had slammed his face. Blood had gushed from his nose. "Make that *well, you sissy."*

He began to search for Glory's doll in Patricia Traymore's bedroom. Opening the closet, he examined the shelves and the floor, but it wasn't there. With sullen anger he observed the many expensive clothes. Silk blouses, and negligées, and gowns, and the kind of suits you see in magazine ads. Glory wore jeans and sweaters most of the time, and she bought them at K-Mart. The people in the nursing home were usually in flannel nightgowns and oversized robes that swaddled their shapeless bodies. One of Patricia Traymore's robes startled him. It was a brown wool tunic with a corded belt. It reminded him of a monk's habit. He took it out of the closet and held it against him. Next he investigated the deep bottom drawers of the dresser. The doll wasn't there either. If the doll was still in the house it was not in her bedroom. He couldn't waste so much time. He glanced into the closets of the empty bedrooms and went downstairs.

Patricia Traymore had left the vestibule light on, as well as a lamp in the library and others in the living room—she had even left on the lights on the Christmas tree. She was sinfully wasteful, he thought angrily. It was unfair to use so much energy, when old people couldn't even afford to heat their own homes. And the tree was already dry. *If a flame touched it, it would ignite and the branches would crackle and the ornaments melt.*

One of the ornaments had fallen from the tree. He picked it up and replaced it. There was really no hiding place in the living room.

The library was the last room he searched. The files were locked—that's where she had probably put it. Then he noticed the carton jammed far back under the library table. And somehow he *knew.* He had to tug hard to get the carton out but when he opened it his heart beat joyfully. There was Glory's precious doll.

The apron was gone, but he couldn't waste time looking for it. He walked through all the rooms, carefully examining them for signs of his presence. He hadn't turned a light on or off or touched a door. He had plenty of experience from his work in the nursing home. Of course if Patricia Traymore looked for the doll, she'd know that someone had come in. But that carton was pushed far under the table. Maybe she wouldn't miss the doll for a while.

He would go out the same way he'd come in—from the second story bedroom window. Patricia Traymore didn't use that bedroom; she probably didn't even glance in it for days at a time.

He had entered the house at five-fifteen. The chimes of the church near the college tolled six as he slid down the tree, made his furtive way through the yard and disappeared into the night.

The Ambassador's house was immense. Stark white walls provided a vivid backdrop for his magnificent art collection. Comfortable, richly upholstered couches and antique Georgian tables caught Pat's eye. A huge Christmas tree decorated with silver ornaments stood in front of the patio doors.

The dining room table was set with an elaborate buffet: caviar and sturgeon, a Virginia ham, turkey en gelée, hot biscuits and salads. Two waiters discreetly refilled the guests' champagne glasses.

Ambassador Cardell, small, trim and whitehaired, welcomed Pat with courtly grace and introduced her to his sister Rowena Van Cleef, who now lived with him. "His baby sister," Mrs. Van Cleef told Pat, her eyes twinkling. "I'm only seventy-four; Edward is eighty-two."

There were some forty other people present. *Sotto voce,* Lila pointed out the most celebrated to Pat. "The British Ambassador and his wife, Sir John and Lady Clemens . . . the French Ambassador . . . Donald Arlen—he's about to be appointed head of the World Bank . . . General Wilkins is the tall man by the mantel—he's taking over the NATO command . . . Senator Whitlock—that's *not* his wife with him . . ."

She introduced Pat to the neighborhood people. Pat was surprised to discover she was the center of attention. Was there any indication of who might have been responsible for the break-in? Didn't it seem as though the President was going to appoint Senator Jennings Vice President? Was the

Senator easy to work with? Did they tape the entire program in advance?

Gina Butterfield, the columnist from *The Washington Tribune*, had drifted over and was listening avidly to what Pat was saying.

"It's so extraordinary that someone broke into your house and left a threatening note," the columnist observed. "Obviously you didn't take it seriously."

Pat tried to sound offhand. "We all feel it was the work of a crank. I'm sorry so much was made of it. It really is unfair to the Senator."

The columnist smiled. "My dear, this is Washington. Surely you don't believe that anything this newsy can be ignored. You seem very sanguine, but if I were in your shoes I'd be quite upset to find my home broken into and my life threatened."

"Especially in that house," another volunteered. "Were you told about the Adams murder-suicide there?"

Pat stared at the bubbles in her champagne glass. "Yes, I'd heard the story. But it was so long ago, wasn't it?"

"Must we discuss that subject?" Lila broke in. "It is Christmas Eve."

"Wait a minute," Gina Butterfield said quickly. "*Adams. Congressman Adams.* Do you mean that Pat is living in the house where he killed himself? How did the press miss that?"

"What possible connection does it have to the break-in?" Lila snapped.

Pat felt the older woman touch her arm in a warning gesture. Was her expression revealing too much?

The Ambassador stopped at their group. "Please, help yourselves to some supper," he urged.

Pat turned to follow him, but the columnist's question to another guest stopped her.

"You were living here in Georgetown at the time of the deaths?"

"Yes, indeed," the woman answered. "Just two houses down

from them. My mother was alive then. We knew the Adams couple quite well."

"That was before I came to Washington," Gina Butterfield explained, "but of course I heard all the rumors. Is it true there was a lot more to the case than came out?"

"Of course it's true." The neighbor's lips parted in a crafty smile. "Renée's mother, Mrs. Schuyler, played the *grande dame* in Boston. She told the press that Renée had realized her marriage was a mistake and planned to divorce Dean Adams."

"Pat, shall we get something to eat?" Lila's arm urged her away.

"Wasn't she getting the divorce?" Gina asked.

"I doubt it," the other snapped. "She was insane about Dean, crazy jealous of him, resentful of his work. A real dud at parties. Never opened her mouth. And the way she'd practice that damn piano eight hours a day. In warm weather we all went wild listening to it. And believe me, she was no Myra Hess. Her playing was altogether pedestrian."

I won't believe this, Pat thought. I don't want to believe it. What was the columnist asking now? Something about Dean Adams having a reputation as a womanizer?

"He was so attractive that women always made a play for him." The neighbor shrugged her shoulders. "I was only twenty-three then, and I had a huge crush on him. He used to walk with little Kerry in the evening. I made it my business to bump into them regularly, but it didn't do me any good. I think we'd better get on that buffet line. I'm starved."

"Was Congressman Adams visibly unstable?" Gina asked.

"Of course not. Renée's mother started that talk. She knew what she was doing. Remember, both their fingerprints were on the gun. My mother and I always thought that Renée was probably the one who flipped and shot up the place. And as far as what happened to Kerry . . . Listen, those bony pianist's hands were mighty powerful! I wouldn't have put it past her to have hit that poor child that night."

20

Sam sipped a light beer as he stared aimlessly across the crowd at the Palm Springs Racquet Club. Turning his head, he glanced at his daughter and smiled. Karen had inherited her mother's coloring; her deep tan only made her blond hair seem that much lighter. Her hand rested on her husband's arm. Thomas Walton Snow, Jr., was a very nice fellow, Sam thought. A good husband; a successful businessman. His family was too boringly social for Sam's taste, but he was happy that his daughter had married well.

Since his arrival, Sam had been introduced to several extremely attractive women in their early forties—widows, grass widows, career types, each ready to select a man for the rest of her life. All of this only caused Sam to feel a cumulative restlessness, an inability to settle down, an aching, pervasive sense of not belonging.

Where in the merry hell *did* he belong?

In Washington. That was where. It was good to be with Karen, but he simply didn't give a damn about the rest of the people she found so intensely satisfying.

My child is twenty-four years old, he thought. She's happily married. She's expecting a baby. I don't want to be introduced to all the eligible forty-plus women in Palm Springs.

"Daddy, will you please stop scowling?"

Karen leaned across the table, kissed him and then settled back with Tom's arm around her. He surveyed the bright, expectant faces of Tom's family. In another day or so they'd start to get fed up. He'd become a difficult guest.

"Sweetheart," he said to Karen, making his voice confidential. "You asked me if you thought the President would appoint Senator Jennings Vice President, and I said I didn't know. I should be more honest. I think she'll get it."

All eyes were suddenly focused on him.

"Tomorrow night the Senator is having a Christmas supper party at her home; you'll see some of it on the television program. She'd like me to be there. If you don't mind, I think I should attend."

Everyone understood. Karen's father-in-law sent out for a timetable. If Sam left L.A. the next morning on the 8 A.M. flight, he'd be at National Airport by four-thirty East Coast time. How interesting to be a guest at the televised dinner party. Everyone was looking forward to the program.

Only Karen was quiet. Then, laughing, she said, "Daddy, cut the baloney. I've heard the rumors that Senator Jennings has her eye on you!"

21

At nine-fifteen, Pat and Lila walked silently together from the Ambassador's party. It was only when they were within reach of their own houses that Lila said quietly, "Pat, I can't tell you how sorry I am."

"How much of what that woman said was true and how much was exaggeration? I must know." Phrases kept running through her mind: neurotic . . . long, bony fingers . . . womanizer . . . We think she hit that poor kid . . . "I really need to know how much is true," she repeated.

"Pat, she's a vicious gossip. She knew perfectly well what she was doing when she started to talk about the background of the house with that woman from *The Washington Tribune.*"

"She was mistaken, of course," Pat said tonelessly.

"Mistaken?"

They were at Lila's gate. Pat looked across the street at her own house. Even though she'd left several lights burning downstairs, it still seemed remote and shadowy. "You see, there's one thing that I'm quite sure I remember. When I ran through the foyer into the living room that night I tripped over my mother's body." She turned to Lila. "So you see what that gets me: a neurotic mother who apparently found me a nuisance and a father who went berserk and tried to kill me. Quite a heritage, isn't it?"

Lila didn't answer. The sense of foreboding that had been nagging at her was becoming acute. "Oh, Kerry, I want to help you."

Pat pressed her hand. "You are helping me, Lila," she said. "Good night."

In the library, the red button on the answering machine was flashing. Pat rewound the tape. There was a single call on the unit. "This is Luther Pelham. It is now seven-twenty. We have a crisis. No matter what time you get in, call me at Senator Jennings' home, 703/555-0143. It is imperative that we meet there tonight."

Her mouth suddenly dry, Pat phoned the number. It was busy. It took three more attempts before she got through. Toby answered.

"This is Pat Traymore, Toby. What's wrong?"

"Plenty. Where are you?"

"At home."

"All right. Mr. Pelham has a car standing by to pick you up. It should be there in ten minutes."

"Toby, what's wrong?"

"Miss Traymore, maybe that's something you're going to have to explain to the Senator."

He hung up.

A half-hour later the network staff car that Luther had sent pulled up in front of Senator Jennings' home in McLean. On the drive over, Pat had worried herself with endless suppositions, but all her thoughts led to the same chilling conclusion: something had happened to further upset or embarrass the Senator, and whatever it was, she was being blamed.

A grim-faced Toby opened the door and led her into the library. Silent shapes were seated around the table in a council of war, the atmosphere oddly at variance with the poinsettia plants flanking the fireplace.

Senator Jennings, icy calm, her sphinxlike expression cast in marble, stared through Pat. Philip was to the Senator's right, his long, thin strands of colorless hair no longer combed carefully over his oval skull.

Luther Pelham's cheekbones were mottled purple. He appeared to be on the verge of a stroke.

This isn't a trial, Pat thought. It's an inquisition. My guilt has already been decided. But for what? Without offering her a seat, Toby dropped his heavy bulk into the last chair at the table.

"Senator," Pat said, "something is terribly wrong and it's quite evident it has to do with me. Will someone please tell me what's going on?"

There was a newspaper in the middle of the table. With one gesture, Philip flipped it over and pushed it at Pat. "Where did they get that picture?" he asked coldly.

Pat stared down at the cover of *The National Mirror.* The headline read: "WILL MISS APPLE JUNCTION BE THE FIRST WOMAN VEEP?" The picture, which took up the entire cover, was of Abigail in her Miss Apple Junction crown standing with her mother.

Enlarged, the picture revealed even more cruelly the massive dimensions of Francey Foster. Bulging flesh strained against the splotchy print of her badly cut dress. The arm around Abigail was dimpled with fat; the proud smile only emphasized the double-chinned face.

"You've seen this picture before," Philip snapped.

"Yes." How horrible for the Senator, she thought. She remembered Abigail's stern observation that she had spent more than thirty years trying to put Apple Junction behind her. Ignoring the others, Pat addressed the Senator directly. "Surely you can't believe I had anything to do with the *Mirror* getting this picture?"

"Listen, Miss Traymore," Toby answered, "don't bother lying. I found out that you were snooping around Apple Junction, including digging up back issues of the newspaper. I was at your place the day Saunders called." There was nothing deferential about Toby now.

"I have told the Senator you went to Apple Junction against my explicit orders," Luther thundered.

Pat understood the warning. She was not to let Abigail Jennings know that Luther had acceded to her trip to Abigail's birthplace. But that didn't matter now. What mattered was Abigail. "Senator," she began, "I understand how you must feel . . ."

The effect of her words was explosive. Abigail jumped to her feet. "Do you indeed? I thought I'd been plain enough, but let me start again. I hated every minute of my life in that stinking town. Luther and Toby have finally gotten around to letting me in on your activities up there, so I know you saw Jeremy Saunders. What did that useless leech tell you? That I had to use the back door and that my mother was the cook? I'll *bet* he did.

"I believe you released that picture, Pat Traymore. And I know why. You're bound and determined you're going to profile me *your* way. You *like* Cinderella stories. In your letters to me you insinuated as much. And when I was bloody fool enough to let myself get talked into this program, you decided that it had to be done *your* way so everyone could talk about that poignant, moving Patricia Traymore touch. Never mind that it could cost me everything I've been working for all my life."

"You believe I would send out that picture to somehow further my own career?" Pat looked from one to the other. "Luther, has the Senator seen the storyboard yet?"

"Yes, she has."

"How about the alternative storyboard?"

"Forget that one."

"What alternative storyboard?" Philip demanded.

"The one I've been begging Luther to use—and I assure you it has no mention of the first beauty contest or picture from it.

Senator, in a way you're right. I do want to see this production done my way. But for the best possible reason. I have admired you tremendously. When I wrote to you, I didn't know there was any chance that you might soon be appointed Vice President. I was looking ahead and hoping you would be a serious contender for the Presidential nomination next year."

Pat paused for breath, then rushed on. "I wish you'd dig out that first letter I sent you. I meant what I said. The one problem you have is that the American public considers you cold and remote. That picture is a good example. Obviously you're ashamed of it. But look at the expression on your mother's face. She's so *proud* of you! She's fat—is that what bothers you? Millions of people are overweight, and in your mother's generation a lot more older people were. So if I were you, when you get inquiries, I'd tell whoever asked me that that was the first beauty contest and you entered because you knew how happy it would make your mother if you won. There isn't a mother in the world who won't like you for that. Luther can show you the rest of my suggestions for the show. But I can tell you this. If you're not appointed Vice President, it won't be because of this picture; it will be because of your reaction to it and your being ashamed of your background.

"I'll ask the driver to take me home," she said. Then, eyes blazing, she turned to Luther. "You can call me in the morning and let me know if you still want me on this program. Good night, Senator."

She turned to go. Luther's voice stopped her. "Toby, get your ass out of that chair and make some coffee. Pat, sit down and let's start fixing this mess."

It was one-thirty when Pat got home. She changed into a nightgown and robe, made tea, brought it into the living room and curled up on the couch.

Staring at the Christmas tree, she reflected on the day. If she accepted what Catherine Graney said, all the talk about the great love between Abigail and Willard Jennings was a lie. If she believed what she had heard at the Ambassador's party, her mother had been a neurotic. If she believed Senator Jennings, everything Jeremy Saunders had told her was a twisted complaint.

It was he who must have sent the picture of Abigail to the *Mirror.* It was just the sort of mean-spirited thing he would do.

She swallowed the last sip of tea and got up. There was no use trying to think about it anymore. Walking over to the Christmas tree, she reached for the switch to turn off the lights, then paused. When she and Lila were having sherry, she thought she'd noticed that one of the ornaments had slipped from its branch and was lying on the floor. My mistake, she thought.

She shrugged and went to bed.

22

At nine-fifteen on Christmas morning, Toby was standing at the stove in Abigail Jennings' kitchen waiting for the coffee to perk. He hoped that he'd be able to have a cup himself before Abby appeared. True, he'd known her since they were kids, but this was one day he couldn't predict what her mood was likely to be. Last night had been some mess. There'd been only two other times he'd seen her so upset, and he never let himself think of either of them.

After Pat Traymore left, Abby and Pelham and Phil had sat around for another hour still trying to decide what to do. Or, rather, Abby had shouted at Pelham, telling him a dozen times that she still thought Pat Traymore was working for Claire Lawrence, that maybe Pelham was too.

Even for her, Abigail had gone pretty far, and Toby was amazed that Pelham had taken it. Later Phil supplied the answer: "Listen, he's the biggest TV news personality in the country. He's made millions. But he's sixty years old, and he's bored stiff. Now he wants to be another Edward R. Murrow. Murrow capped his career as head of the U.S. Information Agency. Pelham wants that job so bad he can taste it. Tremendous prestige and no more competing for ratings. The Senator will deliver for him if he delivers for her. He knows she's got a right to scream about the way this program is going."

Toby had to agree with what Pelham said. Like it or not, the damage was done. Either the program was produced from the angle of including Apple Junction and the beauty contests or it would seem like a farce.

"You can't ignore the fact you're on the cover of *The National Mirror,*" Pelham kept telling Abby. "It's read by four million people and handed away to God knows how many more. That picture is going to be reprinted by every sensational newspaper in this country. You've got to decide what you're going to tell them about it."

"Tell them?" Abby had stormed. "I'll tell them the truth: my father was a lush and the only decent thing he ever did was die when I was six. Then I can say that my fat mother had the viewpoint of a scullery maid and her highest ambition for me was that I'd be Miss Apple Junction and a good cook. Don't you think that's exactly the background a Vice President is supposed to have?" She had cried tears of rage. Abigail was no crybaby. Toby could remember only those few occasions. . . .

He had said his piece. "Abby, listen to me. You're stuck with Francey's picture, so get your act together and go along with Pat Traymore's suggestion."

That had calmed her down. She trusted him.

He heard Abby's steps in the hall. He was anxious to see what she'd be wearing. Pelham had agreed that she should show up at Christmas services at the Cathedral and wear something photogenic but not too luxurious. "Leave your mink home," he'd said.

"Good morning, Toby. Merry Christmas." The tone was sarcastic but under control. Even before he turned around he knew Abby had recovered her cool.

"Merry Christmas, Senator." He swung around. "Hey, you look great."

She was wearing a double-breasted bright red walking suit. The coat came to her fingertips. The skirt was pleated.

"Like one of Santa's helpers," she snapped. But even though

she sounded crabby, there was a sort of joke in her voice. She picked up her cup and held it out in a toast. "We're going to bring this one off too, aren't we, Toby?"

"You bet we are!"

They were waiting for her at the Cathedral. As soon as Abigail got out of the car, a television correspondent held up a microphone to her.

"Merry Christmas, Senator."

"Merry Christmas, Bob." Abby was smart, Toby reflected. She made it her business to know all the press and TV people, no matter how unimportant they were.

"Senator, you're about to go into Christmas services at the National Cathedral. Is there a special prayer you'll be offering?"

Abby hesitated just long enough. Then she said, "Bob, I guess we're all praying for world peace, aren't we? And after that my prayer is for the hungry. Wouldn't it be wonderful if we knew that every man, woman and child on this earth would be eating a good dinner tonight?" She smiled and joined the people streaming through the portal of the Cathedral.

Toby got back into the car. Terrific, he thought. He reached under the driver's seat and pulled out the racing charts. The ponies hadn't been too good to him lately. It was about time his luck changed.

The service lasted an hour and fifteen minutes. When the Senator came out another reporter was waiting for her. This one had some hard questions to ask. "Senator, have you seen *The National Mirror* cover this week?"

Toby had just gotten around the car to open the door. He held his breath, waiting to see how she'd handle herself.

Abby smiled—a warm, happy smile. "Yes, indeed."

"What do you think of it, Senator?"

Abby laughed. "I was astonished. I must say I'm more used

to being mentioned in the *Congressional Record* than in *The National Mirror.*"

"Did the appearance of that picture upset or anger you, Senator?"

"Of course not. Why should it? I suppose that, like most of us, on holidays I think about the people I loved who aren't with me anymore. That picture made me remember how happy my mother was when I won that contest. I entered it to please her. She was widowed, you know, and brought me up alone. We were very, very close."

Now her eyes became moist, her lips trembled. Quickly she bent her head and got into the car. With a decisive snap, Toby closed the door behind her.

The recorder light was blinking when Pat returned from the morning service. Automatically she pressed the rewind button until the tape screeched to a halt, then switched to playback.

The first three calls were disconnects. Then Sam came on, his voice edgy. "Pat, I've been trying to reach you. I'm just boarding a plane for D.C. See you at Abigail's this evening."

How loving can you get? Sam had planned to spend the week with Karen and her husband. And now he's rushing home. Abigail had obviously summoned him to be one of her close and intimate friends at her Christmas supper. There *was* something between them! Abigail was eight years older, but didn't look it. Plenty of men married older women.

Luther Pelham had also phoned. "Continue to work on the second version of the storyboard. Be at the Senator's home at four P.M. If you are called by newspapers about the *Mirror* picture, claim you haven't seen it."

The next message began in a soft, troubled voice: "Miss Traymore—er, Pat—you may not remember me. [A pause.] Of course you will; it's just you meet so many people, don't you? [Pause.] I must hurry. This is Margaret Langley. I am the principal . . . retired, of course . . . of Apple Junction High School."

The message time had run out. Exasperated, Pat bit her lip.

Miss Langley had called back. This time she said hurriedly, "To continue, please call me at 518/555-2460." There were sounds of tremulous breathing. Then Miss Langley burst out, "Miss Traymore, I heard from Eleanor today."

The phone rang only once before Miss Langley answered. Pat identified herself and was interrupted immediately. "Miss Traymore, after all these years I've heard from Eleanor. Just as I came in from church the phone was ringing and she said hello in that sweet, shy voice and we both started to cry."

"Miss Langley, where is Eleanor? What is she doing?"

There was a pause; then Margaret Langley spoke carefully, as though trying to choose exactly the right words. "She didn't tell me where she is. She said she is much better and doesn't want to be hiding forever. She said she is thinking of turning herself in. She knows she'll go back to jail—she did violate her parole. She said that this time she'd like me to visit her."

"Turning herself in!" Pat thought of the stunned, helpless face of Eleanor Brown after her conviction. "What did you tell her?"

"I begged her to call you. I thought you might be able to get her parole reinstated." Now Margaret Langley's voice broke. "Miss Traymore, please don't let that girl go back to prison."

"I'll try," Pat promised. "I have a friend, a Congressman, who will help. Miss Langley, please, for Eleanor's sake, do you know where I can reach her?"

"No, honestly, I don't."

"If she calls back, beg her to contact me before she surrenders. Her bargaining position will be so much stronger."

"I knew you'd want to help. I knew you were a good person." Now Margaret Langley's tone changed. "I want you to know how happy I am that that nice Mr. Pelham phoned and invited me to be on your program. Someone is coming to interview and tape me tomorrow morning."

So Luther had taken that suggestion too. "I'm so glad." Pat tried to sound enthusiastic. "Now, remember to tell Eleanor to call me."

She lowered the receiver slowly. If Eleanor Brown was the timid girl Miss Langley believed her to be, turning herself in would be a tremendous act of courage. But for Abigail Jennings, it could be mortally embarrassing if, in the next few days, a vulnerable young woman was marched back to prison still protesting her innocence of the theft from Abigail's office.

23

As he walked down the corridor of the nursing home, Arthur sensed the tension and was immediately on guard. The place seemed peaceful enough. Christmas trees and Hanukkah candles stood on card tables covered with felt and make-believe snow. All the doors of the patients' rooms had greeting cards taped to them. Christmas music was playing on the stereo in the recreation room. But something was wrong.

"Good morning, Mrs. Harnick. How are you feeling?" She was advancing slowly down the hall on her walker, her birdlike frame bent over, her hair scraggly around her ashen face. She looked up at him without raising her head. Just her eyes moved, sunken, watery, afraid.

"Stay away from me, Arthur," she said, her voice aquiver. "I told them you came out of Anita's room, and I know I'm right."

He touched Mrs. Harnick's arm, but she shrank away. "Of course I was in Mrs. Gillespie's room," he said. "She and I were friends."

"She wasn't your friend. She was afraid of you."

He tried not to show his anger. "Now, Mrs. Harnick . . ."

"I mean what I say. Anita wanted to stay alive. Her daughter, Anna Marie, was coming to see her. She hadn't been East for two years. Anita said she didn't care when she died as long as she saw her Anna Marie again. She didn't just stop breathing. I told them that."

The head nurse, Elizabeth Sheehan, sat at a desk halfway down the corridor. He hated her. She had a stern face, and blue-gray eyes that could turn steel gray when she was angry. "Arthur, before you make your rounds please come to the office."

He followed her into the business office of the nursing home, the place where families would come to make arrangements to jettison their old people. But today there weren't any relatives, only a baby-faced young man in a raincoat with shoes that needed a shine. He had a pleasant smile and a very warm manner, but Arthur wasn't fooled.

"I'm Detective Barrott," he said.

The superintendent of the home, Dr. Cole, was also there.

"Arthur, sit down," he said, trying to make his voice friendly. "Thank you, Nurse Sheehan; you needn't wait."

Arthur chose a straight chair and remembered to fold his hands in his lap and look just a little puzzled, as though he had no idea what was going on. He'd practiced that look in front of the mirror.

"Arthur, Mrs. Gillespie died last Thursday," Detective Barrott said.

Arthur nodded and made his expression regretful. He was suddenly glad he'd met Mrs. Harnick in the hall. "I know. I was so hoping she'd live just a little longer. Her daughter was coming to visit her and she hadn't seen her for two years."

"You knew that?" Dr. Cole asked.

"Of course. Mrs. Gillespie told me."

"I see. We didn't realize she'd discussed her daughter's visit."

"Doctor, you know how long it took to feed Mrs. Gillespie. Sometimes she'd need to rest and we'd just talk."

"Arthur, were you glad to see Mrs. Gillespie die?" Detective Barrott asked.

"I'm glad she died before that cancer got much worse. She would have been in terrible pain. Isn't that right, Doctor?" He looked at Dr. Cole now, making his eyes wide.

"It's possible, yes," Dr. Cole said unwillingly. "Of course one never knows. . . ."

"But I wish Mrs. Gillespie had lived to see Anna Marie. She and I used to pray over that. She used to ask me to read prayers from her *Saint Anthony Missal* for a special favor. That was her prayer."

Detective Barrott was studying him carefully. "Arthur, did you visit Mrs. Gillespie's room last Monday?"

"Oh, yes, I went in just before Nurse Krause made her rounds. But Mrs. Gillespie didn't want anything."

"Mrs. Harnick said she saw you coming out of Mrs. Gillespie's room at about five of four. Is that true?"

Arthur had figured out his answer. "No, I didn't go in her room. I *looked* in her room, but she was asleep. She'd had a bad night and I was worried about her. Mrs. Harnick saw me look in."

Dr. Cole leaned back in his chair. He seemed relieved.

Detective Barrott's voice got softer. "But the other day you said Mrs. Harnick was wrong."

"No, somebody asked me if I'd *gone into* Mrs. Gillespie's room twice. I hadn't. But then, when I thought about it, I remembered I'd looked in. So Mrs. Harnick and I were both right, you see."

Dr. Cole was smiling now. "Arthur is one of our most caring helpers," he said. "I told you that, Mr. Barrott."

But Detective Barrott wasn't smiling. "Arthur, do many of the orderlies pray with the patients or is it just you?"

"Oh, I think it's just me. You see, I was in a seminary once. I was planning to become a priest but got sick and had to leave. In a way I think of myself as a clergyman."

Detective Barrott's eyes, soft and limpid, encouraged confidences. "How old were you when you went into that seminary, Arthur?" he asked kindly.

"I was twenty. And I stayed until I was twenty and a half."

"I see," Detective Barrott said. "Tell me, Arthur, what seminary were you in?"

"I was at Collegeville, Minnesota, with the Benedictine community."

Detective Barrott pulled out a notebook and wrote that down. Too late Arthur realized he had told too much. Suppose Detective Barrott got in touch with the community and they told that after Father Damian's death, Arthur had been requested to leave.

Arthur worried about that all day. Even though Dr. Cole told him to go back to work, he could feel the suspicious glances from Nurse Sheehan. All the patients were looking at him in a peculiar way.

When he went to look in on old Mr. Thoman, his daughter was there and she said, "Arthur, you don't have to worry about my dad anymore. I've asked Nurse Sheehan to appoint another orderly to help him."

It was a slap in the face. Only last week Mr. Thoman had said, "I can't put up with feeling so sick much longer." Arthur had comforted him saying, "Maybe God won't ask you to, Mr. Thoman."

Arthur tried to keep his smile bright as he crossed the recreation room to help Mr. Whelan, who was struggling to his feet. As he walked Mr. Whelan down the hall to the lavatory and back, he realized that he was getting a headache, one of those blinding ones that made lights dance in front of his eyes. He knew what would happen next.

As he eased Mr. Whelan back into his chair, he glanced at the television set. The screen was all cloudy and then a face began to form, the face of Gabriel as he would look on Judgment Day. Gabriel spoke only to him. "Arthur, you are not safe here anymore."

"I understand." He didn't know he'd said the words out loud until Mr. Whelan said, "Shhh."

When he went down to his locker, Arthur carefully packed

his personal effects but left his extra uniform and old shoes. He was off tomorrow and Wednesday, so they might not realize he wouldn't return on Thursday morning unless for some reason they searched his locker and found it empty.

He put on his sports jacket, the brown-and-yellow one he'd bought at J. C. Penney's last year. He kept it here so that if he was meeting Glory for a movie or something, he could look nice.

In the pocket of his raincoat he put the pair of socks that had three hundred dollars stuffed in the toes. He always kept emergency money available, both here and at home, just in case he had to leave suddenly.

The locker room was cold and dingy. There was no one around. They'd given the day off to as many of the staff as possible. *He* had volunteered to work.

His hands were restless and dry; his nerves were screaming with resentment. They had no right to treat him like this. Restlessly his eyes roamed around the barren room. Most of the supplies were locked up in the big storage room, but there was a kind of catchall closet near the stairs. It was filled with opened bottles and cans of cleaning agents and unwashed dust rags. He thought of those people upstairs—Mrs. Harnick accusing him, Mr. Thoman's daughter telling him to stay away from her father, Nurse Sheehan. How dared they whisper about him, question him, reject him!

In the closet he found a half-empty can of turpentine. He loosened the cap, then turned the can on its side. Drops of turpentine began to drip onto the floor. He left the closet door open. Right next to it, a dozen bags of trash were piled together waiting to be carried out to the dump site.

Arthur didn't smoke, but when visitors left packs of cigarettes around the nursing home, he always picked them up for Glory. Now he took a Salem from his pocket, lit it, puffed until he was sure it wouldn't go out, unfastened the tie on one of the trash bags and dropped it in.

It would not take long. The cigarette would smolder; then the whole bag would catch fire; then the other bags would go, and the dripping turpentine would cause the fire to burn out of control. The rags in the closet would cause dense smoke, and by the time the staff tried to get the old people out, the whole building would be gone. It would seem to be a careless accident—an ignited cigarette in the trash; a fire caused by an overturned can of turpentine that had dripped from the shelf—if the investigators could even piece that much together.

He retied the bag as the faint, good burning smell made his nostrils quiver and his loins tighten, then hurried from the building and down the lonely street toward the Metro.

Glory was on the couch in the living room reading a book when Arthur got home. She was wearing a very pretty blue wool housecoat, with a zipper that came up to her neck and long, full sleeves. The book she was reading was a novel on the best-seller list that had cost $15.95. Arthur had never in his life spent more than a dollar for a book. He and Glory would go to secondhand stores and browse and come home with six or seven titles. And it was their pleasure to sit companionably reading. But somehow the dog-eared volumes with the stained covers that they had delighted in purchasing seemed poor and shabby next to this book with the shiny jacket and crisp new pages. The girls in the office had given it to her.

Glory had fixed a roast chicken for him, and cranberry sauce and hot muffins. But it was no pleasure eating Christmas dinner alone. She'd said she wasn't hungry. She seemed to be thinking so deeply. Several times he caught her staring at him, her eyes questioning and troubled. They reminded him of the way Mrs. Harnick had looked at him. He didn't want Glory to be afraid of him.

"I have a present for you," he told her. "I know you'll like it." Yesterday, at the big discount store in the mall, he'd bought a frilly white apron for the Raggedy Ann doll, and except for a few spots on the dress, the doll looked just the same. And he'd bought Christmas paper and wrappings and made it look like a real present.

"And I have a present for you, Father."

They exchanged the gifts solemnly. "You open first," he said. He wanted to see her expression. She'd be so happy.

"All right." She smiled, and he noticed that her hair seemed lighter. Was she coloring it?

She untied the ribbon carefully, pushed back the paper, and the frilly apron showed first. "What . . . oh, Father." She was startled. "You found her. What a pretty new apron." She looked pleased, but not as exquisitely happy as he'd expected. Then her face became very thoughtful. "Look at that poor, sad face. And that's the way I thought of myself. I remember the day I painted it. I was so sick, wasn't I?"

"Will you take her to bed with you again?" he asked. "That's why you wanted her, isn't it?"

"Oh, no. I just wanted to look at her. Open your present. It will make you happy, I think."

It was a handsome blue-and-white wool sweater with a V-neck and long sleeves. "I knitted it for you, Father," Glory told him happily. "Would you believe I finally was able to stick with something and finish it? I guess I'm getting my act together. It's about time, don't you think?"

"I like you just as you are," he said. "I like taking care of you."

"But pretty soon it may be impossible," she said.

They both knew what she meant.

It was time to tell her. "Glory," he said carefully. "Today I was asked to do something very special. There are a number of nursing homes in Tennessee that are badly understaffed and need the kind of help I can give to very sick patients. They want me to go there right away and select one of them to work in."

"Move? Again?" She looked dismayed.

"Yes, Glory. I do God's work, and now it's my turn to ask for your help. You're a great comfort to me. We will leave Thursday morning."

He was sure he'd be safe until then. At the very least, the fire would have caused great confusion. At best, his personnel records might be destroyed. But even if the fire was put out before it burned the place down, it would probably be at least a few days before the police could check his references and find the long gaps between employment, or learn the reason he'd been asked to leave the seminary. By the time that detective wanted to question him again, he and Glory would be gone.

For a long time Glory was silent. Then she said, "Father, if my picture is on that program Wednesday night, I'm going to turn myself in. People all over the country will see it, and I can't go on any longer wondering if someone is staring at me because he or she knows who I am. Otherwise I will go with you to Tennessee." Her lip quivered, and he knew she was near tears.

He went to her and patted her cheek. He could not tell Glory that the only reason he was waiting until Thursday to go away was because of that program.

"Father," Glory burst out, "I've started to be happy here. I don't think it's fair the way they expect you to just pick up and go all the time."

24

At 1:30 P.M. Lila rang Pat's doorbell. She was carrying a small package. "Merry Christmas!"

"Merry Christmas. Come in." Pat was genuinely pleased by the visit. She had been trying to decide whether or not to confide in Luther that Eleanor might turn herself in to the police. And how could she broach the subject of Catherine Graney to him? The prospect of a lawsuit would send him into orbit.

"I won't stay but a minute," Lila said. "I just wanted to give you some fruitcake. It's a specialty of mine."

Pat hugged her impulsively. "I'm glad you did come. It's terribly odd to be so quiet on Christmas afternoon. How about a glass of sherry?"

Lila looked at her watch. "I'll be out of here by quarter of two," she announced.

Pat led her back to the living room; got a plate, a knife and glasses; poured the sherry and cut thin slices of the cake. "Marvelous," she pronounced after sampling it.

"It is good, isn't it?" Lila agreed. Her eyes darted around the living room. "You've changed something in here."

"I switched a couple of paintings. I realized they were in the wrong place."

"How much is coming back to you?"

"Some," Pat admitted. "I was in the library working. Then

something just made me come in here. As soon as I did, I knew that the still life and the landscape should be reversed."

"What else, Pat? There's more."

"I'm so darn edgy," Pat said simply. "And I don't know why."

"Pat, please don't stay here. Move to an apartment, a hotel." Lila clasped her hands imploringly.

"I can't," Pat said. "But help me now. Were you ever in here on Christmas Day? What was it like?"

"That last year, you were three and a half and able to really understand Christmas. They were both so delighted with you. It was a day of genuine happiness."

"I sometimes think I remember a little of that day. I had a walking doll and was trying to make it walk with me. Could that have been true?"

"You did have a walking doll that year, yes."

"My mother played the piano that afternoon, didn't she?"

"Yes."

Pat walked over to the piano, opened it. "Do you remember what she played that Christmas?"

"I'm sure it was her favorite Christmas carol. It's called 'Bells of Christmas.' "

"I know it. Veronica wanted me to learn it. She said my grandmother loved it." Slowly her fingers began to run over the keys.

Lila watched and listened. When the last notes faded away, she said, "That was very much like your mother playing. I told you you resemble your father, but I never realized until this minute how startling the resemblance is. Somebody who knew him well is bound to make the connection."

At three o'clock the television crew from Potomac Cable Network arrived at Senator Jennings' house to tape her Christmas supper.

Toby watched them with a hawk's eye as they set up in the

living and dining rooms, making it his business to be sure nothing got broken or scratched. He knew how much everything in the place meant to Abby.

Pat Traymore and Luther Pelham came within a minute or two of each other. Pat was wearing a white wool dress that showed off her figure. Her hair was twisted in a kind of bun. Toby had never seen her wear it like that. It made her look different and yet familiar. Who the hell did she remind him of? Toby wondered.

She seemed relaxed, but you could tell Pelham wasn't. As soon as he walked in, he started snapping at one of the cameramen. Abigail was uptight, and that didn't help either. Right away she tangled with Traymore. Pat wanted to set the food out on the buffet table and tape the Senator inspecting it and making little changes in the way it was placed. Abigail didn't want to put the food out so early.

"Senator, it takes time to get exactly the feeling we want," Pat told her. "It will be much easier to do now than when your guests are standing around watching."

"I won't have my guests standing around like extras in a B movie," Abigail snapped.

"Then I suggest we photograph the table now."

Toby noticed that Pat didn't back down when she wanted something done. Luther remarked that Abigail had prepared all the food herself, and that was another hassle. Pat wanted a shot of her in the kitchen working.

"Senator, everbody thinks you just phone a caterer when you have a party. That you actually do everything yourself will endear you to all the women who are stuck preparing three meals a day, to say nothing of the men and women whose hobby is cooking."

Abigail flatly rejected the idea, but Pat kept insisting. "Senator, the whole purpose of our being here is to make people see you as a human being."

In the end it was Toby who persuaded Abigail to go along.

"Come on, show them you're a regular Julia Child, Senator," he coaxed.

Abby refused to put an apron over her designer shirt and slacks, but when she began to put hors d'oeuvre together, she made it clear she was a gourmet cook. Toby watched as she rolled batter for pastry shells, chopped ham for quiche, seasoned crabmeat, those long, slender fingers working miraculously. No messy kitchen for Abby. Well, you had to give a tip of the hat to Francey Foster for that.

Once the crew started taping, Abigail began to relax. They had done only a couple of takes when Pat said, "Senator, thank you. I'm sure we have what we want. That came over very well. Now, if you don't mind changing to whatever you're planning to wear at the party, we can get the footage at the table."

Toby was anxious to see what Abigail would wear. She's been hemming and hawing between a couple of outfits. He was pleased when she came back, wearing a yellow satin blouse that matched the yellow in her plaid taffeta skirt. Her hair was soft around her face and neck. Her eye makeup was heavier than usual. She looked stunning. Besides, she had a glow about her. Toby knew why. Sam Kingsley had phoned to say he'd be at the party.

There was no question Abby had set her cap for Sam Kingsley. Toby hadn't missed the way she'd suggested to her friends that they put Sam next to her at dinner parties. There was something about him that reminded Toby of Billy, and of course that was the big attraction for Abby. She'd put on a good show in public, but she'd been a basket case when Billy died.

Toby knew Sam didn't like him. But that wasn't a problem. Sam wouldn't last any longer than the others had. Abby was too domineering for most men. Either they got sick of adjusting to her schedule and moods, or if they knuckled under, she got sick of them. He, Toby, would be part of Abby's life until one or the other of them died. She'd be lost without him, and she knew it.

As he watched her posing at the buffet table, a tinge of regret made him swallow hard. Every once in a while he daydreamed about how it would have been if he'd been smart in school instead of just having the smarts; if he'd gone on to become an engineer instead of a jack-of-all-trades. And if he'd been good-looking like that wimp Jeremy Saunders, instead of rough-faced and burly—well, who knew? Somewhere along the line, Abby might have fallen for him.

He dismissed the thought and got back to work.

Promptly at five the first car drove up. The retired Supreme Court Justice and his wife entered a minute or two later. "Merry Christmas, Madam Vice President," the Justice said.

Abigail returned his kiss warmly. "From your lips to God's ear," she laughed.

Other guests began to flow in. Hired waiters poured champagne and punch. "Keep the hard stuff for later," Luther had suggested. "The Bible Belt doesn't like to be reminded that its public officials serve booze."

Sam was the last to arrive. Abigail opened the door for him. Her kiss on his cheek was affectionate. Luther was directing the other camera toward them. Pat felt her heart sink. Sam and Abigail made a stunning couple—both tall, her ash blond hair contrasting with his dark head, the streaks of gray in his hair a subtle balance to the fine lines around her eyes.

Pat could see everyone clustering around Sam. I only think about him as *Sam,* she thought. I've never seen him in his professional element. Was that the way it had been with her mother and father? They'd met when they were both vacationing on Martha's Vineyard. They'd married within a month, never really knowing or understanding each other's worlds—and then the clash had begun.

Except I wouldn't clash with you, Sam. I like your world.

Abigail must have said something amusing; everyone laughed. Sam smiled at her.

"That's a nice shot, Pat," the cameraman said. "A little sexy—you know what I mean? You never see Senator Jennings with a guy. People *like* that." The cameraman was beaming.

"All the world loves a lover," Pat replied.

"We've got enough," Luther suddenly announced. "Let the Senator and her guests have some peace. Pat, you be at the Senator's office for the taping in the morning. I'll be in Apple Junction. You know what we need." He turned his back, dismissing her.

Did his attitude result from the picture in the *Mirror* or from her refusal to sleep with him? Only time would tell.

She slipped past the guests, down the hallway and into the den, where she'd left her coat.

"Pat."

She turned around. "Sam!" He was standing in the doorway, looking at her. "Ah, Congressman. Season's greetings." She reached for her coat.

"Pat, you're not leaving?"

"No one invited me to stay."

He came over, took the coat from her. "What's this about the *Mirror* cover?"

She told him. "And it seems the senior Senator from Virginia believes I slipped that picture to that rag just to get my way about this program."

He put his hand on her shoulder. "You didn't?"

"That sounds like a question!" Could he really believe she'd had anything to do with the *Mirror* cover? If so, he didn't know her at all. Or maybe it was time she realized that the man she thought she knew didn't exist.

"Pat, I can't leave yet, but I should be able to get away in an hour. Are you going home?"

"Yes, I am. Why?"

"I'll be there as soon as I can. I'll take you to dinner."

"All the decent restaurants will be closed. Stay; enjoy yourself." She tried to pull away from him.

"Miss Traymore, if you give me your keys, I'll bring your car around."

They sprang apart, both embarrassed. "Toby, what the hell are *you* doing here?" Sam snapped.

Toby looked at him impassively. "The Senator is about to ask her guests in to supper, Congressman, and told me to round them up. She particularly told me to look for you."

Sam was still holding Pat's coat. She reached for it. "I can get my own car, Toby," she said. She looked at him directly. He was standing in the doorway, a large, dark mass. She tried to pass him, but he didn't move.

"*May* I?"

He was staring at her, his expression distracted. "Oh, sure. Sorry." He stepped aside, and unconsciously she shrank against the wall to avoid brushing against him.

Pat drove at breakneck speed trying to escape the memory of how warmly Abigail and Sam had greeted each other, of the subtle way in which the others seemed to treat them as a couple. It was a quarter to eight when she got home. Grateful that she'd had the foresight to cook the turkey, she made a sandwich and poured a glass of wine. The house felt dark and empty. She turned on the lights in the foyer, library, dining room and living room, then plugged in the tree.

The other day the living room had somehow seemed warmer, more livable. Now, for some reason, it was uncomfortable, shadowy. Why? Her eye caught a strand of tinsel almost hidden on a brilliant apricot-hued section of the carpet. Yesterday when she and Lila were here, she thought she'd seen an ornament with a piece of tinsel lying on this area of the carpet. Perhaps it had been just the tinsel.

The television set was in the library. She carried the sandwich and the wine there. Potomac Cable had hourly news highlights. She wondered if they'd show Abigail at church.

They did. Pat watched dispassionately as Abigail stepped from the car, the bright red suit dramatic against her flawless skin and hair, her eyes soft as she voiced her prayer for the hungry. This was the woman Pat had revered. The newscaster announced, "Later Senator Jennings was questioned about her picture as a young beauty queen, which is on the cover of this week's *National Mirror*." A postage-stamp-size picture of the *Mirror* cover was shown. "With tears in her eyes the Senator recalled her mother's desire to have her enter that contest. Potomac Cable Network wishes Senator Abigail Jennings a very merry Christmas; and we're sure that her mother, were she aware of her success, would be terribly proud of her."

"Good Lord," Pat cried. Jumping up, she pushed the button that turned off the set. "And Luther has the gall to call that news! No wonder the media are criticized for bias."

Restlessly she began to jot down the conflicting statements she had been hearing all week:

Catherine Graney said that Abigail and Willard were about to divorce.

Senator Jennings claims she loved her husband very much.

Eleanor Brown stole $75,000 from Senator Jennings.

Eleanor Brown swears she did not steal that money.

George Graney was a master pilot; his plane was carefully inspected before takeoff.

Senator Jennings said George Graney was a careless pilot with second-rate equipment.

Nothing adds up, Pat thought, absolutely nothing!

It was nearly eleven o'clock before the door chimes signaled Sam's arrival. At ten-thirty, ready to give up on him, Pat had gone to her room, then told herself that if Sam were not coming, he would have called. She changed to silk pajamas that were comfortable for lounging but technically still suitable for receiving guests. She washed her face, then touched her eyelids lightly with shadow and her lips with gloss. No point looking like a mouse, she thought—not when he'd just left the beauty queen.

Swiftly she hung up the clothes she had left scattered over the room. Was Sam neat? I don't even know that, she thought. The one night they had stayed together certainly hadn't been any barometer of either of their personal habits. When they'd checked into the motel she'd brushed her teeth with the folding toothbrush she always carried in her cosmetic case. "I wish I had one of those," he'd said. She'd smiled up at his reflection in the mirror. "One of my favorite lines from *Random Harvest* was when the minister asks Smithy and Paula if they're so in love they use the same toothbrush." She ran hers under hot water, spread toothpaste across the bristles and handed it to him. "Be my guest."

That toothbrush was now in a velvet jeweler's box in the top drawer of the vanity. Some women press roses or tie ribbons around letters, Pat thought. I kept a toothbrush.

She had just come down the stairs when the chimes rang again. "Come in, come in, whoever you are," she said.

Sam's expression was contrite. "Pat, I'm sorry. I couldn't get away as fast as I'd hoped. And then I cabbed to my place, dropped my bags and picked up my car. Were you on your way to bed?"

"Not at all. If you mean this outfit, it's technically called lounging pajamas and, according to the Saks brochure, is perfect for that evening at home when entertaining a few friends."

"Just be careful which friends you entertain," Sam suggested. "That's a pretty sexy-looking getup."

She took his coat; the fine wool was still cold from the icy wind.

He bent down to kiss her.

"Would you like a drink?" Without waiting for his answer,

she led him into the library and silently pointed to the bar. He poured brandy into snifters and handed one to her. "I assume this is still your after-dinner choice?"

She nodded and deliberately chose the fan-back chair across from the couch.

Sam had changed when he stopped at his apartment. He was wearing an Argyle sweater with a predominantly blue-and-gray pattern that complemented the blueness of his eyes, the touches of gray in his dark brown hair. He settled on the couch, and it seemed to her there was weariness in the way he moved and in the lines around his eyes.

"How did it go after I left?"

"About as you saw it. We did have one high point, however. The President phoned to wish Abigail a merry Christmas."

"*The President phoned!* Sam, does that mean . . . ?"

"My bet is he's milking this for all it's worth. He probably phoned Claire Lawrence as well."

"You mean he hasn't made his decision?"

"I think he's still sending up trial balloons. You saw the way he featured Abigail at the White House dinner last week. But he and the First Lady also went to a private supper in Claire's honor the next night."

"Sam, how badly did that *Mirror* cover hurt Senator Jennings?"

He shrugged. "Hard to say. Abigail has done the Southern-aristocracy scene a little too heavily for a lot of people around here. On the other hand, it just may make her sympathetic. Another problem: that publicity about the threats to you has made for a lot of locker-room jokes on Capitol Hill—and they're all on Abigail."

Pat stared at her untouched brandy. Her mouth suddenly felt dry and brackish. Last week Sam had been worried about *her* because of the break-in. Now he was sharing Abigail's reaction to the publicity. Well, in a way it made things easier. "If this program causes any more unfavorable publicity to Senator Jennings, could it cost her the Vice Presidency?"

"Perhaps. No President, particularly one who's had a spotless administration, is going to risk having it tarnished."

"That's exactly what I was afraid you'd say." She told him about Eleanor Brown and Catherine Graney. "I don't know what to do," she concluded. "Should I warn Luther to keep away from those subjects on the program? If I do, he'll have to tell the Senator the reason."

"There's no way Abigail can take any more aggravation," Sam said flatly. "After the others left she was really wired."

"After the others left!" Pat raised an eyebrow. "You mean you stayed?"

"She asked me to."

"I see." She felt her heart sink. It confirmed everything she had been thinking. "Then I shouldn't tell Luther."

"Try it this way. If that girl . . ."

"Eleanor Brown."

"Yes—if she calls you, persuade her to wait until I see if we can plea-bargain on her parole. In that case there'd be no publicity, at least until the President announces his selection."

"And Catherine Graney."

"Let me look into the records of that crash. She probably doesn't have a leg to stand on. Do you think either one of these women might have made those threats to you?"

"I've never met Eleanor. I'm sure it wasn't Catherine Graney. And don't forget it was a man's voice."

"Of course. He hasn't called again?"

Her eyes fell on the carton under the table. She considered, then rejected, the idea of showing the Raggedy Ann doll to Sam. She did not want him concerning himself about her anymore. "No, he hasn't."

"That's good news." He finished the brandy and set the glass on the table. "I'd better be on my way. It's been a long day and you must be bushed."

It was the opening she was waiting for. "Sam, on the way

home from the Senator's tonight, I did some hard thinking. Want to hear about it?"

"Certainly."

"I came to Washington with three specific and rather idealistic goals in mind. I was going to do an Emmy-winning documentary on a wonderful, noble woman. I was going to find an explanation for what my father did to my mother and me. And I was going to see you and it would be the reunion of the century. Well, none of these turned out as I expected. Abigail Jennings is a good politician and a strong leader, but she isn't a nice person. I was suckered into this program because my preconceived notions about Abigail suited Luther Pelham, and whatever reputation I've achieved in the industry gives credibility to what is essentially P.R. fluff. There's so much about that lady that doesn't hang together that it frightens me.

"I've also been here long enough to know that my mother wasn't a saint, as I'd been led to believe, and very possibly goaded my father into some form of temporary insanity that night. That's not the full story—not yet; but it's close.

"And as for us, Sam, I do owe you an apology. I certainly was terribly naive to think that I was anything more to you than a casual affair. The fact that you never called me after Janice died should have been the tip-off, but I guess I'm not a quick study. You can stop worrying now. I don't intend to embarrass you with any more declarations of love. It's very clear you've got something going with Abigail Jennings."

"I don't have anything going with Abigail!"

"Oh, yes, you do. Maybe you don't know it yet, but you do. That lady *wants* you, Sam. Anyone with half an eye can see that. And you didn't cut short your vacation and come rushing across the country at her summons without good reason. Just forget about having to let me down easy. Really, Sam, all that talk about being worn out and not able to make decisions isn't very becoming. You can drop it now."

"I told you that because it's *true*."

"Then snap out of it. It doesn't become you. You're a handsome, virile man with twenty or thirty good years ahead of you." She managed a smile. "Maybe the prospect of becoming a grandfather is a little shocking to your ego."

"Are you finished?"

"Quite."

"Then if you don't mind, I've overstayed my welcome." He got up, his face flushed.

She reached out her hand. "There's no reason not to be friends. Washington is a small town. That *is* the reason you called me in the first place, isn't it?"

He didn't answer.

With a certain degree of satisfaction, Pat heard him slam the front door as he left.

25

"Senator, they'll probably want you to be anchorwoman on the *Today* show," Toby volunteered genially. He glanced into the rearview mirror to see Abby's reaction. They were on their way to the office. At 6:30 A.M. on December 26 it was still dark and bone-chilling.

"I have no desire to be anchorwoman on the *Today* show or any other show," Abigail snapped. "Toby, what the hell do I look like? I never closed an eye last night. Toby, the President *phoned* me . . . he *phoned* me personally. He said to have a good rest over the Christmas recess because it was going to be a busy year ahead. What could he have meant by that?. . . . Toby, I can taste it. The Vice Presidency. Toby, *why* didn't I follow my instincts? *Why* did I let Luther Pelham talk me into this program? Where was my head?"

"Senator, listen. That picture may be the best thing that ever happened to you. It's for sure that wallflower Claire Lawrence never won any contests. Maybe Pat Traymore is right. That kind of makes you more accessible . . . is that the word?"

They were going over the Roosevelt Bridge, and traffic was picking up. Toby concentrated on the driving. When he looked again into the rearview mirror, Abby's hands were still in her lap. "Toby, I've worked for this."

"I know you have, Abby."

"It isn't fair to lose it just because I've had to claw my way up."

"You're not going to lose it, Senator."

"I don't know. There's something about Pat Traymore that disturbs me. She's managed to give me two bouts of embarrassing publicity in one week. There's more to her than we know."

"Senator, Phil checked her out. She's been touting you since she was in college. She wrote an essay on you her senior year at Wellesley. She's on the level. She may be bad luck, but she's on the level."

"She's trouble. I warn you, there's something else about her."

The car swung past the Capitol and pulled up at the Russell Senate Office Building. "I'll be right up, Senator, and I promise you, I'll keep an eye on Pat Traymore. She won't get in your way." He hopped out of the car to open the door for Abby.

She accepted his hand, got out, then impulsively squeezed his fingers. "Toby, look at that girl's eyes. There's something about them . . . something secretive . . . as though . . ."

She didn't finish the sentence. But for Toby, it wasn't necessary.

At six o'clock Philip was waiting in the office to admit Pat and the network camera crew.

Sleepy-eyed guards and cleaning women with weary, patient faces were the only other people in evidence in the Russell building. In Abigail's office, Pat and the cameramen bent over the storyboard. "We'll only give three minutes to this segment," Pat said. "I want the feeling of the Senator arriving at an empty office and starting work before anyone shows up. Then Philip coming in to brief her . . . a shot of her daily calendar, but don't show the date . . . then office help arriving; the phones starting; a shot of the daily mail; the Senator greeting visitors from her state; the Senator talking to a constituent; Phil in and out with the messages. You know what we want—a sense of behind-the-scenes in a Senator's workday office."

When Abigail arrived, they were ready for her. Pat explained the first shot she wanted, and the Senator nodded and returned to the vestibule. Cameras rolled, and her key turned in the latch. Her expression was preoccupied and businesslike. She slipped off the gray cashmere cape that covered a well-cut but restrained pin-striped gray suit. Even the way she ran her fingers through her hair as she tossed off her hat was natural, the gesture of someone who cares about her appearance but is preoccupied with more important matters.

"Cut," Pat said. "Senator, that's fine, just the feeling I wanted." Her spontaneous praise sounded patronizing even to her own ears.

Senator Jennings' smile was enigmatic. "Thank you. Now what?"

Pat explained the scene with the mail, Phil and the constituent, Maggie Sayles.

The taping went smoothly. Pat quickly realized that Senator Jennings had a natural instinct for presenting herself at the best camera angle. The pin-striped suit gave her an executive, businesslike appearance that would be a nice contrast to the taffeta skirt at the Christmas supper party. Her earrings were silver; she wore a silver tie pin, stark and slim against the ascot of a soft gray silk blouse. It was the Senator's idea to photograph her office in a long shot showing the flags of both the United States and Virginia and then to have only the flag of the United States behind her in close-ups.

Pat watched the camera angle in as Abigail carefully selected a letter from the mound of mail on her desk—a letter in a childish handwriting. Another touch of theater, Pat thought. How smart of her. Then the constituent, Maggie, came in—the one whom Abigail had helped to find a nursing home for her mother. Abigail sprang up to meet her, kissed her affectionately, led her to a chair . . . all animation, warmth, concern.

She does mean the concern, Pat thought. I was here when she got that woman's mother into a home; but there's so much showmanship going on now. Are all politicians like this? Am I simply too damn naive?

By ten o'clock they had finished. Having reassured Abigail that they had everything they needed, Pat and the camera crew got ready to leave. "We'll do the first rough edit this afternoon," Pat told the director. "Then go over it with Luther tonight."

"I think it's going to turn out great," the cameraman volunteered.

"It's turning into a good show. That much I'll grant," Pat said.

26

Arthur's night had been filled with dreams of Mrs. Gillespie's eyes as they'd started to glaze over. In the morning he was heavy-eyed and tired. He got up and made coffee and would have gone out for rolls, but Glory asked him not to. "I won't have any, and after I go to work, you should get some rest. You didn't sleep well, did you?"

"How did you know?" He sat across from her at the table, watching as she perched at the edge of her chair.

"You kept calling out. Did Mrs. Gillespie's death worry you so much, Father? I know how often you used to talk about her."

A chill of fear went through him. Suppose they asked Glory about him? What would she say? Nothing ever to hurt him, but how would she know? He tried to choose his words carefully.

"It's just I'm so sad she didn't get to see her daughter before she died. We both wanted that."

Glory gulped her coffee and got up from the table. "Father, I wish you would take some time off and rest. I think you're working too hard."

"I'm fine, Glory. What was I saying in my sleep?"

"You kept telling Mrs. Gillespie to close her eyes. What were you dreaming about her?"

Glory was looking at him as if she were almost frightened of him, he thought. What did she know, or guess? After she had gone, he stared into his cup, worried and suddenly tired. He was restless and decided to go out for a walk. It didn't help. After a few blocks he turned back.

He had reached the corner of his street when he noticed the excitement. A police car was stopped in front of his home. Instinctively he ducked into the doorway of a vacant house and watched from the foyer. Whom did they want? Glory? Himself?

He would have to warn her. He'd tell her to meet him somewhere and they'd go away again. He had the $300 in cash, and he had $622 in Baltimore in a savings account under a different name. They could make that last until he had a new job. It was easy to get work in a nursing home. They were all desperate for orderlies.

He slipped along the side of the house, cut through the adjacent yard, hurried to the corner and phoned Glory's office.

She was on another line. "Get her," he told the girl angrily. "It's important. Tell her Father says it's important."

When Glory got on the phone, she sounded impatient. "Father, what *is* it?"

He told her. He thought she'd cry or get upset, but there was nothing from her—just silence. "Glory . . . ?"

"Yes, Father." Her voice was quiet, lifeless.

"Leave right now, don't say anything, act like you're going to the ladies' room. Meet me at Metro Central, the Twelfth and G exit. We'll be gone before they have a chance to put out an alert. We'll pick up the money at the bank in Baltimore and then go South."

"No, Father." Now Glory's voice sounded strong, sure. "I'm not running anymore. Thank you, Father. You don't have to run anymore for me. I'm going to the police."

"Glory. No. Wait. Maybe it will be all right. Promise me. *Not yet.*"

A police car was cruising slowly down the block. He could not lose another minute. As she whispered, "I promise," he hung up the phone and ducked into a doorway. When the squad car had passed, he shoved his hands into his pockets and with his stiff, unyielding gait made his way to the Metro station.

It was a subdued Abigail who returned to the car at ten-thirty. Toby started to speak, but something told him to keep his mouth shut. Let Abby be the one to decide if she wanted to get things off her chest.

"Toby, I don't feel like going home yet," Abigail said suddenly. "Take me over to Watergate. I can get a late breakfast there."

"Sure, Senator." He made his voice hearty, as though the request were not unusual. He knew why Abby had selected that place. Sam Kingsley lived in the same building as the restaurant. The next thing, she'd probably phone upstairs and if Sam was in, ask him to join her for coffee.

Fine, but that hadn't been a casual chat in the den between Kingsley and Pat Traymore last night. There was something between those two. He didn't want to see Abby get hurt again. He wondered if he should tip her off.

Glancing over his shoulder, he noticed that Abigail was checking her makeup in her hand mirror. "You look fantastic, Senator," he said.

At the Watergate complex the doorman opened the car door, and Toby noticed the extra-large smile and respectful bow. Hell, there were one hundred Senators in Washington but only one Vice President. I want it for you, Abby, he thought. Nothing will stand in your way if I have anything to say about it.

He steered the car to where the other drivers were parked and got out to say hello. Today the talk was all about Abigail. He overheard a Cabinet member's driver say, "It's practically all sewed up for Senator Jennings."

Abby, you're almost there, girl, he thought exultantly.

Abby was gone more than an hour, so he had plenty of time to read the newspaper. Finally he opened the Style section to glance at the columns. Sometimes he could pick up useful tidbits to pass on to Abby. She was usually too busy to read gossip.

Gina Butterfield was the columnist everyone in Washington read. Today her column had a headline that ran across the two center pages of the section. Toby read it, then read it again, trying to deny what he was seeing. The headline was ADAMS DEATH HOUSE SCENE OF THREATS. SENATOR ABIGAIL JENNINGS INVOLVED. The first couple of paragraphs of the story were in extra-large type:

> Pat Traymore, the fast-rising young television newswoman hired by Potomac Cable to produce a documentary about Senator Jennings, has been harassed by letters, phone calls and a break-in threatening her life if she continues to work on the program.
>
> A guest at the exclusive Christmas Eve supper of Ambassador Cardell, winsome Pat revealed that the house she is renting was the scene of the Adams murder-suicide twenty-four years ago. Pat claims not to be disturbed by the sinister history of the house, but other guests, long-time residents of the area, were not so complacent. . . .

The rest of the column was devoted to details of the Adams murder. On the pages were blown-up file photos of Dean and Renée Adams, the garish picture of the sacks in which their bodies were bundled, a close-up of their small daughter being carried out swathed in bloody bandages. "SIX MONTHS LATER KERRY ADAMS LOST HER VALIANT FIGHT FOR LIFE" was the caption under that picture.

The article hinted at a whitewash in the murder-suicide verdict:

> Aristocratic Patricia Remington Schuyler, mother of the dead woman, insisted that Congressman Adams was unsta-

> ble and about to be divorced by his socialite wife. But many old-timers in Washington think Dean Adams may have been given a bum rap, that it was Renée Adams who held the gun that night. "She was clearly besotted by him," one friend told me, "and he had a roving eye." Did her jealousy reach the breaking point that night? *Who* may have triggered that tragic outburst? Twenty-four years later, Washington still speculates.

Abigail's picture in her Miss Apple Junction crown was prominent. The copy under it read:

> Most specials profiling celebrities are ho-hum material, rehashes of the old Ed Murrow format. But the upcoming program on Senator Abigail Jennings will probably win the Nielsen ratings for the week. After all, the Senator may become our first woman Vice President. The smart money is on her. Now everyone's hoping that the footage will include more pictures of the distinguished senior Senator from Virginia in the rhinestone crown she picked up as a beauty queen along the way. And on the serious side, no one can agree on who hates Abigail Jennings enough to threaten the life of the newswoman who conceived the idea of the program.

Half of the right-hand page was subcaptioned THE PRE-CAMELOT YEARS. It was filled with photographs, most of them informal snapshots.

The accompanying text read:

> In a bizarre coincidence, Senator Abigail Jennings was at one time a frequent guest at the Adams house. She and her late husband, Congressman Willard Jennings, were close friends of Dean and Renée Adams and the John Kennedys. The three stunning young couples could not have guessed that the dark shadow of fate was hovering over that house and all their lives.

There were pictures of the six together and in mixed groups in the garden of the Georgetown house, on the Jennings estate in Virginia and at the Hyannis Port compound. And there were a half-dozen photos of Abigail alone in the group after Willard's death.

Toby uttered a savage, angry growl. He started to crumple the paper between his hands, willing the sickening pages to disintegrate under his sheer physical strength, but it was no use. It wouldn't go away.

He would have to show this to Abby as soon as he got her home. God only knew what her reaction would be. She *had* to keep her cool. Everything depended on that.

When Toby pulled the car up to the curb, Abigail was there, Sam Kingsley at her side. He started to get out, but Kingsley quickly opened the door for Abigail and helped her into the car. "Thanks for holding my hand, Sam," she said. "I feel a lot better. I'm sorry you can't make dinner."

"You promised me a rain check."

Toby drove quickly, frantic to get Abigail home, as though he needed to insulate her from public view until he could nurse her through the first reaction to the article.

"Sam is special," Abby said suddenly, ending the heavy silence. "You know how it's been with me all these years—but Toby, in a crazy way he reminds me of Billy. I have this feeling—just a feeling, mind you—that there could be something developing between Sam and me. It would be like having a second chance."

It was the first time she'd ever talked like this. Toby looked into the rearview mirror. Abigail was leaning against the seat, her body relaxed, her face soft and with a half-smile.

And he was the son-of-a-bitch who was going to have to destroy that hope and confidence.

"Toby, did you buy the paper?"

There was no use lying. "Yes, I did, Senator."

"Let me see it, please."

He handed back the first section.

"No, I don't feel like the news. Where's the section with the columns?"

"Not now, Senator." The traffic was light; they were over Chain Bridge. In a few minutes, they'd be home.

"What do you mean, *not now*?"

He didn't answer, and there was a long pause. Then Abigail said, her tone cold and brittle, "Something bad in one of the columns . . . something that could hurt me?"

"Something you won't like, Senator."

They drove the rest of the way in silence.

27

Over the Christmas holiday official Washington was a ghost town. The President was in his private vacation residence in the Southwest; Congress was in recess; the universities were closed for vacation. Washington became a sleepy city, a city waiting for the burst of activity that signaled the return of its Chief Executive, lawmakers and students.

Pat drove home through the light traffic. She wasn't hungry. A few nibbles of turkey and a cup of tea were as much as she wanted. She wondered how Luther was making out in Apple Junction. Had he turned on the courtly charm he had once used to woo her? All of that seemed long ago.

Apropos of Apple Junction, she wondered if Eleanor Brown had ever called Miss Langley back. *Eleanor Brown.* The girl was a pivotal figure in Pat's growing doubt about the integrity of the television program. What were the facts? It was Eleanor's word against Toby's. *Had* he phoned and requested her to go to the campaign office to look for the Senator's ring? The Senator supported Toby's claim that he had been driving her at the time of the supposed call. And part of the money had been found in Eleanor's storage area. How had she expected to get away with such a flimsy alibi?

I wish I had a transcript of the trial, she thought.

She opened her pad and studied the sentences she had written down the night before. They still didn't add up. On the next page she wrote *Eleanor Brown.* What had Margaret Langley said about the girl? Tapping her pen on the desk and frowning in concentration, she began to jot her impressions of their conversation:

> *Eleanor was timid . . . she never chewed gum in class or talked when the teacher was out of the room . . . she loved her job in the Senator's office . . . she had just been promoted . . . she was taking art classes . . . she was going to Baltimore that day to sketch. . . .*

Pat read and reread her notes. A girl doing well at a responsible job who had just been given a promotion, but so stupid she had hidden stolen money in her own storage room.

Some stolen money. The bulk of it—$70,000—was never found.

A girl as timid as that would be a poor witness in her own defense.

Eleanor had had a nervous breakdown in prison. She would have had to be a consummate actress to fake that. But she had violated her parole.

And what about Toby? He had been the witness who contradicted Eleanor's story. He had sworn he never phoned her that morning. Senator Jennings had confirmed that Toby was driving her at the time of the alleged call.

Would Senator Jennings deliberately lie for Toby, deliberately allow an innocent girl to go to prison?

But suppose someone who *sounded* like Toby had phoned Eleanor? In that case all three—Eleanor, Toby and the Senator—had been telling the truth. Who else would have known about Eleanor's storage space in her apartment building? What about the person who had made the threats, broken in here, left the doll? Could he be the *x* factor in the disappearance of the campaign funds?

The doll. Pat pushed back her chair and reached for the carton jammed under the library table, then changed her mind. There was nothing to be gained by looking at the doll now. The sight of that weeping face was too unsettling. After the program was aired, if there were no more threats, she'd throw it away. If there were any more letters or phone calls or attempted break-ins, she'd have to show the doll to the police.

On the next page in her pad she wrote *Toby*, then fished through the desk drawer for the cassettes of her interviews.

She had recorded Toby in the car that first afternoon. He hadn't realized she was taping him, and his voice was somewhat muffled. She turned the sound as high as possible, pushed the "play" button and began to take notes.

Maybe Abby stuck her neck out for me . . . I was working for a bookie in New York and almost got in trouble . . . I used to drive Abby and Willard Jennings to that house for parties . . . cute little kid, Kerry.

She was glad to switch to the interview with the waitress, Ethel Stubbins, and her husband, Ernie. They had said something about Toby. She found the segment, Ernie saying, "Say hello to him for me. Ask him if he's still losing money on the horses."

Jeremy Saunders had discussed Toby. She listened to his derisive remarks about the joyriding incident, his story about his father's buying off Abigail: "I always thought Toby had a hand in it."

After hearing the last of the cassettes, Pat read and reread her transcriptions. She knew what she had to do. If Eleanor turned herself in and was sent back to prison, Pat vowed she would stay with the case until she had satisfied herself as to Eleanor's guilt or innocence. And if it turns out I believe her story, Pat thought, I'll do everything I can to help her. Let the chips fall where they may—including Abigail Jennings' chips.

Pat wandered from the library into the foyer, and then to

the staircase. She glanced up, then hesitated. *The step above the turn. That's where I used to sit.* Impulsively she hurried up the stairs, sat on that step, leaned her head against the baluster and closed her eyes.

Her father was in the foyer. She had shrunk deeper into the shadows, knowing that he was angry, that this time he would not joke about finding her here. She had run back to bed.

She hurried up the rest of the staircase. Her old room was past the guest room, across the back of the house, overlooking the garden. It was empty now.

She'd walked in here that first morning as the moving men were scurrying through the house, but it had evoked absolutely no memories. Now it seemed she could remember the bed with the frilly white canopy, the small rocking chair near the window with the music box, the shelves of toys.

I came back to bed that night. I was frightened because Daddy was so angry. The living room is right underneath this room. I could hear voices; they were shouting at each other. Then the loud noise and Mother screaming, "No . . . No!"

Mother screaming. After the loud noise. Had she been able to scream after she was shot or had she screamed when she realized she had shot her husband?

Pat felt her body begin to shake. She grasped the door for support, felt the dampness in her palms and forehead. Her breath was coming in short, hard gasps. She thought, I am afraid. But it's over. It was so long ago.

She turned and realized she was running down the hall; she was rushing down the staircase. I am back there, she thought. I am going to remember. "*Daddy, Daddy,*" she called softly. At the foot of the stairs, she turned and began to stumble through the foyer, her arms outstretched. *Daddy . . . Daddy!*

At the living-room door she crumpled to her knees. Vague shadows were around her but would not take form. Burying her face in her hands, she began to sob . . . "Mother, Daddy, come home."

She had awakened and there had been a strange baby-sitter.

Mother. Daddy. I want my mother. I want my daddy. And they had come. Mother rocking her. Kerry, Kerry it's all right. Daddy patting her hair; his arms around both of them. Shhh, Kerry, we're here.

After a while Pat slid into a sitting position and leaned against the wall, staring into the room. Another memory had broken through. She was sure it was accurate. No matter which one was guilty that last night, she thought fiercely, I know that both of them loved me. . . .

28

There was a movie theater on Wisconsin Avenue that opened at ten. Arthur went into a cafeteria near it and dawdled over coffee, then walked around the neighborhood until the box office opened.

Whenever he was upset, he liked to go to the movies. He would choose a seat near the back and against the wall. And he'd buy the tallest bag of popcorn and sit and eat and watch unseeingly as the figures moved on the screen.

He liked the feeling of people near him but not conscious of him, the voices and music on the soundtrack, the anonymity of the darkened auditorium. It gave him a place to think. Now he settled in and stared blankly at the screen.

It had been a mistake to set the fire. There had been no mention of it in the newspaper. When he got off the Metro, he'd phoned the nursing home and the operator had answered at once. He'd muffled his voice: "I'm Mrs. Harnick's son. How serious was the fire?"

"Oh, sir, it was discovered almost at once. A smoldering cigarette in the trash bag. We didn't know any of the guests were even aware of it."

That meant they must have seen the overturned can of turpentine. No one would believe it had tipped accidentally.

If only he hadn't mentioned the monastery. Of course, the

office there might simply say: "Yes, our records indicate Arthur Stevens was with us for a short time."

Suppose they were pressed for details? "He left at the suggestion of his spiritual director."

"May we speak to the spiritual director?"

"He died some years ago."

Would they tell why he had been asked to leave? Would they study the records of the nursing home and see which patients had died in these few years and how many of them he had helped to nurse? He was sure they wouldn't understand that he was only being kind, only alleviating suffering.

Twice before he'd been questioned when patients he had cared for had slipped away to the Lord.

"Were you glad to see them die, Arthur?"

"I was glad to see them at peace. I did everything possible to help them get well or at least be comfortable."

When there was no hope, no relief from pain, when old people became too weak to even whisper or moan, when the doctors and relatives agreed it would be a blessing if God took them, then, and only then, did he help them slip away.

If he had known that Anita Gillespie was looking forward to seeing her daughter, he would have waited. It would have given him so much joy to know Mrs. Gillespie died happy.

That was the problem. She had been fighting death, not reconciled to it. That was why she had been too frightened to understand he was only trying to help her.

It was his concern for Glory that had made him so careless. He could remember the night the worry had begun. They were having dinner at home together, each reading a section of the newspaper, and Glory had cried, "Oh, dear God!" She was looking at the television page of the *Tribune* and had seen the announcement of the Senator Jennings program. It would include the highlights of her career. He had begged Glory not to be upset; he was sure it would be all right. But she hadn't listened. She'd started to sob. "Maybe it's better to face it," she'd said. "I don't want to live my life like this any longer."

Right then her attitude began to change. He stared ahead, heedlessly chewing on the popcorn. He had not been given the privilege of formally taking his vows. Instead, he had sworn them privately. Poverty, chastity, and obedience. Never once had he broken them—but he used to get so lonely. . . .

Then nine years ago he'd met Glory. She'd been sitting in the dreary waiting room of the clinic, clutching the Raggedy Ann doll and waiting her turn to see the psychiatrist. The doll was what had caught his attention. Something made him wait around outside for her.

They'd started walking toward the bus stop together. He'd explained he was a priest but had left parish work to work directly with the sick. She'd told him all about herself, how she'd been in prison for a crime she didn't commit and she was on parole and lived in a furnished room. "I'm not allowed to smoke in my room," she told him, "or even have a hot plate so I can fix coffee or soup when I don't want to go out to the drugstore to eat."

They went for ice cream and it began to get dark. She said she was late and the woman where she lived would be angry. Then she started to cry and said she'd rather be dead than go back there. And he had taken her home with him. "You will be a child in my care," he'd told her. And she was like a helpless child. He gave her his bedroom and slept on the couch, and in the beginning she would just lie in bed and cry. For a few weeks the cops came around the clinic to see if she'd shown up again, but then they lost interest.

They'd gone to Baltimore. That was when he told her he was going to tell everyone that she was his daughter. "You call me Father anyhow," he said. And he had named her Gloria.

Slowly she had started to get better. But for nearly seven years she had left the apartment only at night; she was so sure that a policeman would recognize her.

He'd worked in different nursing homes around Baltimore,

and then two years ago it was necessary to leave and they'd come to Alexandria. Glory loved being near Washington, but she was afraid she might run into people who knew her. He convinced her that was foolish. "None of the people from the Senator's office would ever come near this neighborhood." Even so, whenever Glory went out, she wore dark glasses. Gradually her spells of depression began to ease. She needed less and less of the medicine he brought from the nursing home, and she'd gotten the typing job.

Arthur finished the popcorn. He would not leave Washington until tomorrow night, after he'd seen the program about Senator Jennings. He never helped people slip away until there was absolutely nothing the doctors could do for them, until his voices directed him that their time had come. Neither would he condemn Patricia Traymore without evidence. If she did not talk about Glory on the program or show her picture, Glory would be safe. He would arrange to meet her and they'd go away together.

But if Glory was exposed to the world as a thief, she would give herself up. This time she would die in prison. He was sure of it. He had seen enough people who had lost the will to live. But if it happened, Patricia Traymore would be punished for that terrible sin! He would go to the house where she lived and mete out justice to her.

Three Thousand N Street. Even the house where Patricia Traymore lived was a symbol of suffering and death.

The movie was ending. Where could he go now?

You must hide, Arthur.

"But where?" He realized he had spoken aloud. The woman in the seat ahead of him turned and glanced back.

Three Thousand N Street, the voices whispered. *Go there, Arthur. Go in the window again. Think about the closet.*

The image of the closet in the unused bedroom filled his mind. He would be warm and safe concealed behind the rows of shelves in that closet. The lights went on in the theater and he stood up quickly. He must not draw attention to himself. He would go to another movie now and another after that. By then it would be dark. Where better to spend the hours until the broadcast tomorrow evening than in Patricia Traymore's own home? No one would dream of looking for him there.

She must have her chance to be exonerated, Arthur. You must not be too hasty. The words swirled in the air above his head. "I understand," he said. If there was no reference to Glory on the program, Patricia Traymore would never know that he had been staying with her. But if Glory was shown and identified, Patricia would be punished by the angels.

He would light the avenging torch.

29

At one o'clock Lila Thatcher's maid returned from grocery shopping. Lila was in her study working on a lecture she was planning to give the following week at the University of Maryland. The subject was "Harness Your Psychic Gift." Lila bent over the typewriter, her hands clasped.

The maid knocked on the door. "Miss Lila, you don't look too happy." The maid spoke with the comfortable familiarity of an employee who had become a trusted friend.

"I'm not, Ouida. For someone who's trying to teach people to use their psychic skills, my own are pretty scrambled today."

"I brought in the *Tribune.* Do you want to see it now?"

"Yes, I think so."

Five minutes later, in angry disbelief, Lila was reading the Gina Butterfield spread. Fifteen minutes later, she was ringing Pat's doorbell. With dismay she realized Pat had been weeping. "There's something I have to show you," she explained.

They went into the library. Lila laid the paper on the table and opened it. She watched as Pat saw the headline and the color drained from her face.

Helplessly Pat skimmed the copy, glanced at the pictures. "My God, it makes me sound as though I was blabbing about the break-in, the Senator, this house, *everything.* Lila, I can't tell you how upset they'll all be. Luther Pelham had every single picture of my mother and father edited out of the old films. He didn't want any connection between the Senator and, I quote him, 'the Adams mess.' It's as though there's a force in action I can't stop. I don't know whether to try to explain, to resign or what." She tried to hold back angry tears.

Lila began to fold the newspaper. "I can't advise you about the job, but I can tell you that you must not look at this again, Kerry. I had to show it to you, but I'm taking it home with me. It's not wise for you to see yourself as you were that day, like a broken doll."

Pat grabbed the older woman's arm. "Why did you say that?"

"Say what? You mean why did I call you Kerry? That just slipped out."

"No, I mean why did you compare me to a broken doll?"

Lila stared at her and then looked down at the newspaper. "It's in here," she said. "I just read it. Look." In the lead column Gina Butterfield had reprinted some of the original *Tribune* story about the murder-suicide.

> Police Chief Collins, commenting on the grisly scene, said, "It's the worst I've ever come across. When I saw that poor little kid like a broken doll, I wondered why he hadn't shot her too. It would have been easier for her."

"A broken doll," Pat whispered. "Whoever left it knew me then."

"Left *what*? Pat, sit down. You look as though you're going to faint. I'll get you a glass of water." Lila hurried from the room.

Pat leaned her head against the back of the couch and closed her eyes. When she had looked up the newspaper accounts of the tragedy, she had seen the pictures of the bodies being carried out; of herself, bandaged and bloody on the stretcher. But seeing them juxtaposed against those of the smiling, apparently carefree young couples was worse. She didn't remember reading that quote from the police chief. Maybe she hadn't seen the issue in which it appeared. But it proved that whoever had threatened her knew who she was, had known her then.

Lila came back. She had filled a glass with cold water.

"I'm all right," Pat said. "Lila, the night someone broke in here, he didn't just leave a note." She tugged at the carton to try to get it out from under the library table. It was wedged in so tightly that it wouldn't budge. I can't believe I jammed it in like this, Pat thought. As she struggled, she told Lila about finding the doll.

Shocked, Lila absorbed what she was hearing. The intruder had left a bloodied doll against the fireplace? Pat was in danger here. She had sensed it all along. She was still in danger.

Pat freed the carton. She opened it, going through it rapidly. Lila watched as her expression changed from surprise to alarm. "Pat, what is it?"

"The doll. It's gone."

"Are you sure . . ."

"I put it here myself. I looked at it again just the other day. Lila, I took its apron off. It was sickening to look at. I shoved it way down. Maybe it's still here." Pat fished through the box. "Look, here it is."

Lila stared at the crumpled piece of white cotton, soiled with reddish-brown stains, the strings of the sash hanging limply from the sides.

"When was the last time you saw the doll?"

"Saturday afternoon. I had it out on the table. The Senator's chauffeur came with more of her photograph albums. I hid it in the carton again. I didn't want him to see it." Pat paused.

"Wait. There was something about Toby when he came in. He was brusque and kept eyeing everything in this room. I hadn't answered the bell right away and I think he wondered what I'd been up to. And then he said he'd let himself out. When I heard the door close, I decided to slide the bolt, and Lila, the door was opening again. Toby had something that looked like a credit card in his hand. He tried to pass it off by insinuating that he was just testing the lock for me, and that I should be sure to keep the bolt on.

"He knew me when I was little. Maybe he's the one who's been threatening me. But why?"

It was not yet midafternoon, but the day had turned gray and cloudy. The dark wood paneling and the fading light made Pat seem small and vulnerable. "We must call the police immediately," Lila said. "They'll question the chauffeur."

"I can't do that. Can you imagine what the Senator would think? And it's only a possibility. But I do know someone who can have Toby investigated quietly." Pat saw the distress on Lila's face. "It's going to be all right," she assured her. "I'll keep the bolt on the door—and Lila, if everything that's happened is an attempt to stop the program, it's really too late. We're taping the Senator arriving home this evening. Tomorrow we do some in-studio scenes and tomorrow night it will be aired. After that there won't be any point in trying to scare me. And I'm beginning to think that's what this is about—just an attempt to scare me off."

Lila left a few minutes later. Pat had to be at the studio at four o'clock. She promised she would phone her Congressman friend—Sam Kingsley—and ask him to have the chauffeur investigated. To Lila's consternation, Pat insisted on keeping the newspaper. "I'll have to read it carefully and know exactly what it says. If you don't give me this, I'll go out and buy another one."

Lila's maid had the door open when she came up the steps. "I've been watching for you, Miss Lila," she explained. "You never finished your lunch and you looked real upset when you left."

"You've been watching for me, Ouida?" Lila went into the

dining room and walked over to the windows facing the street. From there she could see the entire frontage and the right side of Pat's house and property. "It won't work," she murmured. "He broke in through the patio doors and I can't see them from here."

"What did you say, Miss Lila?"

"It's nothing. I'm going to keep a stillwatch and I had thought of setting my typewriter on a table just back from the windows."

"A stillwatch?"

"Yes, it's an expression that means if you believe something is wrong, you keep a vigil."

"You think something is wrong at Miss Traymore's? You think that prowler may come back again?"

Lila stared at the unnatural darkness surrounding Pat's house. With an acute sense of foreboding she answered somberly, "That's just what I think."

30

From the moment Father phoned her, Glory had been waiting for the police to come. At ten o'clock it happened. The door of the real estate office opened and a man in his mid-thirties came in. She looked up and saw a squad car parked out front. Her fingers dropped from the typewriter.

"Detective Barrott," the visitor said, and held up a badge. "I'd like to speak with Gloria Stevens. Is she here?"

Glory stood up. Already she could hear his questions: *Isn't your real name Eleanor Brown? Why did you violate parole? How long did you think you could get away with it?*

Detective Barrott came over to her. He had a frank, chubby face with sandy hair that curled around his ears. His eyes were inquisitive but not unfriendly. She realized he was about her own age, and somehow he seemed a little less frightening than the scornful detective who had questioned her after the money was found in her storage room.

"Miss Stevens? Don't be nervous. I wonder if I could speak to you privately?"

"We could go in here." She led the way into Mr. Schuller's small private office. There were two leather chairs in front of Mr. Schuller's desk. She sat in one of them and the detective settled in the other.

"You looked scared," he said kindly. "You have nothing to

worry about. We just want to talk to your dad. Do you know where we can reach him?"

Talk to her dad. Father! She swallowed. "When I left for work he was home. He probably went to the bakery."

"He didn't come back. Maybe when he saw the police car in front of your house, he decided not to. Do you think he might be with some relatives or friends?"

"I . . . I don't know. Why do you want to talk to him?"

"Just to ask a few questions. By any chance has he called you this morning?"

This man thought Arthur was her father. He wasn't interested in her.

"He . . . he did call. But I was on the phone with my boss."

"What did he want?"

"He . . . wanted me to meet him and I said I couldn't."

"Where did he want you to meet him?"

Father's words rang in her ears. *Metro Central . . . Twelfth and G exit . . .* Was he there now? Was he in trouble? Father had taken care of her all these years. She could not hurt him now.

She chose her words carefully. "I couldn't stay on the phone. I . . . I just said I couldn't leave the office and practically hung up on him. Why do you want to talk to him? What's wrong?"

"Well, maybe nothing." The detective's voice was kind. "Does your dad talk to you about his patients?"

"Yes." It was easy to answer that question. "He cares so much about them."

"Has he ever mentioned Mrs. Gillespie to you?"

"Yes. She died last week, didn't she? He felt so bad. Something about her daughter coming to visit her." She thought about the way he had cried out in his sleep, "Close your eyes, Mrs. Gillespie. Close your eyes." Maybe he had made a mistake when he was helping Mrs. Gillespie and they were blaming him for it.

"Has he seemed different lately—nervous or anything like that?"

"He is the kindest man I know. His whole life is devoted to helping people. In fact, they just asked him at the nursing home to go to Tennessee and help out there."

The detective smiled. "How old are you, Miss Stevens?"

"Thirty-four."

He looked surprised. "You don't look it. According to the employment records, Arthur Stevens is forty-nine." He paused, then in a friendly voice added, "He's not your real father, is he?"

Soon he would be pinning her down with questions. "He used to be a parish priest but decided to spend his whole life caring for the sick. When I was very ill and had no one, he took me in."

Now he would ask her real name. But he didn't.

"I see. Miss . . . Miss Stevens, we do want to talk to, er . . . Father Stevens. If he calls you, will you contact me?" He gave her his card. DETECTIVE WILLIAM BARROTT. She could sense him studying her. Why wasn't he asking her more questions about herself, about her background?

He was gone. She sat alone in the private office until Opal came in.

"Gloria, is anything wrong?"

Opal was a good friend, the best friend she'd ever had. Opal had helped her think of herself as a woman again. Opal was always after her to go to parties, saying her boyfriend would fix her up with a blind date. She'd always refused.

"Gloria, what's wrong?" Opal repeated. "You look terrible."

"No, nothing's wrong. I have a headache. Do you think I could go home?"

"Sure; I'll finish your typing. Gloria, if there's anything I can do . . ."

Glory looked into her friend's troubled face. "Not anymore, but thank you for everything."

She walked home. The temperature was in the forties, but

even so, the day was raw with a chill that penetrated her coat and gloves. The apartment, with its shabby, rented furniture, seemed strangely empty, as though it sensed they would not be returning. She went to the hall closet and found the battered black suitcase that Father had bought at a garage sale. She packed her meager supply of clothing, her cosmetics and the new book Opal had given her for Christmas. The suitcase wasn't large, and it was hard to force the locks to snap.

There was something else—her Raggedy Ann doll. At the mental-health clinic the psychiatrist had asked her to draw a picture of how she felt about herself, but somehow she couldn't do that. The doll was with some others on a shelf, and he had given it to her. "Do you think you could show me how this doll would look if it were you?"

It hadn't been hard to paint the tears and to sketch in the frightened look about the eyes and to change the thrust of the mouth so that instead of smiling it seemed about to scream.

"That bad?" the doctor had said when she was finished.

"Worse."

Oh, Father, she thought, I wish I could stay here and wait until you call me. But they're going to find out about me. That detective is probably having me checked right now. I can't run away anymore. While I have the courage, I have to turn myself in. Maybe it will help me get a lighter sentence for breaking parole.

There was one promise she could keep. Miss Langley had begged her to call that television celebrity Patricia Traymore before she did anything. Now she made the call, told what she planned and listened impassively to Pat's emotional pleading.

Finally at three o'clock she left. A car was parked down the street. Two men were sitting in it. "That's the girl," one of them said. "She was lying about not planning to meet Stevens." He sounded regretful.

The other man pressed his foot on the pedal. "I told you she was holding back on you. Ten bucks she'll lead us to Stevens now."

31

Pat sped across town to the Lotus Inn Restaurant on Wisconsin Avenue. Desperately she tried to think of some way she could persuade Eleanor Brown not to surrender herself yet. Surely she could be persuaded to listen to reason.

She had tried to reach Sam, but after five rings had slammed down the phone and run out. Now as she rushed into the restaurant she wondered if she would recognize the girl from her high school picture. Was she using her own name? Probably not.

The hostess greeted her. "Are you Miss Traymore?"

"Yes, I am."

"Miss Brown is waiting for you."

She was sitting at a rear table sipping chablis. Pat slipped into the chair opposite her, trying to collect herself to know what to say. Eleanor Brown had not changed very much from her high school picture. She was obviously older, no longer painfully thin and prettier than Pat had expected, but there was no mistaking her.

She spoke softly. "Miss Traymore? Thank you for coming."

"Eleanor, please listen to me. We can get you a lawyer. You can be out on bail while we work something out. You were in the midst of a breakdown when you violated parole. There are so many angles a good lawyer can work."

The waiter came with an appetizer of butterfly shrimp. "I

used to dream of these," Eleanor said. "Do you want to order something?"

"No. Nothing. Eleanor, did you understand what I said?"

"Yes, I did." Eleanor dipped one of the shrimp in the sweet sauce. "Oh, that's good." Her face was pale but determined. "Miss Traymore, I hope I can get my parole reinstated, but if I can't, I know I'm strong enough now to serve the time they gave me. I can sleep in a cell, and wear a prison uniform, and eat that slop they call food, and put up with the strip searches and the boredom. When I get out I won't have to hide anymore, and I'm going to spend the rest of my life trying to prove my innocence."

"Eleanor, wasn't the money found in your possession?"

"Miss Traymore, half the people in the office knew about that storeroom. When I moved from one apartment to the other, six or eight of them helped. We made a party of it. The furniture I couldn't use was carried down to the storage room. *Some* of the money was found there, but seventy thousand dollars went into someone else's pocket."

"Eleanor, you claim Toby phoned you and he said he didn't. Didn't you think it unusual to be asked to go to the campaign office on Sunday?"

Eleanor pushed aside the shells on her plate. "No. You see the Senator was up for reelection. A lot of mailings were sent from the campaign office. She used to drop by and help just to make the volunteers feel important. When she did that she would take off her big diamond ring. It was a little loose and she really was careless with it. A couple of times she left without it."

"And Toby or someone sounding like Toby said she'd lost or mislaid it again."

"Yes. I knew she'd been in the campaign office on Saturday helping with the mailings, so it sounded perfectly natural that she might have forgotten it again and one of the senior aides might have put it in the safe for her.

"I believe Toby was driving the Senator at the time the call was made. The voice was muffled and whoever spoke to me didn't say much. It was something like, 'See if the Senator's ring is in the campaign safe and let her know.' I was annoyed because I wanted to go to Richmond to sketch and I even said something like 'she'll probably find it under her nose.' Whoever it was who phoned sort of laughed and hung up. If Abigail Jennings hadn't talked so much about the second chance she had given me, called me a convicted thief, I would have had a better chance of reasonable doubt. I've lost eleven years of my life for something I didn't do and I'm not losing another day." She stood up and laid money on the table. "That should cover everything." Bending down, she picked up her suitcase, then paused. "You know what's hardest for me now? I'm breaking my promise to the man I've been living with, and he's been so good to me. He begged me not to go to the police yet. I wish I could explain to him, but I don't know where he is."

"Can I call him for you later? What's his name? Where does he work?"

"His name is Arthur Stevens. I think there's some problem at his job. He won't be there. There's nothing you can do. I hope your program is very successful, Miss Traymore. I was terribly upset when I read the announcement about it. I knew that if even one picture of me was shown I'd be in jail within twenty-four hours. But you know, that made me realize how tired I was of running. In a crazy way, it gave me the courage to face going back to prison so that someday I really will be free. Father, I mean Arthur Stevens, just couldn't accept that. And now I'd better go before I run out of courage."

Helplessly Pat watched her retreating back.

As Eleanor left the restaurant two men at a corner table got up and followed her out.

32

"Abby, it's not as bad as it could be." In the forty years he had known her, it was only the third time he had had his arms around her. She was sobbing helplessly.

"Why didn't you tell me she was staying in that house?"

"There was no reason to."

They were in Abigail's living room. He'd shown her the article when they arrived, then tried to calm the inevitable explosion.

"Abby, tomorrow this newspaper will be lining garbage cans."

"I don't want to line garbage cans!" she'd screamed.

He poured a straight Scotch and made her drink it. "Come on, Senator, pull yourself together. Maybe there's a photographer hiding in the bushes."

"Shut up, you bloody fool." But the suggestion had been enough to shock her. And after the drink, she'd started to cry. "Toby, it looks like the old penny-dreadful scandal sheets. And that picture. Toby, *that picture.*" She didn't mean the one of her and Francey.

He put his arms around her, clumsily patted her back and realized with the dullness of a long-accepted pain that he was nothing more to her than a railing to grab when your feet gave way underneath you.

"If anyone really studies the pictures! Toby, look at *that* one."

"Nobody's going to bother."

"Toby, that girl—that Pat Traymore. How did she happen to lease that house? It can't be a coincidence."

"The house has been rented to twelve different tenants in the past twenty-four years. She's just another one of them." Toby tried to make his voice hearty. He didn't believe that; but on the other hand, Phil still hadn't been able to uncover the details of the rental. "Senator, you gotta hang in there. Whoever made those threats to Pat Traymore . . ."

"Toby, *how do we know there were threats?* How do we know this isn't a calculated attempt to embarrass me?"

He was so startled he stepped back. In a reflex action she pulled away from him, and they stared at each other. "God Almighty, Abby, do you think she *engineered* this?"

The ring of the telephone made them both jump. He looked at her. "You want me . . ."

"Yes." She held her hands up to her face. "I don't give a goddamn who's calling. I'm not here."

"Senator Jennings' residence." Toby put on his butler's voice. "May I take a message for the Senator? She's not available at the moment." He winked at Abby and was rewarded by the trace of a smile. "The President. . . . Oh, just a minute, sir." He held his hand over the mouthpiece. "Abby, the President is calling you. . . ."

"Toby, don't you dare . . ."

"Abby, for chrissake, it's the *President!*"

She clasped her hands to her lips, then came over and took the phone from him. "If this is your idea of a joke . . ." She got on. "Abigail Jennings."

Toby watched as her expression changed. "Mr. President. I'm so sorry. . . . I'm sorry . . . Some reading . . . That's why I left word. . . . I'm sorry. . . . Yes, sir, of course. Yes, I can be at the White House tomorrow evening . . . eight-thirty, of course.

Yes, we've been quite busy with this program. Frankly, I'm not comfortable being the subject of this sort of thing. . . . Why, how kind of you. . . . Sir, you mean . . . I simply don't know what to say. . . . Of course, I understand. . . . Thank you, sir."

She hung up. Dazed, she looked at Toby. "I'm not to tell a soul. He's announcing his appointment of me tomorrow night after the program. He said it isn't a bad idea the whole country gets to know me a little better. He laughed about the *Mirror* cover. He said his mother was a big gal too, but that I'm much prettier now than when I was seventeen. Toby, I'm going to be Vice President of the United States!" She laughed hysterically and flung herself at him.

"Abby, you *did* it!" He lifted her off her feet.

An instant later her face twisted with tension. "Toby, nothing can happen . . . Nothing must stop this. . . ."

He put her down and covered both her hands in his. "Abby, I *swear* nothing will keep this from you."

She started to laugh and then began to cry. "Toby, I'm on a roller coaster. You and that damn Scotch. You know I can't drink. Toby—*Vice President!*"

He had to ease her down. His voice soothing, he said, "Later on we'll take a ride over and just kind of cruise past your new house, Abby. You're finally getting a mansion. Next stop Massachusetts Avenue."

"Toby, shut up. Just make me a cup of tea. I'm going to take a shower and try to collect myself. Vice President! My God, my God!"

He put the kettle on and then, not bothering with a coat, walked to the roadside mailbox and flipped it open. The usual collection of junk—coupons, contests, "You may have won two million dollars". . . . Ninety-nine percent of Abby's personal mail went through the office.

Then he saw it. The blue envelope with the handwritten address. A personal note to Abby. He looked at the upper left-hand corner and felt the blood drain from his face.

The note was from Catherine Graney.

33

Sam drove across town on 7th Street, already a little late for his noon appointment with Larry Saggiotes of the National Transportation Safety Board.

After he left Pat, he'd gone home and lain awake most of the night, his emotions shifting from anger to a sober examination of Pat's charges.

"Can I help you, sir?"

"What? Oh, sorry." Sheepishly Sam realized he'd been so deep in thought, he had arrived in the lobby of the FAA building without realizing he had come through the revolving door. The security guard was looking at him curiously.

He went up to the eighth floor and gave his name to the receptionist. "It will be just a few minutes," she said.

Sam settled into a chair. Had Abigail and Willard Jennings been having a violent argument that last day? he wondered. But that didn't have to mean anything. He remembered there were times when he'd threatened to quit Congress, to get a job that would provide some of the luxuries that Janice deserved. She'd argued with him and stormed at him, and anyone who heard them would have thought they couldn't stand each other. Maybe the pilot's widow did hear Abigail arguing with Willard Jennings that day. Maybe Willard was disgusted about something and ready to give up politics and she didn't want him burning his bridges.

Sam had called his FBI friend Jack Carlson to trace the report of the crash.

"Twenty-seven years ago? That could be a tough one," Jack had said. "The National Transportation Safety Board handles investigations into crashes now, but that many years ago the Civil Aeronautics Administration was in charge. Let me call you back."

At nine-thirty Jack had phoned back. "You're in luck," he'd said laconically. "Most records are shredded after ten years, but when prominent people are involved, the investigation reports are stored in the Safety Board warehouse. They've got the data on accidents involving everyone from Amelia Earhart and Carole Lombard to Dag Hammarskjöld and Hale Boggs. My contact at the board is Larry Saggiotes. He'll get the report sent to his office, look it over. He suggests you come by about noon. He'll review it with you."

"Excuse me, sir. Mr. Saggiotes will see you now."

Sam looked up. He had a feeling the receptionist had been trying to get his attention. I'd better get with it, he thought. He followed her down the corridor.

Larry Saggiotes was a big man whose features and coloring reflected his Greek heritage. They exchanged greetings. Sam gave a carefully edited explanation of why he'd wanted to investigate the crash.

Larry settled back in his chair, frowning. "Nice day here, isn't it?" he commented. "But it's foggy in New York, icy in Minneapolis, pouring in Dallas. Yet in the next twenty-four hours one hundred twenty thousand commercial, military and private planes will take off and land in this country. And the odds against any of them crashing are astronomical. That's why when a plane that's been checked out by an expert mechanic and flown by a master pilot on a day with good visibility suddenly crashes into a mountain and is scattered over two square miles of rocky landscape, we're not happy."

"The Jennings plane!"

"The Jennings plane," Larry confirmed. "I've just read the report. What happened? We don't know. The last contact with George Graney was when he left traffic control in Richmond. There was no suggestion of trouble. It was a routine two-hour flight. And then he was overdue."

"And the verdict was pilot error?" Sam asked.

"*Probable* cause, pilot error. It always ends up like that when we can't come up with other answers. It was a fairly new Cessna twin-engine, so their engineers were around to prove the plane was in great shape. Willard Jennings' widow cried her eyes out about how she'd had a horror of small charter planes, that her husband had complained about rough landings with Graney."

"Did the possibility of foul play ever come up?"

"Congressman, the possibility of foul play is *always* investigated in a case like this. First we look for how it might have been done. Well, there are plenty of ways that are pretty hard to trace. For example, with all the magnetic tape being used today, a strong magnet hidden in the cockpit could screw up all the instruments. Twenty-seven years ago that wouldn't have happened. But if anybody had fooled with the generator of Graney's plane, maybe, frayed or cut a wire, Graney would have had a complete loss of power right as he's flying over a mountain. The chances of recovering usable evidence would have been negligible.

"The fuel switch would be another possibility. That plane had two tanks. The pilot switched to the second tank when the first tank's needle indicated it was empty. Suppose the switch wasn't working? He wouldn't have had a chance to use the second tank. Then, of course, we have corrosive acid. Somebody who doesn't want a plane to make it safely could have put a leaky container of the stuff on board. It could be in the luggage area, under a seat—wouldn't matter. That would eat through the cables within half an hour and there'd be no controlling the plane. But that would be easier to discover."

"Did any of this come up at the hearing?" Sam asked.

"There weren't enough pieces of that plane recovered to play Pick Up Sticks. So the next thing we do is look for motive. And found absolutely none. Graney's charter line was doing well; he hadn't taken out any recent insurance. The Congressman was so poorly insured it was amazing, but when you have family dough, you don't need insurance, I guess. Incidentally, this is the second request I've had for a copy of the report. Mrs. George Graney came in for one last week."

"Larry, if it's at all possible, I'm trying to keep Senator Jennings from being embarrassed by having this rehashed—and of course I'll study the report myself, but let me get this straight: was there any suggestion that George Graney was an inexperienced or careless pilot?"

"Absolutely none. He had an impeccable record, Congressman. He had been in air combat through the Korean War, then worked for United for a couple of years. This kind of flying was child's play to him."

"How about his equipment?"

"Always in top shape. His mechanics were good."

"So the pilot's widow has a valid reason to be upset that the blame for the crash got laid at George Graney's doorstep."

Larry blew a smoke ring the size of a cruller. "You bet she does—*more* than valid."

34

At ten minutes past four, Pat managed to reach Sam from the lobby of the Potomac Cable Network building. Without mentioning their quarrel, she told him about Eleanor Brown. "I couldn't stop her. She was determined to turn herself in."

"Calm down, Pat. I'll send a lawyer to see her. How long will you be at the network?"

"I don't know. Have you seen the *Tribune* today?"

"Just the headlines."

"Read the second section. A columnist I met the other night heard where I lived and rehashed everything."

"Pat, I'll be here. Come over when you finish at the network."

Luther was waiting for her in his office. She had expected to be treated as a pariah. Instead, he was fairly restrained. "The Apple Junction shooting went well," he told her. "It snowed there yesterday and that whole cruddy backwoods looked like the American dream. We caught the Saunders house, the high school with the crèche in front and Main Street with its Christmas tree. We put a sign in front of the town hall: 'Apple Junction, Birthplace of Senator Abigail Foster Jennings.'"

Luther puffed on a cigarette. "That old lady, Margaret Langley, was a good interview. Kind of classy-looking and quaint. Nice touch having her talk about what a dedicated student the Senator was and showing the yearbook."

Pat realized that somehow it had become *Luther's* idea to do background shots in Apple Junction. "Have you seen the footage from last night and this morning?" she asked.

"Yes. It's okay. You might have gotten a little more of Abigail actually working at her desk. The sequence at Christmas dinner was fine."

"Surely you've seen today's *Tribune*?"

"Yes." Luther ground his cigarette into the ashtray and reached for another one. His voice changed. Telltale red spots appeared in his cheeks. "Pat, would you mind laying your cards on the table and explaining why you gave out that story?"

"Why I *what*?"

Now the restraint in Luther's manner disappeared. "Maybe a lot of people would consider it coincidence that so much has happened this week to give the Senator sensational publicity. I happen not to believe in coincidence. I agree with what Abigail said after that first picture came out in the *Mirror*. You've been out from day one to force us to produce this program *your* way. And I think you've used every trick in the books to get personal publicity for yourself. There isn't anyone in Washington who isn't talking about Pat Traymore."

"If you believe that, you ought to fire me."

"And give you more headlines? No way. But just as a matter of curiosity, will you answer a few questions for me?"

"Go ahead."

"The first day in this office, I told you to edit out any reference to Congressman Adams and his wife. Did you know you were renting their house?"

"Yes, I did."

"Wouldn't it have been natural to mention it?"

"I don't think so. I certainly edited out every single picture of them from the Senator's material—and incidentally, I did a damn good job of it. Have you run through all those films?"

"Yes. You did do a good job. Then suppose you tell me your reasoning for the threats. Anyone who knows the business would realize that whether or not you worked on the program it was going to be completed."

Pat chose her words carefully. "I think the threats were just that—*threats.* I don't think anyone ever meant to harm me, just scare me off. I think that someone is afraid to have the program made and thought that if I didn't do it the project would be dropped." She paused, then added deliberately, "That person couldn't know I'm just a figurehead in a campaign to make Abigail Jennings Vice President."

"Are you trying to insinuate . . .?"

"No, not insinuate: state. Look, I fell for it. I fell for being hired so fast, for being rushed down here to do three months' work in a week, for having the material for the program spoon-fed to me by you and the Senator. The little claim this program will have to being an honest documentary is because of the segments I had to force down your throats. It's only because of the rotten publicity I've inadvertently caused Abigail Jennings that I'm going to do my best to make this program work for her. But I warn you, when it's over, there are some things I intend to investigate."

"Such as . . .?"

"Such as Eleanor Brown, the girl who was convicted of embezzling the campaign funds. I saw her today. She was about to turn herself in to the police. And she swears she never touched that money."

"Eleanor Brown turned herself in?" Luther interrupted. "We can make a plus out of that. As a parole violater, she won't get bail."

"Congressman Kingsley is trying to have bail set."

"That's a mistake. I'll see that she stays put until the President makes his appointment. After that, who cares? She had a fair trial. We'll talk about the case on the program just as we've written it, only we'll add the fact that because of the program she turned herself in. That'll spike her guns if she wants to make trouble."

Pat felt that somehow she had betrayed her trust. "I happen to think that girl is innocent, and if she is, I'll fight to get her a new trial."

"She's guilty," Luther snapped. "Otherwise why did she break parole? She's probably gone through that seventy thousand bucks now and wants to be able to stop running. Don't forget: a panel of jurors convicted her unanimously. You still believe in the jury system, I hope? Now, is there anything else? Any single thing that you know that could reflect badly on the Senator?"

She told him about Catherine Graney.

"So she's talking about suing the network?" Luther looked immensely pleased. "And you're worried about that?"

"If she starts gossiping about the Jennings marriage . . . the very fact that the Senator wasn't left a penny by her mother-in-law. . . ."

"Abigail will have the wholehearted support of every woman in America who's put up with a miserable mother-in-law. As far as the Jennings marriage goes, it's this Graney woman's word against the Senator and Toby . . . don't forget he was a witness to their last time together. And what about the letter you gave me that the Senator wrote to her husband? That's dated only a few days before he died."

"We *assume* that. Someone else could point out that she never filled in the *year*."

"She can fill it in now if necessary. Anything else?"

"To the best of my knowledge those are the only two places where the Senator might have unfavorable publicity. I'm prepared to give my word of honor on that."

"All right." Luther seemed appeased. "I'm taking a crew to tape the Senator going into her home this evening—that end-of-the-day working scene."

"Don't you want me at that taping?"

"I want you as far away from Abigail Jennings as you can get until she has time to calm down. Pat, have you read your contract with this network carefully?"

"I think so."

"Then you do realize we have the right to cancel your employment here for a specified cash settlement? Frankly, I don't buy the cock-and-bull story that someone is trying to keep this program from being made. But I almost admire you for having made yourself a household word in Washington, and you've done it by piggybacking onto a woman who's dedicated her whole life to public service."

"Have *you* read my contract?" Pat asked.

"I wrote it."

"Then you do know you gave me creative control of the projects to which I'm assigned. Do you think you've fulfilled my contract this week?" She opened the door of Luther's office, sure that everyone in the newsroom was listening to them.

Luther's last words echoed through the room: "By this time next week the terms of your contract will be moot."

It was one of the few times in her life that Pat slammed a door.

Fifteen minutes later she was giving her name to the desk clerk in Sam's apartment building.

Sam was waiting in the hallway when the elevator stopped at his floor. "Pat, you look bushed," he told her.

"I am." Wearily she looked up at him. He was wearing the same Argyle sweater he'd had on the night before. With a stab of pain she noted again how it brought out the blueness of his eyes. He took her arm and they walked down the long corridor.

Inside the apartment, her immediate impression was surprise at the decor. Charcoal gray sectional furniture was grouped in the center of the room. The walls had a number of good prints and a few first-class paintings. The carpet was wall-to-wall in a tweedy gray-black-and-white combination.

Somehow in Sam's home she'd expected a more traditional look—a couch with arms, easy chairs, family pieces. An Oriental, however worn, would have been a distinct improvement over the carpet. He asked her what she thought of the place and she told him.

Sam's eyes crinkled. "You sure know how to get invited back, don't you? You're right, of course. I wanted to make a clean sweep, start over, and naturally outdid myself. I agree. This place does look like a motel lobby."

"Then why stay here? I gather you have other options."

"Oh, the apartment is fine," Sam said easily. "It's just the furniture that bugs me. I rang out the old but didn't know exactly what the new was supposed to be."

It was a half-joking statement that suddenly assumed too much weight. "By any chance, do you have a Scotch for a tired lady?" she asked.

"Sure do." He went over to the bar. "Lots of soda, one ice cube, twist of lemon if possible, but don't worry if you're out of lemon." He smiled.

"I'm sure I don't sound that wimpy."

"Not wimpy, just considerate." He mixed the drinks and placed them on the cocktail table. "Sit down and don't be so fidgety. How did the studio go?"

"By this time next week I probably won't have a job. You see, Luther really thinks I'm pulling all this as a publicity stunt and he rather admires my moxie for trying it."

"I think Abigail has somewhat the same view."

Pat raised an eyebrow. "I'm sure you'd be the first to know. Sam, I hardly expected to call you so quickly after last night. In fact, my guess would have been a nice three-month cooling-off period before we met as disinterested friends. But I do need some help fast, and I certainly can't look to Luther Pelham for it. So I'm afraid you're elected."

"Not exactly the reason I'd choose to hear from you, but I'm glad to be of service."

Sam was different today. She could feel it. It was as though that vacillating aimlessness were missing. "Sam, there was something else about the break-in." As calmly as possible, she told him about the Raggedy Ann doll. "And now the doll is gone."

"Pat, are you telling me that someone has been back in your house without you knowing it?"

"Yes."

"Then you're not going to spend another minute there."

Restlessly she got up and walked over to the window.

"That isn't the answer. Sam, in a crazy way the fact that the doll is gone is almost reassuring. I don't think whoever has been threatening me really intends to hurt me. Otherwise he certainly would have done it. I think he's afraid of what the program might do to *him*. And I've got some ideas." Quickly she explained her analysis of the Eleanor Brown case. "If Eleanor Brown wasn't lying, Toby was. If Toby was lying, the Senator was covering up for him, and that seems incredible. But suppose another person was involved who could imitate Toby's voice, who knew about Eleanor's storeroom and planted just enough of the money to make her look guilty?"

"How do you explain the doll and the threats?"

"I think someone who knew me when I was little, and may have recognized me, is trying to scare me and stop this program. Sam, what do you make of this? *Toby* knew me when I was little. Toby has become truly hostile toward me. I thought at first it was because of the Senator and all the bad publicity, but the other day he kept eyeing the library as though he was casing it. And after he left, he let himself back in. He didn't realize I intended to follow him to slide the safety bolt. He tried to say he was just testing the lock and that anyone could get in and I should be careful. I fell for that—but Sam, I really am nervous about him. Could you have him checked out and see if he's ever been in trouble? I mean real trouble?"

"Yes, I can. I never liked that bird myself." He came up behind her, put his arms around her waist. In an instinctive reaction she leaned back against him. "I've missed you, Pat."

"Since last night?"

"No, since two years ago."

"You could have fooled me." For a moment she gave herself up to the sheer joy of being close to him; then she turned and faced him. "Sam, a little residual affection doesn't add up to what I want. So why don't you just . . ."

His arms were tight around her. His lips were no longer tentative. "I'm fresh out of residual affection."

For long moments they stood there, silhouetted against the window.

Finally Pat stepped back. Sam let her go. They looked at each other. "Pat," he said, "everything you said last night was true except one thing. There is absolutely nothing between Abigail and me. Can you give me a little time to find myself again? I didn't know until I saw you this week that I've been functioning like a zombie."

She tried to smile. "You seem to forget, I need some time too. Memory Lane isn't as simple as I expected it to be."

"Do you think you're getting honest impressions of that night?"

"Honest, perhaps, but not particularly desirable. I'm beginning to believe my mother may have been the one who went crazy that night, and somehow that's harder."

"Why do you think that?"

"It's not why I *think* it, but why she may have snapped that interests me now. Well, one more day and 'The Life and Times of Abigail Jennings' will be presented to the world. And at that point I start doing some real investigating. I just wish to God this whole thing wasn't so rushed. Sam, there's too much that doesn't hang together. And I don't care what Luther Pelham thinks. That segment about the plane crash is going to blow up in Abigail's face. Catherine Graney means business."

She declined his invitation to dinner. "This has been a grueling day. I was up at four o'clock to get ready for the Senator's office, and tomorrow we finish taping. I'm going to fix a sandwich and be in bed by nine o'clock."

At the door, he held her once more. "When I'm seventy, you'll be forty-nine."

"And when you're one hundred and three, I'll be eighty-two. You'll get a trace on Toby and you'll let me know when you hear anything about Eleanor Brown?"

"Of course."

When Pat left, Sam phoned Jack Carlson and quickly told him what Pat had confided.

Jack whistled. "You mean that guy's been back? Sam, you really have a loony. Sure we can check this Toby character, but do me a favor. Get me a sample of his handwriting, can you?"

35

Detective Barrott was kind. He believed she was telling the truth. But the older detective was hostile. Over and over Eleanor answered the same questions from him.

How could she tell them where she was keeping seventy thousand dollars that she'd never even seen?

Was she angry at Patricia Traymore for preparing the program that might force her out of hiding? No, of course not. At first she was afraid and then she knew she couldn't hide anymore, that she'd be glad if it were over.

Did she know where Patricia Traymore lived? Yes, Father had told her that Patricia Traymore lived in the Adams house in Georgetown. He'd shown her that house once. He'd been on the ambulance squad of Georgetown Hospital when that awful tragedy had happened. Break into that house? Of course not. How could she?

In the cell she sat on the edge of the bunk wondering how she could have thought she was strong enough to go back into this world. The steel bars and the insulting intimacy of the open toilet, the sense of entrapment, the haunting depression that like a black fog was beginning to envelop her.

She lay on the bunk and wondered where Father had gone. It was impossible that they seemed to be suggesting he would deliberately hurt anyone. He was the kindest man she had ever known. But he had been terribly nervous after Mrs. Gillespie died.

She hoped he wouldn't be angry that she had given herself up. They would have arrested her anyway. She was sure Detective Barrott was planning to investigate her.

Had Father gone away? Probably. With growing concern Eleanor thought of the many times he had changed jobs. Where was he now?

Arthur had an early dinner in a cafeteria on 14th Street. He chose beef stew, lemon meringue pie and coffee. He ate slowly and carefully. It was important that he eat well now. It might be days before he had a hot meal again.

His plans were made. After dark he would go back to Patricia Traymore's house. He'd slip in through the upstairs window. He'd settle himself in the closet in the guest room. He'd bring cans of soda; he still had one of the Danish pastries and two of the rolls from this morning in his pocket. He'd better pick up some cans of juice too. And maybe he should get some peanut butter and rye bread. That would be enough to hold him over until he saw the program the next night.

He had to spend ninety of his precious dollars on a miniature black-and-white TV with a headset. That way he could watch the program right in Patricia Traymore's house.

On the way to her house, he'd buy caffeine pills in the drugstore. He couldn't take the chance of crying out in his sleep. Oh, she'd probably never hear him from her room, but he couldn't risk it.

Forty minutes later he was in Georgetown, two streets from Patricia Traymore's home. The whole area was quiet, more quiet than he would have liked. Now that the Christmas shopping was over, a stranger was more likely to be noticed. The police might even be keeping a watch on Miss Traymore's house. But the fact that she had the corner property helped. The house behind hers was dark.

Arthur slipped into the yard of the unlighted house. The wooden fence that separated the backyards wasn't high. He dropped his shopping bag over the fence, making sure that it slid down onto a snowbank, and then easily climbed over.

He waited. There wasn't a sound. Miss Traymore's car wasn't in the driveway. Her house was totally dark.

It was awkward getting up the tree with the shopping bag. The trunk was icy and hard to grasp; he could feel its rough coldness through his gloves. Without the tiers of branches, he could not have made it. The window was stiff and hard to raise. When he stepped over the sill into the room, the floorboards creaked heavily.

For agonizing minutes he waited by the window, ready to bolt out again, to clamber down the tree and run across the yard. But there was only silence in the house. That and the occasional rumble of the furnace.

He began to organize his hiding place in the closet. To his satisfaction he realized that the shelves were not attached to the walls. If he spread them out just a little, they would look as though they were touching the walls and no one would realize how much space he had in the triangular area behind him.

Carefully he began to set up his secret place. He selected a thick quilt and laid it on the floor. It was large enough to use as a sleeping bag. He set up his supplies of food and his television set. There were four king-size pillows on the lowest shelf.

In a few minutes he was settled. Now he needed to explore.

Unfortunately, she hadn't left any lights on. It meant he could move around only by holding his flashlight very low to the floor so no gleam could show out the window. Several times he practiced going back and forth between the guest bedroom and the master suite. He tested the floorboards and found the one that creaked.

It took him twelve seconds to make his way down the hall from his closet to Pat's room. He crept into her room and over to the vanity table. He had never seen such pretty objects. Her comb and mirror and brushes were all decorated with ornate silver. He took the stopper from the perfume bottle and inhaled the subtle fragrance.

Then he went into the bathroom, noticed her negligee on the back of the door and tentatively touched it. Angrily he thought that this was the kind of clothing Glory would enjoy.

Had the police gone to Glory's office to question her? She should be home now. He wanted to talk to her.

He made his way over to the bed, found the phone on the night table and dialed. After the fourth ring he began to frown. She had talked about turning herself in to the police, but she would never do that after having promised she'd wait. No, she was probably lying in bed, trembling, waiting to see if her picture was shown on the program tomorrow night.

He replaced the phone on the night table but sat crouched by Pat's bed. Already he missed Glory. He was keenly aware of the solitary quiet of the house. But he knew that soon his voices would come to join him.

36

"That was fine, Senator," Luther said. "Sorry I had to ask you to change. But we did want the look of a single working day, so you had to be wearing the same outfit coming home as going out."

"It's all right. I should have realized that," Abigail said shortly.

They were in her living room. The camera crew were packing their equipment. Toby could see that Abigail had no intention of offering Pelham a drink. She just wanted to be rid of him.

Luther was obviously getting the message. "Hurry up," he snapped at the crew. Then he smiled ingratiatingly. "I know it's been a long day for you, Abigail. Just one more session in the studio tomorrow morning and we'll wrap it up."

"That will be the happiest moment in my life."

Toby wished Abigail could relax. They'd gone for a drive and passed the Vice President's mansion a couple of times. Abby had even joked about it: "Can you imagine what the columnists would say if they saw me casing the place?" But as soon as the camera crew arrived, she'd tensed up again.

Pelham was putting on his coat. "The President has called a news conference for nine P.M. in the East Room tomorrow night. Are you planning to be there, Abigail?"

"I believe I've been invited," she said.

"That makes our timing excellent. The program will run between six-thirty and seven, so there won't be a schedule conflict for the viewers."

"I'm sure all of Washington is fainting with anticipation," Abigail said. "Luther, I really am terribly tired."

"Of course. Forgive me. I'll see you in the morning. Nine o'clock, if that's all right."

"One minute more and I'd have gone mad," Abigail said when she and Toby were finally alone. "And when I think all this is absolutely unnecessary . . ."

"No, it's not unnecessary, Senator," Toby said soothingly. "You still have to be confirmed by Congress. Sure, you'll get a majority, but it would be nice if a lot of people sent telegrams cheering your nomination along. The program can do that for you."

"In that case it will be worth it."

"Abby, is there anything more you want me for tonight?"

"No, I'm going to bed early and read until I fall asleep. It's been a long day." She smiled, and he could see she was starting to unwind. "Which waitresses are you chasing now? Or is it a poker game?"

Pat got home at six-thirty. She switched on the foyer light, but the stairs past the turn remained in shadow.

Her father's angry words suddenly echoed in her ears: "You shouldn't have come."

That last night the bell had rung insistently; her father had opened the door; someone had brushed past him; that person had been looking up—that is why she was so scared; Daddy was angry and she was afraid she'd been seen.

Her hand shook as she placed it on the banister. There's no use getting upset, she thought. It's just that I'm overtired and it's been a rough day. I'll get comfortable and fix some dinner.

In her bedroom she undressed quickly and reached for the robe on the back of the door, then decided she would wear the brown velour caftan instead. It was warm and comfortable.

At her dressing table she tied back her hair and began to cream her face. Mechanically her fingertips moved over her skin, rotating in the pattern the beautician had taught her, pressing for an instant against her temples, touching the faint scar near her hairline.

The furniture behind her was reflected in the mirror; the posts of the bed seemed like tall sentinels. She looked intently into the mirror. She had heard that if you picture an imaginary dot on your forehead and stare into it you can hypnotize yourself and retreat back into the past. For a full minute she concentrated on the imaginary dot, and had the odd sensation of watching herself walking backward into a tunnel . . . and it seemed she was not alone. She had a sense of another presence.

Ridiculous. She was getting lightheaded and fanciful.

Going downstairs to the kitchen, she fixed an omelette, coffee and toast and forced herself to eat.

The kitchen had a cozy, calming warmth. She and her mother and father must sometimes have eaten together here. Did she have a vague recollection of sitting on her father's lap at this table? Veronica had shown her their last Christmas card. It was signed Dean, Renée and Kerry. She said the names aloud, "Dean, Renée and Kerry" and wondered why the cadence seemed wrong.

Rinsing the dishes and putting them in the dishwasher was a reason for delaying what she knew must be done. She had to study that newspaper article and see if it divulged any new facts about Dean and Renée Adams.

The paper was still on the library table. Opening it to the center spread, she forced herself to read every line of the text. Much of it she already knew but that did not help to deaden the pain . . . "The gun smeared with both their fingerprints . . . Dean Adams had died instantly from the bullet wound in his forehead . . . Renée Adams might have lived a short time. . . ."

One column emphasized the rumors her neighbors had gleefully picked up at the party: the marriage was clearly unhappy, Renée had urged her husband to leave Washington, she despised the constant round of receptions, she was jealous of the attention her husband attracted from other women. . . .

That quote from a neighbor: "She was clearly besotted with him—and *he* had a roving eye."

There were persistent rumors that Renée, not Dean, had fired the gun. At the inquest, Renée's mother had attempted to squelch that speculation. "It is not a mystery," she said, "it is a tragedy. Only a few days before she was murdered, my daughter told me she was coming home with Kerry and would file for divorce and custody. I believe that her decision triggered his violence."

She could have been right, Pat thought. I remember tripping over a body. Why am I sure it was Mother's, not his? *She wasn't sure.*

She studied the informal snapshots that covered most of the second page. Willard Jennings was so scholarly-looking. Catherine Graney had said that he wanted to give up Congress and accept a college presidency. And Abigail had been an absolutely beautiful young woman. There was one rather blurred snapshot sandwiched in among the others. Pat glanced at it several times, then moved the paper so that the light shone directly on it.

It was a candid shot that had been taken on the beach. Her father, her mother and Abigail were in a group with two other people. Her mother was absorbed in a book. The two strangers were lying on blankets, their eyes closed. The camera had caught her father and Abigail looking at each other. There was no mistaking the air of intimacy.

There was a magnifying glass in the desk. Pat found it and held it over the picture. Magnified, Abigail's expression became rapturous. Her father's eyes were tender as they looked down at her. Their hands were touching.

Pat folded the newspaper. What did the pictures mean? A

casual flirtation? Her father had been attractive to women, probably encouraged their attention. Abigail had been a beautiful young widow. Maybe that was all it amounted to.

As always when she was troubled, Pat turned to music. In the living room she plugged in the Christmas-tree lights and impulsively switched off the chandelier. At the piano she let her fingers rove over the keys until she found the soft notes of Beethoven's *Pathétique.*

Sam had been himself again today, the way she'd remembered him, strong and confident. He needed time. Of course he did. So did she. Two years ago they'd felt so torn and guilty about their relationship. Now it could be different.

Her father and Abigail Jennings. Had they been involved? Had she just been one in a string of casual affairs? Her father might have been a ladies' man. Why not? He was certainly attractive, and it was the style among rising young politicians then—look at the Kennedys. . . .

Eleanor Brown. Had the lawyer been able to arrange bail for her? Sam hadn't phoned. Eleanor is innocent, Pat told herself—I am sure of it.

Liszt's *Liebestraum.* That was what she was playing now. And the Beethoven. She had unconsciously chosen both those pieces the other night as well. Had her mother played them here? The mood of both of them was the same, plaintive and lonely.

"Renée, listen to me. Stop playing and listen to me." "I can't. Let me alone." The voices—his troubled and urgent, hers despairing.

They quarreled so much, Pat thought. After the quarrels she would play for hours. But sometimes, when she was happy, she'd put me on the bench next to her. "*No, Kerry, this way. Put your fingers here. . . . She can pick out the notes when I hum them. She's a natural.*"

Pat felt her hands beginning the opening notes of Mendelssohn's *Opus 30, Number 3,* another piece that suggested pain. She stood up. There were too many ghosts in this room.

Sam phoned just as she was starting up the stairs again. "They won't release Eleanor Brown. They're afraid she'll jump bail. It seems the man she's living with is a suspect in some nursing-home deaths."

"Sam, I can't stand thinking of that girl in a cell."

"Frank Crowley, the lawyer I sent, thinks she's telling the truth. He's getting a transcript of her trial in the morning. We'll do what we can for her, Pat. It may not be much, I'm afraid. . . . How are you?"

"Just about to turn it."

"The place locked up?"

"Bolted tight."

"Good. Pat, it may be all over but the shouting. Quite a few of us have been invited to the White House tomorrow night. The President's making an important announcement. Your name is on the media list. I checked."

"Sam, do you think . . . ?"

"I just don't know. The money's on Abigail, but the President is really playing it close. None of the possible appointees has been given Secret Service protection yet. That's always a tip-off. I guess the President wants to keep everyone guessing until the last minute. But no matter who gets it, you and I will go out and celebrate."

"Suppose you don't agree with his choice?"

"At this point I don't give a damn whom he chooses. I've got other things in mind. I want to celebrate just being with you. I want to catch up on the last two years. After we stopped seeing each other, the only way I could get over missing you was to tell myself why it wouldn't have worked even if I was free. After a while, I guess I started to believe my own lies."

Pat's laugh was shaky. She blinked back the sudden moisture in her eyes. "Apology accepted."

"Then I want to talk about not wasting any more of our lives."

"I thought you needed more time. . . ."

"Neither of us does." Even his voice was different—confident, strong, the way she had remembered it all those nights she had lain awake thinking about him. "Pat, I fell hopelessly in love with you that day on Cape Cod. Nothing will ever change that. I'm so damn grateful you waited for me."

"I had no choice. Oh, God, Sam, it's going to be marvelous. I love you so."

For minutes after they said goodbye, Pat stood with her hand resting on the telephone as though by touching it, she could hear again every single word Sam had uttered. Finally, still smiling softly, she started up the stairs. A sudden creaking sound overhead startled her. She knew what it was. That one board on the upstairs landing which always moved when she stepped on it.

Don't be ridiculous, she told herself.

The hallway was poorly lit by flame-shaped bulbs in wall sconces. She started to go into her bedroom, then impulsively turned and walked toward the back of the house. Deliberately she stepped on the loose board and listened as it responded with a distinct creaking. I'd swear that's the sound I heard. She went into her old bedroom. Her footsteps echoed on the uncarpeted floor. The room was stuffy and hot.

The door of the guest bedroom was not quite closed. It was much cooler in there. She felt a draft and walked over to the window. The window was open from the top. She tried to close it, then realized the sash cord was broken. That's what it is, she thought; there's probably enough draft to make the door sway. Even so, she opened the closet and glanced at the shelves of bedding and linen.

In her room she undressed quickly and got into bed. It was ridiculous to still feel so jittery. Think about Sam; think about the life that they would have together.

Her last impression before she began to doze was the strange feeling that she was not alone. It didn't make sense, but she was too tired to think about it.

* * *

With a sigh of relief, Catherine Graney reversed the sign on the shop door from "OPEN" to "CLOSED." For the day after Christmas, business had been unexpectedly brisk. A buyer from Texas had bought the pair of Rudolstadt figura candelabra, the marquetry game tables and the Stouk carpet. It had been a most impressive sale.

Catherine turned off the lights in her shop and went upstairs to her apartment, Sligo at her heels. She had laid a fire that morning. Now she touched a match to the paper under the kindling. Sligo settled in his favorite spot.

Going into the kitchen, she began to fix dinner. Next week when young George was here she'd enjoy cooking big meals. But a chop and a salad were all she wanted now.

George had called her the day before to wish her a merry Christmas and to tell her the news. He'd been promoted to major. "Twnety-seven years old and an oak leaf already!" she'd exclaimed. "By God, would your Dad be proud."

Catherine put her chop under the broiler. One more good reason not to let Abigail Jennings smear George senior's name any longer. She wondered what Abigail had thought of the letter. She had worked and reworked it before mailing it Christmas Eve.

> *I must insist you take the opportunity on the upcoming program to publicly acknowledge that there has never been a shred of proof to indicate that pilot error caused your husband's fatal accident. It is not enough to no longer smear George Graney's reputation: you must set the record straight. If you do not, I will sue you for libel and reveal your true relationship with Willard Jennings.*

At eleven o'clock she watched the news. At eleven-thirty Sligo nuzzled her hand. "I know," she groaned. "Okay, get your leash."

The evening was dark. Earlier there'd been some stars, but

now the sky was clouded over. The breeze was raw, and Catherine pulled up the collar of her coat. "This is going to be one quick walk," she told Sligo.

There was a path through the woods near her house. Usually she and Sligo cut through there and then walked back around the block. Now he strained at the leash, rushing her through the path to his favorite bushes and trees. Then he stopped abruptly and a low growl came from his throat.

"Come on," Catherine said impatiently. All that she'd need would be for him to go after a skunk.

Sligo leaped forward. Bewildered, Catherine watched as a hand shot out and grabbed the old animal in a lock around the neck. There was a sickening cracking sound, and Sligo's limp body dropped onto the hardened snow.

Catherine tried to scream, but no sound came. The hand that had snapped Sligo's neck was raised over her head, and in the instant before she died, Catherine Graney finally understood what had happened that long-ago day.

37

On the morning of December 27, Sam got up at seven, reread the transcript of the CAA investigation into the crash that had killed Congressman Willard Jennings, underlined a particular sentence and phoned Jack Carlson. "How are you coming with that report on Toby Gorgone?"

"I'll have it by eleven."

"Are you free for lunch? I have something to show you." It was the sentence from the transcript: "*Congressman Jennings' chauffeur, Toby Gorgone, placed his luggage on the plane.*" Sam wanted to read the report on Toby before discussing it.

They agreed to meet at the Gangplank Restaurant at noon.

Next Sam phoned Frank Crowley, the attorney he'd hired to represent Eleanor Brown, and invited him to the same lunch. "Can you have the transcript of Eleanor Brown's trial with you?"

"I'll make sure I have it, Sam."

The coffee was perking. Sam poured a cup and turned on the kitchen radio. Most of the nine-o'clock news was over. The weatherman was now promising a partly sunny day. The temperature would be in the low thirties. And then the headlines were recapped, including the fact that the body of a prominent antiques dealer, Mrs. Catherine Graney of Richmond, had been founded in a wooded area near her home. Her dog's neck had been broken. Police believed the animal had died trying to defend her.

Catherine Graney dead! Just as she'd been about to blow open a potential scandal involving Abigail. "I don't believe in coincidence," Sam said aloud. "I just don't believe in it."

For the rest of the morning he agonized over his suspicions. Several times he reached for the phone to call the White House. Each time he withdrew his hand.

He had absolutely no proof that Toby Gorgone was anything but what he appeared to be, a devoted bodyguard-chauffeur for Abigail. Even if Toby was guilty of the crime, he had absolutely no proof that Abigail was aware of his activities.

The President would announce the appointment of Abigail that night. Sam was sure of it. But the confirmation hearings were several weeks away. There would be time to launch a thorough investigation. And this time I'll make sure there's no whitewash, he thought grimly.

Somehow Sam was sure that Toby was responsible for the threats to Pat. If he had anything to hide, he wouldn't want her digging into the past.

If he turned out to be the one who had threatened her . . .

Sam clenched his hands into fists. He was no longer thinking of himself as a grandfather-to-be.

Abigail twisted her hands nervously. "We should have left earlier," she said, "we're in all the traffic. Step on it."

"Don't worry, Senator," Toby said soothingly. "They can't start taping without you. How did you sleep?"

"I kept waking up. All I could think of was 'I am going to be Vice President of the United States.' Turn on the radio. Let's see what they're saying about me. . . ."

The eight-thirty CBS news was just beginning. "Rumors persist that the reason the President has called a news conference for this evening is to announce his choice of either Senator Abigail Jennings or Senator Claire Lawrence as Vice President of the United States, the first woman to be so honored." And then: "In a tragic coincidence, it has been learned that Mrs. Catherine Graney, the Richmond antiques dealer found murdered while walking her dog, is the widow of the pilot who died twenty-seven years ago in a plane crash with Congressman Willard Jennings. Abigail Jennings began her political career when she was appointed to complete her husband's term. . . ."

"Toby!"

He glanced into the rearview mirror. Abigail looked shocked. "Toby, how awful."

"Yeah, it's lousy." He watched as Abigail's expression hardened.

"I'll never forget how Willard's mother went to that woman and sat with her when the plane was overdue. She never even called to see how *I* was."

"Well, they're together now, Abby. Look how fast the traffic is moving. We'll be at the studio right on time."

As they pulled into the private parking area, Abigail asked quietly, "What did you do last night, Toby—play poker or have a date?"

"I saw the little lady from Steakburger and spent the evening with her. Why? You checking on me? You want to talk to her, Senator?" Now his tone had an indignant edge.

"No, of course not. You're welcome to your cocktail waitresses, on your own time. I hope you enjoyed yourself."

"I did. I haven't been taking much personal time lately."

"I know. I've kept you awfully busy." Her voice was conciliatory. "It's just . . ."

"Just *what*, Senator?"

"Nothing . . . nothing at all."

At eight o'clock Eleanor was taken for a lie-detector test. She had slept surprisingly well. She remembered that first night in a cell eleven years ago when she had suddenly started to scream. "You expressed acute claustrophobia that night," a psychiatrist had told her after the breakdown. But now there was a curious peacefulness about not running anymore.

Could Father have hurt those old people? Eleanor racked her brain, trying to remember a single example of his being anything but kind and gentle. There was none.

"This door." The matron led her into a small room near the cellblock. Detective Barrott was reading the newspaper. She was glad he was there. He didn't treat her as though she were a liar. He looked up at her and smiled.

Even when another man came in and hooked her to the lie-detector machine, she didn't start to cry the way she had after her arrest for stealing from the Senator. Instead, she sat in the chair, held up her doll and a little embarrassed, asked if they'd mind if she kept it with her. They didn't act as though it were a crazy request. Frank Crowley, that nice fatherly-looking man who was her lawyer, came in. She had tried to explain to him yesterday that she couldn't pay him more than the nearly five hundred dollars she'd saved, but he told her not to worry about it.

"Eleanor, you can still refuse to take this test," he told her now, and she said that she understood.

At first the man who was giving her the test asked simple, even silly, questions about her age and education and her favorite food. Then he started asking the ones she'd been gearing herself to hear.

"Have you ever stolen anything?"

"No."

"Not even anything small, like a crayon or a piece of chalk when you were little?"

The last time she'd been asked that, she'd started sobbing, "I'm not a thief. I'm *not* a thief." But now it wasn't that hard. She pretended she was talking to Detective Barrott, not this brusque, impersonal stranger. "I've never, ever stolen anything in my life," she said earnestly. "Not even a crayon or a piece of chalk. I couldn't take anything that belonged to anyone else."

"What about the bottle of perfume when you were in high school?"

"*I did not steal it.* I swear to you. I forgot to give it to the clerk!"

"How often do you drink? Every day?"

"Oh, no. I just have wine sometimes, and not very much. It makes me sleepy." She noticed that Detective Barrott smiled.

"Did you take the seventy-five thousand dollars from Senator Jennings' campaign office?"

Last time during the test, she'd gotten hysterical at that question. Now she simply said, "No, I did not."

"But you put five thousand dollars of that money in your storage room, didn't you?"

"No, I did not."

"Then how do you think it got there?"

The questions went on and on. "Did you lie when you claimed Toby Gorgone phoned?"

"No, I did not."

"You're sure it was Toby Gorgone?"

"I thought it was. If it wasn't, it sounded just like him."

Then the incredible questions began: "Did you know Arthur Stevens was a suspect in the death of one of his patients, a Mrs. Anita Gillespie?"

She almost lost control. "No, I did not. I can't believe that." Then she remembered the way he'd yelled in his sleep: "*Close your eyes, Mrs. Gillespie. Close your eyes!*"

"You do believe it's possible. It shows up right in this test."

"No," she whispered. "Father could never have hurt anyone, only help them. He takes it so to heart when one of his patients is in pain."

"Do you think he might try to stop the pain?"

"I don't know what you mean."

"I think you do. Eleanor, Arthur Stevens tried to set fire to the nursing home on Christmas Day."

"That's impossible."

The shock of what she was hearing made Eleanor blanch. Horrified, she stared at the interrogator as he asked his last question: "Did you ever have any reason to suspect that Arthur Stevens was a homicidal maniac?"

During the night Arthur swallowed caffeine pills every two hours. He could not risk falling asleep and calling out. Instead he sat crouched in the closet, too tense to lie down, staring into the dark.

He'd been so careless. When Patricia Traymore came home, he'd listened at the door of the closet to the sounds of her moving around the house. He'd heard the roar of the pipes when she showered; she'd gone back downstairs and he'd smelled coffee perking. Then she had begun playing the piano. Knowing it was safe to go out, he'd sat on the landing listening to the music.

That was when the voices started talking to him again, telling him that when this was over he must find a new nursing home where he could continue his mission. He'd been so deep in meditation that he hadn't realized that the music had stopped, hadn't thought about where he was until he heard Patricia Traymore's footsteps on the stairs.

In his rush to get to his hiding place he'd stepped on the loose board, and she had known something was wrong. He hadn't dared to breathe when she opened the door of the closet. But of course it never occurred to her to look behind the shelves.

And so he had kept watch all night, straining for the sounds of her awakening, glad when she finally left the house, but afraid to leave the closet for more than a few minutes at a time. A housekeeper might come in and hear him.

The long hours passed. Then the voices directed him to take the brown robe from Patricia Traymore's closet and put it on.

If she had betrayed Glory, he would be suitably clothed to mete out her punishment.

38

Pat arrived at the network building at nine thirty-five and decided to have coffee and an English muffin in the drugstore. She wasn't ready for the charged atmosphere, underlying irritability and explosive nerves that she knew would be waiting on this final day of taping and editing. Her head was vaguely throbbing, her whole body sore. She knew that she had slept restlessly and that her dreams had been troubled. At one point she had cried out, but she couldn't remember what she had said.

In the car she had turned on the news and learned about Catherine Graney's death. She couldn't put the image of the woman out of her mind. The way her face had brightened when she talked about her son; the affectionate pat she had given her aging Irish setter. Catherine Graney would have followed through on her threat to sue Senator Jennings and the network after the program was aired. Her death had ended that threat.

Had she been the random victim of a mugger? The report had said she was walking her dog. What was his name? Sligo? It seemed unlikely that a criminal would choose to attack a woman with a large dog.

Pat pushed back the English muffin. She wasn't hungry. Only three days ago she had shared coffee with Catherine Graney. Now that attractive, vibrant woman was dead.

When she reached the studio, Luther was already on the set, his face mottled, his lips bloodless, his eyes constantly roving, hunting for flaws. "I said to get rid of those flowers!" he was shouting. "I don't give a damn whether they were just delivered or not. They look dead. Can't anybody do anything right around here? And that chair isn't high enough for the Senator. It looks like a goddamn milking stool." He spotted Pat. "I see you're finally here. You heard about that Graney woman? We'll have to redo the segment of Abigail talking about traffic safety. She comes across a little too heavy on the pilot. There's bound to be backlash when people find out his widow is a crime victim. We start taping in ten minutes."

Pat stared at Luther. Catherine Graney had been a good and decent person and all this man cared about was that her death had caused a setback in the taping. Wordlessly she turned and went into the dressing room.

Senator Jennings was seated in front of a mirror, a towel wrapped around her shoulders. The makeup artist was anxiously hovering over her, dabbing a touch of powder on her nose.

The Senator's fingers were tightly locked together. Her greeting was cordial enough. "This is it, Pat. Will you be as glad to be finished as I?"

"Yes, I think so, Senator."

The makeup girl picked up the can of hair spray and tested it.

"Don't use that stuff on me," the Senator snapped. "I don't want to look like a Barbie doll."

"I'm sorry." The girl's tone faltered. "Most people . . ." Her voice trailed off.

Aware that Abigail was watching her in the mirror, Pat deliberately avoided eye contact.

"There are a few points we should discuss." Now Abigail's tone was brisk and businesslike. "I'm just as glad we're redoing the air-safety segment, even though of course it's terrible about

Mrs. Graney. But I want to come off more emphatically on the necessity for better facilities at small airports. And I've decided we should talk more about my mother. There's no use not meeting that *Mirror* picture and that spread in yesterday's *Tribune* head on. And we should certainly emphasize my role in foreign affairs. I've prepared some questions for you to ask me."

Pat put down the brush she was holding and turned to face the Senator. "*Have* you?"

Four hours later, over sandwiches and coffee, a small group sat in the projection room viewing the completed tape. Abigail was in the first row, Luther and Philip on either side of her. Pat sat several rows behind them with the assistant director. In the last row, Toby kept his solitary vigil.

The program opened with Pat, Luther and the Senator sitting in a semicircle. "Hello, and welcome to the first program in our series *Women in Government*. . . ." Pat studied herself critically. Her voice was huskier than usual; there was something in the rigid way she was sitting that suggested tension. Luther was totally at ease, and on the whole, the opening sounded all right. She and Abigail complemented each other well. Abigail's blue silk dress had been a good choice; it expressed femininity without frills. Her smile was warm, her eyes crinkled. Her acknowledgment of the flattering introduction had no hint of coyness.

They discussed her position as senior Senator from Virginia. Abigail: "It's a tremendously demanding and satisfying job. . . ." The montage of shots of Apple Junction. The shot of Abigail with her mother. Pat watched the screen as Abigail's voice became tender. "My mother faced the same problem as so many working mothers today. She was widowed when I was six. She didn't want to leave me alone and so she took a job as a housekeeper. She sacrificed a hotel-management career so that she'd be there when I came home from school. We were very close.

She was always embarrassed about her weight. She had a glandular problem. I guess a lot of people can understand. When I tried to get her to live with Willard and me, she'd laugh and say, 'No way is the mountain coming to Washington.' She was a funny, dear lady." At that point Abigail's voice trembled. And then Abigail explained the beauty contest: "Talk about win it for the Gipper . . . I won that for Mommy. . . ."

Pat found herself caught in the spell of Abigail's warmth. Even the scene in Abigail's den when the Senator had called her mother a fat tyrant seemed unreal now. But it *was* real, she thought. Abigail Jennings is a consummate actress. The clips of the reception and the first campaign. Pat's questions to Abigail: "Senator, you were a young bride; you were completing your last year in college and you were helping your husband campaign for his first seat in Congress. Tell us how you felt about that." Abigail's answer: "It was wonderful. I was very much in love. I'd always pictured myself getting a job as an assistant to someone in public office. To be there right at the beginning was thrilling. You see, even though a Jennings had always held that seat, Willard's competition was stiff. The night we heard Willard had been elected—I can't describe it. Every election victory is exciting, but the first one is unforgettable."

The clip with the Kennedys at Willard Jennings' birthday party . . . Abigail said, "We were all so young. . . . There were three or four couples who used to get together regularly and we'd sit around for hours talking. We were all so sure we could help to change the world and make life better. Now those young statesmen are gone. I'm the only one left in government and I often think of the plans Willard and Jack and the others were making."

And my father was one of the "others," Pat reflected as she watched the screen.

There were several genuinely touching scenes. Maggie in the office with Abigail thanking her for finding her mother a place in the nursing home; a young mother tightly holding her three-year-old daughter and telling how her ex-husband had kidnapped the child. "No one would help me. No one. And then someone said, 'Call Senator Jennings. She gets things done.' "

Yes, she does, Pat agreed.

But then, with Luther interviewing her, Abigail discussed the embezzled campaign funds. "I'm so glad that Eleanor Brown has turned herself in to complete her debt to society. I only hope that she may also be honest enough to return whatever is left of that money, or tell who shared in spending it."

Something made Pat turn around. In the semi-darkness of the screening room, Toby's thick bulk loomed in his chair, his hands folded under his chin, the onyx ring gleaming on his finger. His head was nodding approval. Quickly she looked back at the screen, not wanting to meet his gaze.

Luther questioned Abigail about her commitment to airline safety. "Willard was constantly asked to speak at colleges and he accepted every possible date. He said that college was the time when young people were beginning to form mature judgments about the world, about government. We were living on a Congressman's salary and had to be very careful. I am a widow today because my husband chartered the cheapest plane he could find. . . . Do you know the statistics on how many army pilots bought a second-hand plane and tried to start a charter airline on a shoestring? Most of them went out of business. They hadn't the funds to keep the planes in proper condition. My husband died over twenty-five years ago and I've been fighting ever since to bar those small planes from busy fields. And I've always worked closely with the Airline Pilots Association to tighten and maintain rigid standards for pilots."

No mention of George Graney, but once again the implied reason for Willard Jennings' death. After all these years Abigail won't stop underscoring the blame for that accident, Pat thought. As she watched herself on the screen, she realized that the documentary had turned out exactly as she had planned it; it portrayed Abigail Jennings as a sympathetic human being and a dedicated public servant. The realization brought no satisfaction.

The program ended with Abigail walking into her home in the near-dark and Pat's commentary that like so many single adults, Abigail was going home alone, and she would spend the evening at her desk studying proposed legislation.

The screen went dark, and as the room brightened, they all stood up. Pat watched for Abigail's reaction. The Senator turned to Toby. He nodded approvingly, and with a relaxed smile Abigail pronounced the program a success.

She glanced at Pat. "In spite of all the problems, you've done a very good job. And you were right about using my early background. I'm sorry I gave you so much grief. Luther, what do you think?"

"I think you come across terrific. Pat, what's your feeling?"

Pat considered. They were all satisfied, and the ending was technically all right. Then what was it that was forcing her to press for an additional scene? The letter. She wanted to read the letter Abigail had written to Willard Jennings. "I have one problem," she said. "The personal aspects of this program are what make it special. I wish we hadn't ended on a business note."

Abigail raised her eyes impatiently. Toby frowned. The atmosphere in the room suddenly became strained. The projectionist's voice came over the loudspeaker. "Is that a wrap?"

"No. Run the last scene again," Luther snapped.

The room darkened and an instant later the closing two minutes of the program were replayed.

They all watched intently. Luther was the first to comment. "We can leave it, but I think Pat may be right."

"That's wonderful," Abigail said. "What are you going to do about it? I've got to be at the White House in a few hours and I don't intend to arrive there at the last second."

Can I get her to go along with me? Pat wondered. For some reason she desperately wanted to read the "Billy darling" letter and she wanted the Senator's spontaneous reaction to it. But Abigail had insisted on seeing every inch of the storyboard before they taped. Pat tried to sound casual. "Senator, you've been very generous in opening your personal files to us. In the last batch Toby brought over I found a letter that might just give the final personal touch we want. Of course you can read it before we tape, but I think it would have a more natural quality if you don't. In any case, if it doesn't work, we'll go with the present close."

Abigail's eyes narrowed. She looked at Luther. "Have you read this letter?"

"Yes, I have. I agree with Pat. But it's up to you."

She turned to Philip and Toby. "You two went over everything you released for possible use on the program?"

"Everything, Senator."

She shrugged. "In that case . . . Just make sure you don't read a letter from someone saying she was Miss Apple Junction the year after me."

They all laughed. There is something changed about her, Pat thought. She's surer of herself.

"We'll shoot in ten minutes," Luther said.

Pat hurried into the dressing room. She dabbed fresh powder on the beads of perspiration that had formed on her forehead. What is the matter with me? she asked herself fiercely.

The door opened and Abigail came in. She opened her purse and pulled out a compact. "Pat, that program is pretty good, isn't it?"

"Yes, it is."

"I was so against it. I had such a bad feeling about it. You've done a great job making me look like a pretty nice person." She smiled. "Seeing the tape, I liked myself better than I have in a long time."

"I'm glad." Here again was the woman she had admired so much.

A few minutes later they were back on the set. With her hand, Pat was covering the letter she was about to read. Luther began to speak. "Senator, we want to thank you for sharing your time with us in this very personal way. What you have accomplished is certainly an inspiration to everyone and surely an example of how good can come from tragedy. When we were planning this program, you gave us many of your private papers. Among them we found a letter you wrote to your husband, Congressman Willard Jennings. I think this letter sums up the young woman you were and the woman you became. May I allow Pat to read it to you now?"

Abigail tilted her head, her expression questioning.

Pat unfolded the letter. Her voice husky, she read it slowly. "Billy, darling." Her throat tightened. She had to force herself to go on. Again her mouth was hopelessly dry. She glanced up. Abigail was staring at her, the color draining from her face. "You were splendid in the hearings this afternoon. I am so proud of you. I love you so and look forward to a lifetime of being with you, of working with you. Oh, my dearest, we really are going to make a difference in this world."

Luther interjected, "That note was written on May thirteenth, and on May twentieth Congressman Willard Jennings died and you went on alone to make a difference in this world. Senator Abigail Jennings, thank you."

The Senator's eyes were shining. A tender half-smile played at the corners of her mouth. She nodded and her lips formed the words "Thank you."

"Cut," the director called.

Luther jumped up. "Senator, that was perfect. Everybody will . . ."

He stopped in mid-sentence as Abigail lunged forward and grabbed the letter from Pat's hand. "Where did you *get* that?" she shrieked. "What are you trying to *do* to me?"

"Senator, I told you, we don't have to use it," Luther protested.

Pat stared as Abigail's face twisted into a mask of anger and pain. Where had she seen that expression, on *that* face, once before?

A bulky figure rushed past her. Toby was shaking the Senator, almost shouting at her: "Abby, get hold of yourself. That was a great way to end the program. *Abby, it's okay to let people know about your last letter to your husband.*"

"My . . . last . . . letter?" Abigail raised one hand to cover her face as though she were trying to remold her expression. "Of course . . . I'm sorry . . . It's just that Willard and I used to write little notes to each other all the time. . . . I'm so glad you found—the last one. . . ."

Pat sat immobilized. "Billy darling, Billy darling . . ." The words had a drumroll cadence, hammering in her mind. Gripping the arms of the chair, she looked up and met Toby's savage stare. She shrank back in mindless terror.

He turned back to Abigail and, with Luther and Phil assisting, escorted her from the studio. One by one the floodlights were turned off. "Hey, Pat," the cameraman called. "That's a wrap, isn't it?"

At last she was able to get up. "It's a wrap," she agreed.

39

Whenever Sam was wrestling with a problem, a long walk had a way of clearing his head and helping him think. That was why he elected to walk the several miles from his apartment to the Southwest section of the District. The Gangplank Restaurant was on the Washington Channel, and as he neared it, he studied the restless pattern of the whitecaps.

Cape Cod. Nauset Beach. Pat walking beside him, her hair tossed by the wind, her arm tucked in his, the incredible sense of freedom, as though it were just the two of them and sky and beach and ocean. Next summer we'll go back, he promised himself.

The restaurant resembled a ship moored to the dock. He hurried up the gangplank, enjoying the faint undulating feeling.

Jack Carlson was already seated at a window table. Several crushed cigarettes were in the ashtray in front of him, and he was sipping a Perrier. Sam apologized for being late.

"I'm early," Jack said simply. He was a trim, gray-haired man with bright, inquisitive eyes. He and Sam had been friends for more than twenty years.

Sam ordered a gin martini. "Maybe that will quiet me down or pick me up," he explained with an attempt at a smile. He felt Jack's eyes studying him.

"I've seen you looking more cheerful," Jack commented.

"Sam, what made you ask us to check on Toby Gorgone?"

"Only a hunch." Sam felt himself tense. "Did you come up with anything interesting?"

"I'd say so."

"Hello, Sam." Frank Crowley, his normally pale face ruddy from the cold, his heavy white hair somewhat disheveled, joined them. He introduced himself to Jack, adjusted his silver-rimmed glasses, opened his briefcase and pulled out a bulky envelope. "I'm lucky to be here," he announced. "I started going through the trial transcript and almost forgot the time." The waiter was at his elbow. "Vodka martini, very dry," he ordered. "Sam, you seem to be the only one I know who can still drink gin martinis."

Without waiting for a reply, he continued. "*United States* versus *Eleanor Brown.* Makes interesting reading and boils down to one simple issue: which member of Senator Jennings' official family was lying, Eleanor or Toby? Eleanor took the stand in her own defense. A big mistake. She started talking about the shoplifting connection and the prosecutor blew it up until you'd think she'd robbed Fort Knox. The Senator's testimony didn't help any. She talked too damn much about giving Eleanor a second chance. I've marked the most relevant pages." He handed Carlson the transcript.

Jack took an envelope from his pocket. "Here's the fact sheet you wanted on Gorgone, Sam."

Sam skimmed it, raised his eyebrows and reread it carefully.

> Apple Junction: Suspect in car theft. Police chase resulted in death of three. No indictment.
> Apple Junction: Suspect in bookmaking operation. No indictment.
> New York City: Suspect in firebombing of car resulting in death of loan shark. No indictment. Thought to be on fringe of Mafia.
> May have settled gambling debts by performing services for mob.
> Other relevant fact: Exceptional mechanical aptitude.

"A perfectly clean record," he said sarcastically.

Over sliced-steak sandwiches they discussed, compared and evaluated the fact sheet on Toby Gorgone, Eleanor Brown's trial transcript, the CAA findings on the plane crash and the news of Catherine Graney's murder. By the time coffee was served, they had separately and jointly arrived at disturbing possibilities: Toby was a mechanical whiz who had left a suitcase on the Jennings plane minutes before takeoff and the plane had crashed under mysterious circumstances. Toby was a gambler who might have been in debt to bookies at the time the campaign funds disappeared.

"It seems to me that Senator Jennings and this character Toby take turns exchanging favors," Crowley commented. "She alibis for him and he pulls her chestnuts out of the fire."

"I can't believe Abigail Jennings would deliberately send a young girl to prison," Sam said flatly. "And I certainly don't believe she'd be party to the murder of her husband." He realized they were all whispering now. They were talking about a woman who in a few hours might become Vice President–designate of the United States.

The restaurant was starting to empty. The diners, most of them government people, were hurrying back to their jobs. Probably at one point during lunch every one of them had speculated about the President's conference tonight.

"Sam, I've seen dozens of characters like this Toby," Jack said. "Most of them in the mob. They're devoted to the head guy. They smooth his path—and take care of themselves at the same time. Perhaps Senator Jennings wasn't involved in Toby's activities. But look at it this way: Let's say Toby knew Willard Jennings wanted to give up his seat in Congress and get a divorce from Abigail. Jennings wasn't worth fifty thousand bucks in his own right. Mama held the purse strings. So Abigail would have been out of the political scene, dropped by Willard Jennings' circle of friends and back to being an ex–beauty queen from a hick town. And Toby decided not to let that happen."

"Are you suggesting she returned the favor by lying for him about the campaign money?" Sam asked.

"Not necessarily," Frank said. "Here—read the Senator's testimony on the stand. She admitted that they stopped at a gas station around the time Eleanor received the call. The engine had developed a knock and Toby wanted to check it. She swears he was never out of her sight. But she *was* on her way to deliver a speech and probably studying her notes. One minute she probably saw Toby in front of the car tinkering at the engine; the next maybe he was behind it getting a tool out of the trunk. How long does it take to scoot around to the public phone, dial a number and leave a two-second message? I'd have torn that testimony apart. But even assuming we're right, I can't understand why Toby picked Eleanor."

"That's easy," Jack said. "He knew about her record. He knew how sensitive she was. Without that open-and-shut case, there'd have been a full-blown investigation into the missing funds. He'd have been a suspect and his background investigated. He's smart enough to have gotten away with another 'no indictment' on his fact sheet, but the Senator would have been pressured by the party to get rid of him."

"If what we believe about Toby Gorgone checks out," Sam concluded, "Catherine Graney's death becomes too timely, too convenient to be a case of random murder."

"If Abigail Jennings gets the nod from the President tonight," Jack said, "and it comes out that her chauffeur murdered the Graney woman, those confirmation hearings will be a worldwide scandal."

The three men sat at the table, each somberly reflecting on the possible embarrassment to the President. Sam finally broke the silence.

"One bright note is if we can prove Toby wrote those threatening notes and arrest him, I can stop worrying about Pat."

Frank Crowley nodded at Jack. "And if your people get enough on him, Toby might be persuaded to tell the truth about the campaign funds. I tell you, to see that poor girl Eleanor Brown taking that lie-detector test this morning and swearing she'd never even stolen a piece of chalk would break your heart. She doesn't look eighteen, never mind thirty-four. That prison experience almost killed her. After her breakdown a shrink had her paint a doll's face to show how she felt. She still carries that doll around with her. The damn thing would give you the creeps. It looks like a battered child."

"A doll!" Sam exclaimed. "She has a *doll*. By any chance, is it a Raggedy Ann doll?"

At Frank's astonished nod, he signaled for more coffee. "I'm afraid we're barking up the wrong tree," he said wearily. "Let's start all over again."

40

Toby poured a Manhattan into the chilled cocktail glass and set it down in front of Abigail. "Drink this, Senator. You need it."

"*Toby where did she get that letter? Where did she get it?*"

"I don't know, Senator."

"It couldn't have been in anything you gave her. I never saw it again after I wrote it. *How much does she know?* Toby, if she could prove I was there that night . . ."

"She can't, Senator. No one can. And no matter what she may have dug up, she hasn't any proof. Come on, she did you a favor. That letter will clinch sympathy for you. Wait and see."

He finally appeased her the only way that worked. "*Trust* me! Don't worry about it. Have I ever let you down?" He calmed her a little, but even so, she was still a bundle of nerves. And in a few hours she was due at the White House.

"Listen, Abby," he said. "While I fix you something to eat, I want you to belt two Manhattans. After that have a hot bath and sleep for an hour. Then get yourself in your best-looking outfit. This is the biggest night of your life."

He meant it. She had reason to be upset—plenty of reason. The minute he heard the letter being read, he'd been on his feet. But as soon as Pelham said, "Your husband was lost a week later," he'd known it would be all right.

Abby almost blew it. Once again he'd been there to stop her from making a terrible mistake.

Abby reached for her glass. "Bottoms up," she said, and a touch of a smile lingered around her lips. "Toby, in a little while we'll have it."

The Vice Presidency. "That's right, Senator." He was sitting on a hassock across from the couch.

"Ah, Toby," she said. "What would I have become without you?"

"State assemblywoman from Apple Junction."

"Oh, sure." She tried to smile.

Her hair was loose around her face and she didn't look more than thirty years old. She was so slim. Slim the way a woman should be. Not a bag of bones, but firm and sleek.

"Toby, you look as though you're thinking. That would be a first."

He grinned at her, glad she was starting to loosen up. "You're the smart one. I leave the thinking to you."

She sipped the drink quickly. "The program turned out all right?"

"I keep telling you . . . it wouldn't have made sense for you to carry on about the letter. She did you a favor."

"I know. . . . It's just . . ."

The Manhattan was hitting her. He had to get some food into her. "Senator, you relax. I'll fix a tray for you."

"Yes . . . that would be a good idea. Toby, do you realize that a few hours from now I'm going to be Vice President–designate of the United States?"

"I sure do, Abby."

"We all know how ceremonial the office is. But Toby, if I do a good job, they may not be able to deny me the top spot next year. That's what I intend to have happen."

"I know that, Senator." Toby refilled her glass. "I'm going to fix you an omelette. Then you're going to take a nap. This is your night."

Toby got up. He couldn't look anymore at the naked yearning on her face. He'd seen it the day she got the news that she wouldn't be eligible for a scholarship to Radcliffe. She'd come over to where he was mowing the lawn and shown him the letter, then sat on the porch steps, hugged her legs and dropped her head in her lap. She'd been eighteen years old. "Toby, I want to go there so bad. I can't rot in this stinking town. I can't. . . ."

And then he'd suggested she romance that jerk Jeremy Saunders. . . .

He'd helped her other times, helped her to find her destiny.

And now, once again, somebody was trying to ruin everything for her.

Toby went into the kitchen. As he prepared the dinner he tried to envision how interesting it would be when Abby was one heartbeat away from the Presidency.

The phone rang. It was Phil. "The Senator okay?"

"She's fine. Look, I'm getting her dinner."

"I have a piece of information you wanted. Guess who owns Pat Traymore's house."

Toby waited.

"Pat Traymore, that's who. It's been in trust for her since she was four years old."

Toby whistled soundlessly. Those eyes, that hair, a certain look about her . . . Why hadn't he figured it out before this? He could have blown everything by being so dumb.

Phil's voice was querulous. "Did you hear me? I said . . ."

"I heard you. Just keep it under your hat. What the Senator don't know won't hurt her."

A short time later he went back to his apartment above the garage. Under his urging, Abigail decided to watch the program while resting in her room. At eight o'clock he would bring the car around and they'd leave for the White House.

He waited until the program had been on a few minutes, then quietly left his apartment. His car, a black Toyota, was in the driveway. He pushed it until he could roll it down to the street. He didn't want Abby to know he was going out. He had a little less than an hour and a half for the round trip to Pat Traymore's house.

It was enough to do what was needed.

41

Pat drove across Massachusetts Avenue, up Q Street, over the Buffalo Bridge and into Georgetown. Her head was aching now—a steady throbbing. She drove by rote, observing traffic lights subconsciously.

Presently she was on 31st Street, turning the corner, pulling into her driveway. She was on the steps, the slap of the wind on her face. Her fingers were fumbling in her purse for her key. The lock was clicking; she was pushing the door open, going into the shadowy quiet of the foyer.

In a reflex action, she closed the door and leaned against it. The coat was heavy on her shoulders. She shrugged it off, tossed it aside. She raised her head; her eyes became riveted on the step at the bend of the staircase. *There was a child sitting there. A child with long reddish-brown hair, her chin leaning on the palms of her hands; her expression curious.*

I wasn't asleep, she thought. I heard the doorbell ring and I wanted to see who was coming. *Daddy opened the door and someone pushed past him. He was angry. I ran back to bed.* When I heard the first shot, I didn't come right down. I stayed in bed and screamed for Daddy.

But he didn't come. And I heard another loud bang and ran down the stairs to the living room. . . .

And then . . .

She realized she was trembling and light-headed. Going into the library, she poured brandy into a tumbler and sipped it quickly. Why had Senator Jennings been so devastated by that letter? She'd been panicky, furious, frightened.

Why?

It didn't make sense.

And why did I get so upset reading it? Why has it upset me every time I've read it?

The way Toby looked at me as though he hated me. The way he shouted at the Senator. He wasn't trying to calm her down. He was trying to warn her about something. But what?

She sat huddled in the corner of the sofa, her arms clasped around her knees. I used to sit in here like this when Daddy was working at his desk. "You can stay, Kerry, as long as you promise to be quiet." Why was her memory of him so vivid now? She could see him, not as he'd looked in the film clips but as he'd been here in this room, leaning back in the chair, tapping his fingers on the desk when he was concentrating.

The newspaper article was still open on the desk. On a sudden impulse she went over to it, reread it carefully. Her eyes kept coming back to the picture of her father and Abigail Jennings on the beach. There was an undeniably intimate quality there. A summer-afternoon flirtation or more? Suppose her mother had looked up and caught that glance between them?

Why was she so afraid? She'd slept so badly last night. A hot bath and a brief rest would help calm her down. Slowly she went upstairs to her room. Again she had the eerie feeling she was being watched. She had had the same sensation the night before, before she fell asleep, but again she brushed it from her mind.

The phone rang just as she reached her room. It was Lila.

"Pat, are you all right? I'm worried about you. I don't want to alarm you, but I must. I sense danger around you. Won't you please come over here now and stay with me?"

"Lila, I think the impression you're getting is that I'm really quite close to a breakthrough in remembering that night. Something happened today, during the final taping, that seems to be triggering it. But don't worry—no matter what it is, I can handle it."

"Pat, *listen* to me. You shouldn't be in that house now!"

"It's the only way I'll be able to piece it together."

She's nervous because of the break-ins, Pat told herself as she lay in the tub. She's afraid I can't face the truth. She slipped on her terry-cloth robe. Sitting at the dressing table, she unpinned her hair and began to brush it. She'd been wearing it in a chignon most of the week. She knew Sam liked it best when it was loose. Tonight she'd wear it that way.

She got into bed and turned the radio on low. She hadn't expected to doze, but she soon drifted off. The sound of Eleanor's name startled her into consciousness.

The bedside clock read six-fifteen. The program would be on in fifteen minutes.

"Giving as her motive that she could no longer endure the fear of being recognized, Miss Brown has surrendered and was taken into custody. She still steadfastly maintains her innocence of the theft for which she was convicted. A police spokesman said that in the nine years since she violated parole, Miss Brown had been living with a paramedic Arthur Stevens. Stevens is a suspect in a series of nursing-home deaths and a warrant has been issued for his arrest. A religious fanatic, he has been dubbed the 'nursing home angel.' "

"The Nursing Home Angel!" The first time he phoned, the caller had referred to himself as an angel of mercy, of deliverance, of vengeance. Pat bolted up and grabbed the phone. Frantically she dialed Sam's number, let the phone ring ten, twelve, fourteen times before she finally replaced it. If only she had realized what Eleanor was saying when she talked about Arthur Stevens! *He had begged Eleanor not to give herself up. To save Eleanor he might have tried to stop the program.*

Could Eleanor have been aware of those threats? No, I'm

sure she wasn't, Pat decided. Her lawyer should know about this before we tell the police.

It was twenty-five past six. She got out of bed, tightened the belt of her robe and put on her slippers. As she hurried down the stairs, she wondered where Arthur Stevens was now. Was he aware that Eleanor was under arrest? Would he see the program and blame her when Eleanor's picture was shown? Blame her because Eleanor had not kept her promise to wait before going to the police?

In the living room she turned the chandelier to the brightest setting and took a moment to light the Christmas tree before switching on the set. Even so, the room had an oddly cheerless quality. Settling herself on the couch, she watched intently as the credits rolled after the six-o'clock news.

She had wanted the chance to watch the program alone. In the studio she'd been conscious of tuning into everyone else's reactions to it. Even so, she realized she was dreading seeing it again. It was much more than the usual apprehension of launching a new series.

The furnace rumbled and a hissing of air came from the heat risers. The sound made her jump. It's crazy what this place is doing to me, she thought.

The program was beginning. Critically Pat studied the three of them—the Senator, Luther and herself, sitting in the semicircle. The background was good. Luther had been right about changing the flowers. Abigail showed none of the tension she'd exhibited off-camera. The footage on Apple Junction was well chosen. Abigail's reminiscences about her early life had just the right touch of human interest. And it's all such a lie, Pat thought.

The films of Abigail and Willard Jennings at their wedding reception, at parties on the estate, during his campaigns. Abigail's tender memories of her husband as the clips were shown. "Willard and I . . . ," "My husband and I . . ." Funny she never once referred to him as Billy.

With growing awareness, Pat realized that the films of Abigail as a young woman had an oddly familiar quality. They were evoking memories that had nothing to do with her having viewed them so many times. Why was that happening now?

There was a commercial break.

The segment about Eleanor Brown and the embezzled funds would come next.

Arthur heard Patricia Traymore go down the stairs. Cautiously he tiptoed until he was sure he was listening to the faint sounds of the television broadcast coming from downstairs. He had been afraid that friends might join her to view the program. But she was alone.

For the first time in all these years he felt as though he were dressed in the garb God intended him to wear. With moist, open palms, he smoothed the fine wool against his body. This woman even defiled sacred garments. What right had she to wear the raiment of the chosen?

Returning to his secret place, he put on the earphones, turned on the set and adjusted the picture. He had tapped into the cable antenna, and the screen was remarkably clear. Kneeling as before an altar, his hands locked in the posture of prayer, Arthur began to watch the program.

Lila sat watching the documentary, her dinner on a tray before her. It was hard to make even a pretense of eating. Her absolute certainty that Pat was in serious danger only heightened as she saw Pat's image on the screen.

Cassandra's warnings, she thought bitterly. Pat won't listen to me. She simply has to get out of that house *or she will suffer a death more violent than her parents endured. She is running out of time.*

Lila had met Sam Kingsley just once and liked him very much. She sensed that he was important to Pat. Would it be of any use to try to talk to Congressman Kingsley, share her apprehension with him? Could she possibly persuade him to insist that Pat leave her home until this dark aura around it dissolved?

She pushed the tray aside, got up and reached for the Green book. She would call him immediately.

Sam went directly to his office from the restaurant. He had several meetings scheduled, but found it impossible to concentrate on any of them. His mind kept returning to the luncheon discussions.

They had built a strong circumstantial case against Toby Gorgone, but Sam had been a prosecutor long enough to know that strong circumstantial evidence can be upset like a house of cards. And the Raggedy Ann doll was upsetting the case against Toby. If Toby was innocent of involvement in the plane crash and the embezzled funds, if Catherine Graney had been the victim of a random mugging, then Abigail Jennings was what she seemed to be—above reproach and a worthy candidate for the job most people expected her to get. But the more Sam thought about Toby, the more uneasy he got.

At twenty after six he was finally free and immediately dialed Pat. Her phone was busy. Quickly he locked his desk. He wanted to get home in time to watch the documentary.

The sound of the telephone stopped him as he was rushing out of the office. Some instinct warned him not to ignore it.

It was Jack Carlson. "Sam, are you alone?"

"Yes."

"We have some new developments in the Catherine Graney case. Her son found a draft of a letter she wrote to Senator Jennings. A letter that probably arrived at the Senator's house yesterday. It's pretty strong stuff. Mrs. Graney intended to attack Senator Jennings' version of her relationship with her husband, and she was going to sue her for libel if she didn't retract her statements about pilot error on the program."

Sam whistled. "Are you saying that Abigail may have received that letter yesterday?"

"Exactly. But that isn't the half of it. Mrs. Graney's neighbors had a party last night. We got a list of the guests and checked them all out. One young couple who came late, about eleven-fifteen or so, had trouble locating the exact street. They'd asked directions from a guy who was getting in his car two blocks away. He brushed them off fast. The car was a black Toyota, with Virginia plates. They described someone who sounds like Gorgone. The girl even remembers he was wearing a heavy, dark ring. We're picking Toby up for questioning. Do you think you ought to phone the White House?"

Toby might have been seen near the site of Catherine Graney's murder. If he had killed Catherine Graney, everything else they suspected of him was possible, even logical.
"Abigail has to know about this immediately," Sam said. "I'll go to her now. She should have the chance to withdraw her name from consideration. If she refuses, I'll call the President myself. Even if she had no idea of what Toby was up to, she's got to accept the moral responsibility."

"I don't think that lady has ever worried about moral responsibility. If J. Edgar were alive, she wouldn't have gotten this far toward the Vice Presidency. You saw that article in the *Trib* the other day about what great pals she was with Congressman Adams and his wife."

"I saw it."

"Like the paper said, there was always a rumor that another woman was the direct cause of the fatal quarrel. I was new in the Bureau when that case broke, but when I read that article, something started bugging me. On a hunch I pulled the Adams file. We have a memo in it about a freshman Congresswoman named Abigail Jennings. All the indications were that *she* was that other woman."

* * *

Try as she would, Abigail couldn't rest. The knowledge that in a few hours she would be nominated to be Vice President of the United States was too exhilarating to bear.

Madam Vice President. *Air Force Two* and the mansion on the grounds of the old Naval Observatory. Presiding over the Senate and representing the President all over the world.

In two years the Presidential nomination. I'll win, she promised herself. Golda Meir. Indira Gandhi. Margaret Thatcher. Abigail Jennings.

The Senate had been a mighty step up. The night she was elected Luther had said, "Well, Abigail, you're a member of the world's most exclusive club."

Now another vast step was impending. No longer one of one hundred Senators, but the second-highest official in the land.

She had decided to wear a three-piece outfit, a silk blouse and skirt with a knitted jacket, in tones of pink and gray. It would show up well on the television sets.

Vice President Abigail Jennings . . .

It was six-fifteen. She got up from the chaise, went over to her dressing table and brushed her hair. With deft strokes she applied a touch of eye shadow and mascara. Excitement had flushed her cheeks; she didn't need blush. She might as well get dressed now, watch the program and practice her acceptance speech until it was time to leave for the White House.

She slipped into the suit and fastened a gold-and-diamond sunburst pin to her jacket. The library television set had the biggest screen. She'd watch her program in there.

"Stay tuned for *Women in Government.*"

She had already seen everything but the last few minutes of the program. Even so, it was reassuring to watch it again. Apple Junction under a fresh coating of snow had a down-home country look that concealed its shabby dreariness. Thoughtfully she studied the Saunders home. She remembered when Mrs. Saunders had ordered her to retrace her steps and take the path to the service entrance. She'd made that miserable witch pay for that mistake.

If it weren't for Toby's figuring out how to get the money for Radcliffe, where would she be now?

The Saunderses *owed* me that money, she told herself. Twelve years of humiliations in that house!

She watched the clips of the wedding reception, the early campaigns, Willard's funeral. She remembered the exultation she had felt when in the funeral car Jack Kennedy had agreed to urge the Governor to appoint her to complete Willard's term.

The insistent ring of the doorbell startled her. No one ever dropped in. Could someone from the press be brazen enough to ring like that? She tried to ignore it. But the peal became a steady, unbroken intrusion. She hurried to the door. "Who is it?"

"Sam."

She pulled open the door. He stepped in, his face grim, but she barely glanced at him. "Sam, why aren't you watching *This Is Your Life?* Come on." Grabbing his hand, she ran ahead into the library. On the program, Luther was asking her about her commitment to airline safety.

"Abigail, I have to talk to you."

"Sam, for heaven's sake. Don't you want me to see my own program?"

"This won't wait." Against the background of the documentary, he told her why he had come. He watched the disbelief grow in her eyes.

"You're trying to say Toby may have killed the Graney woman? You're crazy."

"Am I?"

"He was out on a date. That waitress will vouch for him."

"Two people described him accurately. The letter Catherine Graney wrote you was the motive."

"What letter?"

They stared at each other, and her face paled.

"He picks up your mail, doesn't he, Abigail?"

"Yes."

"Did he get it yesterday?"

"Yes."

"And what did he bring in?"

"The usual junk. Wait a minute. You can't make these accusations about him. You make them *to* him."

"Then call him in here now. He's going to be picked up for questioning anyway."

Sam watched as Abigail dialed the phone. Dispassionately he observed the beautiful outfit she was wearing. She was dressed up to become Vice President, he thought.

Abigail held the receiver to her ear, listening to the bell ring. "He's probably just not answering. He certainly wouldn't expect me to be calling." Her voice trailed off, then became resolutely brisk. "Sam, you can't believe what you're saying. Pat Traymore put you up to this. She's been out to sabotage me from the beginning."

"Pat has nothing to do with the fact that Toby Gorgone was seen near Catherine Graney's home."

On the television screen Abigail was discussing her leadership in airline safety regulations. "I am a widow today because my husband chartered the cheapest plane he could find."

Sam pointed to the set. "That statement would have been enough to send Catherine Graney to the newspapers tomorrow morning, and Toby knew it. Abigail, if the President has called this news conference tonight to introduce you as Vice President–designate, you've got to ask him to postpone the announcement until this is cleared up."

"Have you taken leave of your senses? I don't care if Toby was two blocks from where that woman was killed. What does it prove? Maybe he has a girlfriend or a floating card game in Richmond. He's probably just not answering the phone. I wish to God I hadn't bothered to answer the door."

A sense of urgency overwhelmed Sam. Yesterday Pat had told him that she felt Toby had become hostile to her; that she was becoming nervous when he was around. Only a few minutes ago Abigail had said that Pat was trying to sabotage her. Did Toby believe that? Sam grasped Abigail's shoulders. "Is there any reason that Toby might consider Pat a threat to you?"

"Sam, stop it! Let go of me! He was just as upset as I about the publicity she's caused, but even that turned out all right. In fact, he thinks that in the long run she did me a favor."

"Are you *sure?*"

"Sam, Toby never laid eyes on Pat Traymore before last week. You're not being rational."

He never laid eyes on her before last week? That wasn't true. Toby had known Pat well as a child. Could he have recognized her? Abigail had been involved with Pat's father. Was Pat becoming aware of that? Forgive me, Pat, he thought. I have to tell her. "Abigail, Pat Traymore is Dean Adams' daughter, Kerry."

"Pat Traymore is—Kerry?" Abigail's eyes widened with shock. Then she shook herself free. "You don't know what you're talking about. Kerry Adams is dead."

"I'm telling you Pat Traymore is Kerry Adams. I've been told that you were involved with her father, that you may have triggered that last quarrel. Pat is starting to remember bits and pieces of that night. Would Toby try to protect you or himself from anything she might find out?"

"No," Abigail said flatly. "I don't care if she remembers seeing me. Nothing that happened was my fault."

"*Toby*—what about *Toby*? Was he there?"

"She never saw him. When he went back for my purse he told me she was already unconscious."

The implications of what she had said burst upon both of them. Sam ran for the door, Abigail stumbling behind him.

* * *

Arthur watched the film clips of Glory in handcuffs being led from the courtroom after the Guilty verdict. There was one close-up of her. Her face was dazed and expressionless, but her pupils were enormous. The uncomprehending pain in her eyes brought tears to his own. He buried his face in his hands as Luther Pelham talked about Glory's nervous breakdown, her parole as a psychiatric outpatient, her disappearance nine years ago. And then, not wanting to believe what he was hearing, he listened as Pelham said, "Yesterday, citing her overwhelming fear of being recognized, Eleanor Brown surrendered to the police. She is now in custody and will be returned to federal prison to complete her sentence."

Glory had surrendered to the police. She had broken her promise to him.

No. She had been *driven* to break her promise—driven by the certainty that this program would expose her. He knew he would never see her again.

His voices, angry and vengeful, began speaking to him. Clenching his fists, he listened intently. When they were silent, he tore off the headset. Without bothering to push the shelves together to conceal his hiding place, he hurried out to the landing and descended the stairs.

Pat sat motionless, studying the program. She watched herself begin to read the letter. "Billy, darling."

"Billy," she whispered. "Billy."

Raptly she studied Abigail Jennings' shocked expression, the involuntary clenching of her hands before she managed with iron control to assume a pleasant misty-eyed demeanor as the letter was read to her.

She had seen that anguished expression on Abigail's face before.

"Billy, darling. Billy, darling."

"You must not call Mommy 'Renée.' "

"But Daddy calls you 'Renée' . . ."

The way Abigail had lunged at her when the cameras stopped rolling. "*Where did you get that letter? What are you trying to do to me?*"

Toby's shout: "It's all right, Abby. It's all right to let people hear the last letter you wrote your husband." "*Your husband.*" That's what he'd been trying to tell her.

The picture of Abigail and her father on the beach, their hands touching.

Abigail was the one who had rung the bell that night, who had pushed past her father, her face ravaged with grief and anger.

"*You must not call me 'Renée,' and you must not call Daddy 'Billy.'* "

Dean *Wilson* Adams. Her *father*—not Willard Jennings—was Billy!

The letter! She had found it on the floor in the library the day she had tried to hide her father's personal papers from Toby. That letter must have fallen from *his* files, not Abigail's.

Abigail had been here that night. She and Dean Adams—*Billy* Adams—had been lovers. Had she precipitated that final quarrel?

A little girl was crouched in bed, her hands over her ears to drown out the angry voices.

The shot.

"*Daddy! Daddy!*"

Another loud bang.

And then I ran downstairs. I tripped over Mother's body. Someone else was there. Abigail? Oh, God, could Abigail Jennings have been there when I ran into the room?

The patio door had opened.

The phone began to ring, and in the same instant, the chandeliers went off. Pat jumped up and spun around. Illuminated by the twinkling lights of the Christmas tree an apparition was rushing toward her, the tall, gaunt figure of a monk with a vacant unlined face and silvery hair that fell forward over glittering china blue eyes.

Toby drove toward Georgetown, careful to keep his car below the speed limit. This was one night he didn't need a ticket. He'd waited until the documentary was on before he left. He knew Abby would be glued to the set for that half-hour. If she did phone him after the program, he could always say he'd been outside checking the car.

From the beginning he'd known there was something weirdly familiar about Pat Traymore. Years ago he hadn't shed any tears when he'd read that Kerry Adams had "succumbed to her injuries." Not that anything a three-or-four-year-old kid said stood up in court; but even so, it wasn't the kind of grief he needed.

Abby had been right. Pat Traymore had been out to put the screws on them from the beginning. But she wasn't going to get away with it.

He was on M Street in Georgetown. He turned onto 31st Street and drove to N, then turned right. He knew where to park. He'd done it before.

The right side of the property extended halfway down the block. He left the car just around the next corner, walked back and ignoring the padlocked gate, easily scaled the fence. Silently he melted into the shadowy area beyond the patio.

It was impossible not to think about the other night in this place—dragging Abby out, holding his hand over her mouth to keep her from crying out, laying her on the back seat of the car, hearing her terrified moan, "My purse is in there" and going back.

Edging his way under cover of the tree trunks, Toby pressed against the back of the house until he was on the patio a few inches from the doors. Turning his head, he glanced cautiously inside.

His blood froze. Pat Traymore was lying on the couch, her

hands and legs tied behind her. Her mouth was taped. A priest or monk, his back to the door, was kneeling beside her and lighting the candles in a silver candelabrum. What in hell was he up to? The man turned, and Toby had a better chance to see him. He wasn't a real priest. That wasn't a habit—it was some sort of robe. The look on his face reminded Toby of a neighbor who years before had gone berserk.

The guy was yelling at Pat Traymore. Toby could barely make out the words. "You did not heed my warnings. You were given the choice."

Warnings. They thought Pat Traymore had made up that story about the phone calls and the break-in. But if she hadn't . . . As Toby watched, the man carried the candelabrum over to the Christmas tree and set it under the lowest branch.

He was setting fire to the place! Pat Traymore would be trapped in there. All he had to do was get back into the car and go home.

Toby flattened against the wall. The man was heading toward the patio doors. *Suppose he was found in there?* Everyone knew Pat Traymore had been getting threats. If this place burned and she was found with the guy who had been threatening her, that would be the end of it. No more investigations, no possibility that someone would talk about having seen a strange car parked in the neighborhood.

Toby listened for the click of the lock. The robed stranger pushed open the patio doors, then turned back to look into the room.

Silently Toby moved over and stood behind him.

As the closing credits of the program rolled onto the screen, Lila redialed Sam's number. But it was useless. There was still no answer. Again she tried to phone Pat. After a half-dozen rings she hung up and walked over to the window. Pat's car was still in the driveway. Lila was positive she was home. As

Lila watched, it seemed there was a reddish glow behind the dark aura surrounding the house.

Should she call the police? Suppose Pat was simply coming close to the memory of the tragedy; suppose the danger Lila was sensing was of an emotional not physical nature. Pat wanted so desperately to understand how one of her parents had hurt her so badly. Suppose the truth was even worse than she had envisioned?

What could the police do if Pat simply refused to answer the door? They would never break it down just because Lila had told them about her premonitions. Lila knew exactly how scornful of parapsychology the policemen could be.

Helplessly she stood at the window staring at the whirling clouds of blackness which were enveloping the house across the street.

The patio doors. They had opened that night. She had looked up and seen him and run to him, wrapping her arms around his legs. Toby, her friend who always gave her piggyback rides. And he had picked her up and thrown her . . .

Toby. . . it had been *Toby.*

And he was there now, standing behind Arthur Stevens. . . .

Arthur sensed Toby's presence and whirled around. The blow from Toby's hand caught him directly on the throat, sending him reeling backward across the room. With a gasping, strangling cry he collapsed near the fireplace. His eyes closed; his head lolled to the side.

Toby came into the room. Pat shrank from the sight of the thick legs in the dark trousers, the massive body, the powerful hands, the dark square of the onyx ring.

He bent over her. "You know, don't you, Kerry? As soon as I figured out who you were, I was sure you'd get around to doping it out. I'm sorry about what happened, but I had to take care of Abby. She was crazy about Billy. When she saw your mother shoot him, she fell apart. If I hadn't come back for her purse, I swear I wouldn't of touched you. I just wanted to shut you up for a while. But now you're out to get Abby, and that can't happen.

"You made it easy for me this time, Kerry. Everyone knows you've been getting threats. I didn't expect to be so lucky. Now this kook will be found with you and no more questions asked. You ask too many questions—you know that?"

The branches directly above the candelabrum suddenly ignited. They began to crackle, and gusts of smoke surged toward the ceiling."The whole room will be gone in a few minutes, Kerry. I've got to get back now. It's a big night for Abby."

He patted her cheek. "Sorry."

The entire tree burst into flame. As she watched him closing the patio doors behind him, the carpet began to smolder. The pungent odor of evergreen mingled with the smoke. She tried to hold her breath. Her eyes stung so painfully that it was impossible to keep them open. She'd suffocate here. Rolling to the edge of the couch, she threw herself to the floor. Her forehead banged against the leg of the cocktail table. Gasping at the sudden pain, she began to wriggle toward the hall. With her hands tied behind her, she could barely move. She managed to flip over onto her back, brace her hands under her and use them to propel herself forward. The heavy terry-cloth robe hampered her. Her bare feet slid helplessly over the carpet.

At the threshhold of the living room, she stopped. If she could manage to close the door, she'd keep the fire from spreading, at least for a few minutes. She dragged herself over the doorsill. The metal plate broke the skin on her hands. Squirming around the door, she propped herself against the wall, wedged her shoulder behind the door and leaned backward until she heard the latch click. The hallway was already filling with smoke. She couldn't tell any longer which way she was going. If she made a mistake and wandered into the library, she wouldn't have a chance.

Using the baseboard for guidance, she inched her way toward the front door.

42

Lila tried once again to reach Pat. This time she asked the operator to check the number. The phone was in working order.

She could not wait any longer. Something was terribly wrong. She dialed the police. She could ask them to check Pat's house, tell them she thought she had seen the prowler. But when the desk sergeant answered, she could not speak. Her throat closed as though she was choking. Her nostrils filled with the smell of acrid smoke. Pain shot through her wrists and ankles. Her body suffused with heat. The sergeant repeated his name impatiently. At last Lila found her voice.

"Three thousand N Street," she shrieked. "Patricia Traymore is dying! Patricia Traymore is dying!"

Sam drove at a frenzied pace, running red lights, hoping to pick up a police escort. Beside him Abigail sat, her clenched hands pressing against her lips.

"Abigail, I want the truth. What happened the night Dean and Renée Adams died?"

"Billy had promised he'd get a divorce. . . . That day he called me and said he couldn't do it. . . . That he had to make a go of his marriage . . . That he couldn't leave Kerry. I thought Renée was in Boston. I went there to plead with him. Renée went wild when she saw me. She had found out about us. Billy kept a gun in the desk. She turned it on herself. . . . He tried to get it from her . . . the gun went off. . . . Sam, it was a nightmare. He died before my eyes!"

"Then who killed *her*?" Sam demanded. "Who?"

"She killed herself," Abigail sobbed. "Toby knew there'd be trouble. He was watching from the patio. He dragged me out to the car. Sam, I was in shock. I didn't know what was happening. The last I saw was Renée standing there, holding the gun. Toby had to go back for my purse. Sam, I heard that second shot before he went back into the house. I swear it. He didn't tell me about Kerry until the next day. He said she must have come down right after we left, that Renée must have shoved her against the fireplace to get her out of the way. But he didn't realize she'd been seriously injured."

"Pat remembers tripping over her mother's body."

"No. That's impossible. She can't have."

The tires screeched as they turned onto Wisconsin Avenue.

"You've always believed Toby," he accused her, "because you *wanted* to believe him. It was better for you that way. Did you believe the plane crash was an accident, Abigail—a fortunate accident? Did you believe Toby when you alibied for him for the campaign funds?"

"Yes . . . yes. . . ."

The streets were packed with pedestrians. Wildly he honked the horn. The dinner crowd was drifting into the restaurants. He raced the car down M Street, across 31st Street to the corner of N and floored the brake pedal. They were both thrown forward.

"Oh, my God," Abigail whispered.

An elderly woman, screaming for help, was banging her fists against the front door of Pat's house. A police car, its siren wailing, was racing down the block.

The house was in flames.

* * *

Toby hurried through the yard toward the fence. It was all over now. No more loose ends. No pilot's widow to stir up trouble for Abigail. No Kerry Adams to remember what happened in the living room that night.

He'd have to hurry. Pretty soon Abby would be looking for him. She was due at the White House in an hour. *Someone was yelling for help. Someone must have spotted smoke.* He heard the police siren and he began to run.

He'd just reached the fence when a car roared past, spun around the corner and screeched to a stop. Car doors slammed and he heard a man shouting Pat Traymore's name. Sam Kingsley! He had to get out of here. The whole back of the house was starting to go. Someone would see him.

"Not the front door, Sam, back here, back here." Toby dropped from the fence. Abby. It was Abby. She was running along the side of the house, heading for the patio. He ran to her, overtook her. "Abby, for Christ sake, stay away from there."

She looked at him wildeyed. The smell of smoke permeated the night air. A side window blew out and flames whooshed across the lawn.

"Toby, is Kerry in there?" Abby grabbed his lapels.

"I don't know what you're talking about."

"Toby, you were seen near the Graney woman's house last night."

"Abby, shut up! Last night I had dinner with my Steakburger friend. You saw me come in at ten-thirty."

"No I didn't."

"Yes, you did, Senator!"

"Then it's true. . . . What Sam told me . . ."

"Abby, don't pull that shit on me. I take care of you. You take care of me. It's always been like that, and you know it."

A second police car, its dome light blinking, sped past. "Abby, I've got to get out of here." There was no fear in his voice.

"Is Kerry in there?"

"I didn't start the fire. I didn't do a thing to her."

"Is she in there?"

"Yes."

"You oaf! You stupid, homicidal oaf! Get her *out* of there!" She pounded on his chest. "You heard me. Get her out of there." Flames shot through the roof. "Do as I say," she shouted.

For several seconds they stared at each other. Then Toby shrugged, giving in, and ran clumsily along the snow-covered side lawn, through the garden and onto the patio. The sound of fire engines wailed down the street as he kicked in the patio doors.

The heat inside was withering. Pulling off his coat, Toby wrapped it around his head and shoulders. She had been on the couch, somewhere to the right of the doors. It's because she's Billy's girl, he thought. It's all over for you, Abby. We can't pull this one off now. . . .

He was at the couch, running his hands along it. He couldn't see. She wasn't there.

He tried to feel the floor around the couch. A crackling sound exploded overhead. He had to get out of here—the whole place was going to cave in.

He stumbled toward the doors, guided only by the cold draft. Pieces of plaster fell on him and he lost his balance and fell. His hand touched human flesh. A face, but not a woman's face. It was the crazy.

Toby pulled himself up, felt himself shaking, felt the room shaking. A moment later the ceiling collapsed.

With his last breath he whispered, "Abby!" But he knew she couldn't help him this time. . . .

In a pushing, crawling motion, Pat moved inch by inch along the hallway. The tightly knotted rope had cut off the circulation in her right leg. She had to drag her legs, use only her fingers and palms to propel herself. The floorboards were becoming unbearably hot. The acrid smoke stung her eyes and skin. She couldn't feel the baseboard any longer. She was disoriented. It was hopeless. She was choking. She was going to burn to death.

Then it began . . . the pounding . . . the voice . . . Lila's voice shouting for help. . . . Pat twisted her body, tried to move toward the sound. A roar from the back of the house shook the floor. The whole house was collapsing. She felt herself losing consciousness. . . . She had been meant to die in this house.

As blackness overwhelmed her, she heard a cacophony of hammering, splintering noises. They were trying to break the door down. She was so near it. A rush of cold air. Funnels of flames and smoke roaring toward the draft . . . Men's angry voices shouting, "*It's too late. You can't go in there.*" Lila's screams: "*Help her, help her.*" Sam's desperate, furious "*Let go of me.*"

Sam . . . Sam . . . Footsteps running past her . . . Sam yelling her name. With the last of her strength, Pat lifted her legs and smashed them against the wall.

He turned. In the light of the flames, he saw her, scooped her up, and ran out of the house.

The street was crowded with fire engines and squad cars. Onlookers huddled together in shocked silence. Abigail stood statuelike as the ambulance attendants worked over Pat. Sam was kneeling at the side of the stretcher, his hands caressing Pat's arms, his face bleak with apprehension. A trembling, ashen-faced Lila was standing a few feet away, her eyes riveted on Pat's still body. Around them, hot sooty debris drifted from the wreckage of the house.

"Her pulsebeat is getting stronger," the attendant said.

Pat stirred, tried to push aside the oxygen mask. "Sam . . ."

"I'm here, darling." He looked up as Abigail touched his shoulder. Her face was smudged with grimy smoke. The suit she had planned to wear to the White House was soiled and wrinkled. "I'm glad Kerry's all right, Sam. Take good care of her."

"I intend to."

"I'll get a policeman to drive me to a phone. I don't feel quite up to telling the President in person that I must resign from public life. Let me know what I need to do to help Eleanor Brown."

Slowly she began to walk to the nearest police car. Recognizing her, the onlookers broke into astonished comments and parted to open a path for her. Some of them began clapping. "Your program was great, Senator," someone yelled. "We love you." "We're rooting for you to be Vice President," another one shouted.

As she stepped into the car, Abigail Jennings turned, and with a tortured half-smile forced herself to acknowledge their greetings for the last time.

43

On December 29 at 9 P.M. the President strode into the East Room of the White House for the news conference he had summarily postponed two nights earlier. He walked to the lecturn where the microphones had been placed. "I wonder why we're all here," he remarked. There was a burst of laughter.

The President expressed regret at the untimely resignation of the former Vice President. Then he continued, "There are many outstanding legislators who would fill the role with great distinction and could complete my second term in office if for any reason I were unable to. However, the person I have chosen to be Vice President, with the hearty approval of the leaders of all branches of the government and subject to confirmation by the Congress, is one who will fill a unique place in the history of this country. Ladies and gentlemen, it is my pleasure to present to you the first woman Vice President of the United States, Senator Claire Lawrence of Wisconsin."

A roar of applause erupted as the White House audience jumped to its feet.

Nestled together on the couch in his apartment, Sam and Pat watched the news conference. "I wonder if Abigail is seeing this," Pat said.

"I imagine she is."

"She never needed Toby's kind of help. She could have done it on her own."

"That's true. And it's the saddest part of it."

"What will happen to her?"

"She'll leave Washington. But don't count her out. Abigail's tough. She'll fight her way back. And this time without that goon in the background."

"She did so much good," Pat said sadly. "In so many ways, she *was* the woman I believed her to be."

They listened to Claire Lawrence's acceptance speech. Then Sam helped Pat to her feet. "With your eyebrows and lashes singed, you have the most incredible surprised look." He cupped her face in his hands. "Feel good to be out of the hospital?"

"You know it!"

He had come so close to losing her. Now she was looking up at him, her face trusting but troubled.

"What will happen to Eleanor?" she asked. "You haven't said anything and I've been afraid to ask."

"I didn't mean *not* to tell you. The revised statement from Abigail coupled with everything else we have on Toby will exonerate her. How about you? Now that you know the truth, how do you feel about your mother and father?"

"Happy that it wasn't my father who pulled the trigger. Sorry for my mother. Glad that neither one of them hurt me that night. They were absolutely wrong for each other, but so much that happened was nobody's fault. Maybe I'm starting to understand people better. At least I hope so."

"Think about this. If your parents hadn't gotten together, you wouldn't be around, and I might be spending the rest of my life in a place that's decorated . . . how did you put it . . . like a motel lobby?"

"Something like that."

"Have you decided about the job?"

"I don't know. Luther does seem sincere about wanting me to stay. I guess for what it's worth the program was well received. He's asked me to start planning one on Claire Lawrence and thinks we might even be able to get the First Lady. It's mighty tempting. He swears this time I'll have creative control of my projects. And with you around, he certainly won't try any more passes at me."

"He'd better not!" Sam put his arm around her and saw the faint beginning of a smile. "Come on. You like a water view." They walked to the window and looked out. The night had clouded over but the Potomac gleamed in the lights of the Kennedy Center.

"I don't think I've ever experienced anything like seeing that house on fire, knowing you were inside," he said. His arm tightened around her. "I can't lose you, Pat, not now, not ever." He kissed her. "I'm dead serious about not wasting any more time. Would a honeymoon in Caneel Bay next week suit you?"

"Save your money. I'd rather go back to the Cape."

"And the Ebb Tide?"

"You guessed it. With just one change." She looked up at him and her smile became radiant. "This time when we leave we'll take the same plane home."